FARRAH ROCHON
TERRA LITTLE
VELVET CARTER

HOT
Christmas
NIGHTS

HARLEQUIN® KIMANI ARABESQUE®

HOT CHRISTMAS NIGHTS
ISBN-13: 978-0-373-09160-7

Copyright © 2014 by Harlequin Books S.A.

The publisher acknowledges the copyright holders of the individual works as follows:

TUSCAN NIGHTS
Copyright © 2014 by Farrah Roybiskie

CHRISTMAS TANGO
Copyright © 2014 by Terra Little

TIED UP IN TINSEL
Copyright © 2014 by Danita Carter

PLEASE RECYCLE
THIS PRODUCT IS RECYCLABLE

Recycling programs for this product may not exist in your area.

HARLEQUIN®
www.Harlequin.com

Printed in U.S.A.

CONTENTS

Dedicated to my sister-in-law, Ayeshia Roybiskie.
I love having you as a sister.

And over all these virtues put on love, which binds
them all together in perfect unity.
—*Colossians* 3:14

TUSCAN NIGHTS

Chapter 1

Aiden Williams buried his chin deeper into his wool scarf as he shifted from one foot to the other on the cobblestones in front of Forno Leoncini. Cursing himself for leaving his gloves in the car, he blew into his cupped hands before shoving them into the pockets of his corduroys.

What had previously been a light snowfall had gained strength over the past few minutes, the thick flakes swirling around him as the wind kicked up. He knew he couldn't stand out here forever, but he wasn't ready to make his presence known. Not yet.

Despite the cold, his skin grew hot as he peered through the bakery's garland-framed windowpane. His eyes focused on the woman standing before a rectangular stone table, her flour-covered fist punching a ball of dough. The last time he'd seen her in the flesh, she was standing in a church vestibule, wearing a wedding gown, preparing to marry his older brother, Cameron.

Three years later, Aiden was still conflicted over how he felt about Cameron being a no-show for his own wedding. On the one hand, he was grateful he had not been forced to endure years of seeing Nyla and his brother living as man and wife. Aiden doubted he would have been able to stomach it, knowing that she was only pretending.

Yet Cameron's decision to stand her up at the altar had been the catalyst that prompted Nyla's hasty move to Europe. She'd left Atlanta a week after the aborted nuptials and had not been back since.

But here she was, a mere twenty feet away. And she was as sexy as ever. More gorgeous than he remembered, if that was even possible.

Aiden turned up his coat collar as the snow began to fall in earnest. Uncertainty, entwined with a heavy dose of nervousness, kept him rooted where he stood, just outside the warm glow cast by the bakery's interior lights. He was unsure how Nyla would react to him tracking her down to this small town tucked away in the hills of the Siena region in Tuscany.

He'd debated the entire drive here whether to contact her but decided against giving Nyla any notice. Aiden was convinced she'd make an excuse for why he shouldn't come, just as she had done the previous three times he'd suggested they meet in the month since he'd been in Zurich, Switzerland, consulting on an IT project for a worldwide banking giant—a job he only accepted because it brought him to Europe.

No, he wasn't giving her a chance to back out this time. He'd come too far to find her—he'd crossed a damn ocean.

Yet Aiden still couldn't bring himself to take these last few steps. Because worse than having Nyla make excuses about why she couldn't see him would be to have her flat-out reject him to his face.

His gut clenched with a sharp ache. Nyla wouldn't do that.

Even though she had.

Aiden mentally blocked the words she'd spoken the last time he saw her face-to-face, as he had more times than he could count over the past three years. He never believed them anyway. Guilt and fear had forced her to say the things she'd said that day. He knew what was in Nyla's heart.

Which was why, when she mentioned on Facebook that she would be spending Christmas alone, he canceled his nonstop flight to Atlanta and rented a car instead. He'd made the six-and-a-half-hour drive from Zurich to San Gimignano, Italy, in just under eight hours. If not for the snow, which he'd never driven in before, and the road signs written in a language he didn't understand, he would have been here much sooner.

Once he'd made the decision to finally go to her, Aiden couldn't get here fast enough. Now he just needed to take this final step.

Not yet.

His eyes remained focused on Nyla as she labored over the dough, punching it down, flipping it over and reshaping it. Memories of the countless hours he'd spent perched on the kitchen counter at his parents' home, or—later, as they became closer—at Nyla's house in Kirkwood, watching her do this very same thing, had his chest tightening with a mercifully sweet ache.

His favorite fantasy of all time was imagining Nyla

coming to him, sweaty from the kitchen heat, with that sexy smile that used to curve up the corner of her mouth. She would crook her finger and he would obey. He would take her then and there, on the kitchen table, up against the counter. Anywhere he damn well pleased.

Aiden shut his eyes against the onslaught of wanting that crashed through him.

Why had he let her pretend that the attraction between them was one-sided? Why had he let her get away without fighting for her?

None of that mattered anymore. She was here now, and Aiden wasn't letting her get away.

He straightened his spine.

He hadn't come all this way to stare at Nyla through a window. He'd come with one goal in mind, to convince her that *he* was the Williams brother she should have been with all along.

"You can do this," he whispered.

He *had* to do this. He was tired of living without her.

Aiden sucked in a deep breath of the frigid air, opened the bakery's front door and walked inside.

Nyla Thompson held the crayon drawing she'd received in the mail yesterday close to her face while she held her phone out in front of her with the other hand.

"I love the Christmas card you made for me, Angelique. It's the most beautiful drawing I've ever seen in my entire life," she told her niece through her phone's web-chat app.

"It's me, Mommy, Daddy, Landon and the Christmas tree," the four-year-old said. "Jack is behind me," she tacked on, referring to the old beagle Nyla's sister

Rae had owned long before she became a wife and the mother of two.

"Your aunt Nyla needs to get back to work," Nyla heard just before Rae came back into view. Her sister took the electronic tablet from her daughter and smiled at Nyla. "I don't want to keep you too long, but she demanded to talk to you before we left for the cabin," Rae said. "She was so afraid her Christmas card wouldn't arrive before Christmas."

Nyla's heart melted. "She's such a sweetie. You have to bring both her and Landon the next time you come here."

"A four-year-old and a two-year-old on a nine-hour flight across the Atlantic? You must be delusional," Rae said. "I think it's high time you made it back to Atlanta for a visit. Patrick and Lana will soon have another niece for you to meet. I'm hoping for a New Year's Day baby."

Their brother's wife was due with their first child in just a matter of days. The desire to be there to welcome her newest niece into the world was so overwhelming that Nyla had seriously contemplated doing something she had not done in almost three years—return to the United States.

"I'll think about it," Nyla said.

The sarcastic look on her sister's face spoke volumes. "Sure you will," Rae said. "We have to get on the road, so I'll talk to you later."

"Drive safely," Nyla said. "And tell everyone I said hello when you get to the cabin. I'll call you all Christmas morning."

"Make sure it's Christmas morning *our* time, not yours."

"Yes, I know," Nyla said with a laugh. She waved goodbye to her sister and ended the face-to-face Web chat.

Pocketing her phone, Nyla pushed back at the wave of melancholy that threatened to wash over her. She had become an expert at battling homesickness, but it was always worse during the holidays. That was the one time of the year that her scattered family came together. The tradition had started when they were kids, when her parents would take them to a cabin in the Smoky Mountains to enjoy the holiday. For the third year in a row, she was missing it.

She thought about the legal pad sitting next to her computer, upstairs in the apartment over the bakery that she sublet from Murano Leoncini, the bakery owner's eldest son. The pad had a list of properties that could possibly house a high-end bakery. She'd started her search for available retail space in the Atlanta area the same day Murano emailed to say that he planned to return to San Gimignano and finally fulfill his father's dream for him to take over the family business.

Maybe it was time she started thinking about her dreams again. But was she ready to take that next step? To go back home to Atlanta?

Dread coiled within her belly just at the thought.

"Stop it." She punched the bread dough with more force than it warranted before flipping it over and kneading it. She worked the dough for another minute, then transferred it to a bowl.

The bell above the bakery's front entrance clanged.

"Dammit," Nyla whispered. She'd been meaning to turn the sign to closed for the past twenty minutes.

"Solo un minuto," she called. She draped a moistened

linen cloth over the bowl of dough and set it on the ledge of the wood-fired stone oven so the heat could help the dough rise. Wiping her hands on the apron tied around her waist, she walked over to the old CD player boom box Guido Leoncini kept in the kitchen and turned the volume down on her favorite holiday album, *A Motown Christmas*. Then she walked over to the retail area of Leoncini's.

"Posso aiutarlo?" she asked the gentleman who stood with his hands in his pockets, his eyes fixed on the few loaves that remained on the shelves that lined the bakery's right wall.

He turned and Nyla gasped.

"Aiden?"

She tried to close her mouth, but her slacked jaw wouldn't cooperate. It was as if the pathway between her brain and the rest of her body was blocked, because despite telling herself to move, or at least say something else, for God's sake, all she could do was openly stare.

An apprehensive smile lifted one corner of his mouth. "Hey," he said.

"Hey," she replied.

Hey? After three years, that's all two highly intelligent people could come up with? The absurdity of it nearly drew a hysterical laugh from her, or maybe it was just anxiety over the fact that he was actually standing here in front of her.

"You're here," she said, shifting from one foot to the other. She folded her arms over her chest and then quickly dropped her hands to her sides. Her nerves were so jumbled she didn't know what to do with herself. "What are you doing here?"

With that trace of nervousness still evident in his

eyes, he lifted one shoulder in an easy shrug. "I asked a couple of people on the street where I could find a good loaf of bread. Everyone pointed me to this place."

A sharp, shocked laugh shot out of Nyla's mouth, and, just like that, the trepidation that had caused her muscles to tense upon seeing him began to ease.

"I see your sense of humor is as healthy as ever," Nyla said.

"You always said it was my best asset."

She nodded. It was. Though he rarely let others see it. It was when he'd gradually started to reveal that side of himself to her that Nyla realized he saw *her* differently, as someone he could trust enough to share the real Aiden with. Her downfall had come when she began to reciprocate those feelings.

"So?" He tilted his head to the side and rubbed his jaw. "Do I at least get a hug?"

She hesitated for the briefest second before she closed the short distance between them and wrapped her arms around the man who, in what seemed like a lifetime ago, nearly became her brother-in-law.

If only he had not started to become so much more...

Nyla quickly released him and took a step back. She struggled to maintain her composure under his direct gaze, her hand self-consciously brushing a wayward strand of hair off her forehead.

"So, really, what are you doing here? Didn't you mention that you were going back home for the holidays?"

A knowing grin eased up the corner of his lips. "So you *do* check out my Facebook page more often than you've been letting on."

She cursed the heat that instantly rushed to her cheeks.

"Occasionally," she admitted. "How else am I supposed to keep up with your asinine *Doctor Who* commentary?"

His smile broadened and Nyla's lungs suddenly had the hardest time functioning. That smile had come to mean so much to her in such a short amount of time. And she'd missed it. She'd missed it *so* much more than she'd allowed herself to admit.

"I considered going home," he said. "But I decided it didn't make much sense to fly all the way to Atlanta when I have to be back in Zurich just after New Year's Day. I figured I'd take these few days off to see a bit more of the continent." His shrug was casual, but his deep brown eyes held a hint of uncertainty. "Is it okay that I'm here?"

Nyla considered his inquiry for a moment. He'd contacted her on several occasions over the past few weeks, asking if she would be willing to meet with him. She'd given the idea lip service, even going so far as to suggest lunch at her favorite café in Milan, halfway between Zurich and San Gimignano. But she'd already had excuses waiting in the wings for if and when he ever brought it up again.

There were no excuses to buy her any more time. Aiden was *here*.

"Of course it's okay that you came," Nyla finally said.

But even as the words left her mouth, a prickle of unease traveled along her nerve endings.

Since fleeing Atlanta three years ago she had worked to maintain a certain distance from anything that reminded her of the single most painful part of her past. Other than Rae, who had visited once since Nyla moved to Europe, she had not been near anyone else who had witnessed the humiliation she'd suffered on what should have been the happiest day of her life, her wedding day.

Her stomach clutched with the pain that never failed to strike whenever she thought about that day.

Her wedding day *should* have been the happiest of her life, but it wasn't, and unlike what many probably suspected, it had nothing to do with her groom deciding not to show up. It was because, for months before her wedding day ever arrived, she had been living a lie.

It had taken Nyla a long time to acknowledge the feelings she'd denied for so long, feelings she'd started to have toward Aiden months before she'd fled from Georgia. While she was still engaged to his brother.

But that was a long time ago. She had worked through those issues and had come to terms with the mistakes she'd made. She could handle seeing Aiden again.

Reaching for his hands, Nyla captured them both and gave them a gentle but firm squeeze. "It really is good to see you again," she said.

And she meant it. The price she'd paid for falling in love with him had been steep—it had upended her entire life. But she could not deny that the feelings had been real.

"It's good to see you, too, Nyla."

The earnestness in his voice, the sincerity in his eyes, the way he tightened his hold on her hands—it confirmed the one thing she feared she would find if they ever came face-to-face again. After three long years, nothing had changed. They were both still caught up in this forbidden love that had caused so much pain for so many.

Nyla dragged in a steadying breath as she extracted her hands from his hold.

Despite the warmth the stone oven delivered to the entire bakery, she rubbed up and down her arms. She was a heartbeat away from bursting out of her skin with the bevy of conflicting emotions that suddenly overwhelmed her.

She pointed to the door. "I should lock up. We're actually closed."

Mentally cursing the self-consciousness that made her hyperaware of every single move she made, she walked over to the door and flipped the open sign to closed.

In an attempt to steal a few moments to catch her breath, she stared out the window at the people making their way through the narrow street leading to the Piazza della Cisterna in the very heart of San Gimignano.

"The snow is coming down pretty hard out there," she said.

"It is," Aiden said from just behind her.

Nyla jumped and turned, covering her chest, which she was certain would crack wide-open from her rampant heartbeats. She tried to play off her nervousness with a breathy laugh, but it came out sounding forced.

"I didn't realize you were right there," she said, her hand still to her chest.

Aiden's deep brown eyes bored into hers, seeing more than she wanted him to see.

"You're not okay with me being here," he said. "I shouldn't have just shown up out of the blue like this. I can tell I've caught you off guard."

"Just a bit," she admitted.

"I'm sorry. That wasn't my intent in coming here."

He pulled his bottom lip between his teeth, a telling sign of irritation. The fact that she remembered that idiosyncrasy about him was both alarming and revealing. She'd learned so much about him in the short time she'd known him.

He blew out a frustrated breath. "I should go. It was wrong to just drop in on you without any warning."

He took a step toward the door.

"Aiden, no," she said. "You came all this way. You don't have to go anywhere. Please stay."

"Are you sure? I don't want there to be any awkwardness between us, Nyla." Dipping his head to her eye level, he said, "If you really don't want me here, if you think it's still too soon, I'll leave."

He brought his hand up as if to caress her cheek but pulled back before touching her. Instead he stuffed his hands into his pockets.

This was what she'd loved most about him. In her thirty years, Nyla had yet to find anyone as selfless as Aiden Williams.

"I don't want you to go," she said.

Profound relief washed over his face. His shoulders relaxed as a gentle smile traveled across his lips. "Good, because driving in all that snow would suck."

The laugh that broke free felt like her first genuine laugh in months, years even. Count on Aiden to be the one to elicit it. He seemed to be the one person who could make her laugh, even when she was trying her hardest to wallow.

She motioned for him to follow her into the kitchen.

"So, how are you enjoying Switzerland?" she called over her shoulder.

"It's okay, I guess. Just being in another country is cool." He shrugged one shoulder before leaning it against the arching brick entryway that separated the kitchen from the retail shop. "Other than a trip down to Cabo San Lucas for spring break, this is my first time abroad."

"Zurich and Cabo are two very different experiences," she said.

"Yeah." He chuckled. "Honestly, I've been too swamped with work to do much sightseeing, but I plan to extend my trip by at least a week or two once the project I'm setting up is complete."

"What exactly are you doing there?" she asked as she peeked under the towel to check on her dough.

"Boring computer stuff."

Nyla's brow arched. "I think I could have figured that out on my own. Care to elaborate?"

"No, I don't," he said. He took off his coat and draped it over his arm. "If memory serves correctly, your eyes will start to glaze over after about thirty seconds."

Her lips twitched in amusement. He'd probably called that one correctly. No matter how hard she'd tried—and she *had* tried—she could not feign interest in the techie things he loved so much.

Back when she would visit his parents' home, when she and Cameron first started dating, Nyla was convinced that Aiden was permanently attached to his computer. It didn't matter what he was doing: grabbing a soda from the fridge, answering the landline phone, even making a sandwich. His laptop computer was in his hand.

As she looked at him now, he hardly resembled that skinny college senior he'd been when she left the States.

His lean, lanky body had filled out in a way she never would have imagined three years ago. He was still slim, but Nyla could make out the outline of muscles underneath his moss-green wool sweater and the plaid scarf still wrapped loosely around his neck. Gone was the close-cropped haircut. He now wore his hair in long, neat dreads that were gathered in a band at the base of his head and reached the middle of his back.

Aiden had always seemed old beyond his years, intellectually. It looked as if his body had finally caught up with that brain of his.

"Whatever it is that you're doing with your fancy computers, I really am happy it brought you to my part of the world," she said. "So, now that you're staying in Europe for Christmas, what are your plans for the holiday?"

"Well, that's where you come in," he said.

"Me?"

"Like I said, I have the next several days off, and I've never been to Italy before. I was hoping that the only resident of the country I know would be willing to play tour guide for a couple of days."

His expression held a subtle apprehensiveness that told her he wasn't as relaxed as he was trying to appear.

"What did you have in mind?" Nyla asked.

"I'd like to go down to Rome, see the Colosseum, maybe reenact my favorite scene from *Gladiator*." He curled his biceps. "I think I could have filled in for Russell Crowe as Maximus Meridius. What do you think?"

She couldn't help it; she burst out laughing. "I'm sorry."

"Yeah, I know. I'm not really gladiator material. But I'd still like to see it." His voice took on a more serious note. "Look, Nyla. I know this is last minute, and I *did* just show up out of the blue. And as much as we're trying to pretend that it's just like old times, before…well… you know." He shook his head. "We're both aware of the eight-hundred-pound gorilla in the room. If it makes you too uncomfortable to do this, just say the word."

As she stared at him, Nyla told herself that enough time had passed since she'd had that horrible slip in judgment that had changed everything. She might not be ready to talk about it just yet, but she would hope that she had undergone enough personal growth that she could put her past mistakes behind her and just enjoy a few days with this person who had meant so much to her.

Maybe it would help to think about the girl she'd spotted in several of the pictures on his Facebook page. Young, petite and with obvious adoration toward Aiden, she looked like his perfect match.

Then again, maybe it wasn't such a good idea to think of Aiden's other woman.

She walked over to where he still leaned against the archway. Aiden straightened as she approached, the apprehension that colored his expression just a few seconds ago replaced with cautious hope.

"I'm not sure I'm ready to tackle that eight-hundred-pound gorilla yet, but if you're willing to ignore it for now, so am I."

"You're sure about this?" he asked. "You did say on Facebook that you didn't have any special plans for the holidays, but I don't want you to feel obligated to do this just because I came all the way from Zurich. In the snow. Without knowing how to read a lick of Italian. And did I mention the snow?"

The grin twitching at the corner of his mouth wrung a laugh out of her.

"I am happy to do it," Nyla said. "Honestly, I was planning to spend a quiet Christmas at home, but it's been a while since I took a trip down to Rome. Besides, every man should have the chance to live out his gladiator fantasy."

Nyla fought to ignore the tingles his rich, warm laugh generated along her nerve endings. She held up one finger. "However, there is a catch."

Aiden's smooth forehead creased with a frown. "What's that?"

She grabbed an apron from the peg on the wall and tossed it to him. "I'll play tour guide if you play baker's assistant."

Chapter 2

Aiden sprinkled coarse sea salt over the balls of dough lined along the slab of cold marble. "Is this too much?" he asked.

Nyla looked up from the dough she was stretching into a long rope. "It's perfect." With a grin, she said, "Someone must have taught you well."

"I wonder who that could have been." He let out a soft chuckle as he cupped the small mounds of dough in his hands, making sure they were evenly rounded. "I still remember when you found me hunched over my computer during midterms. I was ready to throw the thing out the window. You dragged me into my mom's kitchen and showed me the therapeutic benefits of beating the crap out of bread dough instead."

"Much cheaper and less damaging than beating the crap out of your computer. Tastier, too."

"In more ways than one."

The moment the words left his mouth Aiden wished he could rein them back in.

Nyla's hands stilled, her shoulders stiffened. "Aiden," she said, a hint of reprimand in her soft voice.

Every trace of the delicate camaraderie that had surfaced over the past half hour vanished in the uncomfortable silence that settled around them.

Aiden swallowed the groan of frustration that nearly escaped his throat. He couldn't believe they were back to this, dancing around the attraction that had always hummed between them.

As if it hadn't been hard enough to fight the first time.

In the beginning he really had tried to fight it, because Aiden figured any acknowledgment of his attraction to Nyla was a lost cause that would only lead to him looking like a fool for falling for his older brother's girl. Who in their right mind would ever think a woman like Nyla—beautiful, successful, damn near a goddess in her own right—would take a second glance at a scrawny computer geek? Especially after she'd already caught the eye of his richer, handsomer, ex–professional NBA player older brother?

But she *had* looked his way.

As much as Cameron had tried to play the victim, Aiden laid some of the blame for the relationship that had developed between him and Nyla at his brother's feet. It had been at Cameron's request that Nyla would often come over to their parents' home in Druid Hills, which was halfway between where Cameron lived in Buckhead in North Atlanta, and Kirkwood, where Nyla lived, south of the city.

At first Aiden wanted to call his brother out for being

an inconsiderate ass, making his woman meet him half-way so that he wouldn't have to drive too far to pick her up. For purely selfish reasons, Aiden had decided to keep his mouth shut. He wanted her at his house. He'd started to fall in love with Nyla with a swiftness that, to this day, still shocked him.

He'd found himself spending more time studying at home than at the library on the off chance that Nyla would show up. Thoughts of her had occupied his brain every waking hour. He was lucky he'd passed a single class that final semester.

He was far from a ladies' man, especially when compared to Cameron, but he'd had a couple of girlfriends by the time he met Nyla. It was only with considerable effort that Aiden could now recall those other girls' names. Nyla's hold on his heart was unyielding, leaving no room for anyone else. Even after she'd left and he'd finished school and moved out on his own, she was still the ideal by which all other women had been measured, and he had yet to find one that even came close.

He had finally decided to stop looking. She had never been his—not officially—but he was determined to change that. It might take a Christmas miracle, but one way or another he was going to convince her that they belonged together.

He just had to figure out how to make that happen.

He looked up to find her wiping her brow with the arm of her long-sleeved T-shirt. Her shoulder-length hair was pulled back into a ponytail holder, but several pieces had fallen out and now framed her face. She had the uncanny ability to look even more beautiful in a plain white shirt with a light dusting of flour on her forehead than she had dressed in a flowing wedding gown.

Of course, his memory of how she looked in that wedding gown was marred by the fact that she had been on the verge of marrying his brother. And that, prior to seeing her in that gown, his last encounter with her had been at her wedding rehearsal dinner, where she'd told him that the kiss that had been the most meaningful of his life had been the biggest regret of hers.

Hearing those words from her had been difficult, but he'd been just as wounded by the way she'd looked at him that night, as if he were a lovesick boy that she had somehow led on, instead of a man she had begun to have feelings for. It made him question everything about the time the two of them had shared.

Aiden shook those thoughts from his head. Dealing with the repercussions of everything that had happened back then was never easy.

He was not going to think about that now. It was water under the proverbial bridge. He'd grown a lot over these past three years. He no longer questioned the time he'd spent with Nyla. He was just grateful to have found her again.

Though he was surprised to have found her in a place like this.

"So, how did you end up baking bread in a tiny family bakery?" Aiden asked. "You completed one of the top pastry programs in all of France. Why aren't you making cream puffs and macarons?"

"I spent nearly a year working at an exclusive hotel in Paris after I finished my training at Leôntre, but when I vacationed in Tuscany two years ago I fell instantly in love with it. Especially San Gimignano, with all its medieval towers and its rich history. I just had to be here."

"I understand," he said.

Nyla looked up from the dough she was braiding and smiled that soft smile that used to make his breath catch. Apparently it still did. He had to remind himself to pull in some oxygen.

In a quiet voice, she said, "I knew you would."

A mutual love of history was just one of the things they'd discovered they had in common, which had led to exploring other interests they shared. Which had then led to Nyla breaking dates with Cameron so that the two of them could attend museum exhibits, foreign film showings at the Lefont Theater and quiet meals at her home.

Which had then led to Aiden falling so deeply in love with her that he ached with it.

"Nyla, I know you don't want to talk about it, but we can't pretend it isn't there."

"Aiden, please." She slipped a wooden paddle underneath the two loaves of sourdough she'd put in the stone oven twenty minutes ago and transferred them to the countertop. "I just… I can't right now. Please."

His fingers clenched the sides of the marble table. He hated that they were back here, tiptoeing around each other. There was a time, only a few years ago, when she had been his best friend. How could one kiss change everything?

But it had. And if he wasn't careful, he would scare her away again. He wasn't willing to lose any of the ground he'd made in reclaiming the friendship they once shared.

It had been hard enough to get to this point. When he finally found her on Facebook, nearly two years after she'd left Atlanta, Aiden had debated for weeks whether to make contact. She'd made herself clear when she left—she didn't want anything to do with him.

When he finally gathered up the nerve to contact her, she ignored his friend request for six months. *Six* months. He'd given up hope of ever speaking to her again.

And then, one day, there she was.

He could still feel the shock and desire that gripped his chest with every breath he took as he stared at her profile picture sitting in his friends list. He spent hours scrolling along her Facebook page, going through her photos, learning everything he could about the life she'd led in the two and a half years since he'd last seen her.

Gradually, their online friendship began to resemble the real-life one they'd shared. Nyla began to leave comments here and there. Aiden found himself scouring the Web for stories he figured she would find interest in—outdoor festivals, restaurant openings—with the sole purpose of garnering her attention. That's just how desperate he was to have her back in his life again, that he was willing to resort to high-school crush tactics.

It didn't seem all that pathetic right now. Just look what it had gotten him. Here they were, enjoying a pastime the two of them had engaged in more times than he could count.

As Nyla transferred the rolls he'd made into the stone oven, she told him about the history of the family bakery—both the business itself and the building that housed it, which was once rumored to be a boarding-house for ladies of ill repute.

"Everything is aboveboard these days," she said with a laugh. "Being so close to the Piazza della Cisterna, we get heavy foot traffic, but this rare snow has kept many of the tourists inside for the last couple of days."

"So, if the bakery is closed until after Christmas, why are we baking all this bread?" Aiden asked.

"It's for the 'Concert of Good Wishes' at Sant'Agostino Church," she answered. "It's a huge event for the holidays. Several schools sell refreshments to benefit their music programs and Leoncini's donates the bread to help defray the cost. Yet another reason I love San Gimignano—the locals are always willing to pitch in to help each other."

Even though it made him feel like an ass, Aiden couldn't help the resentment slowly building within him toward the town. With its quaint little shops and rich history, it seemed like the perfect fit for Nyla. But it was half a world away from Atlanta, which made it the exact opposite of perfect in his eyes.

"Do you think the concert will still go on, even with the heavy snow?"

"Oh, yeah," Nyla answered. "I don't care how much it snows, there's going to be a crowd." She started filling several brown paper bags with long loaves of crusty bread. Then she nodded to a spot just beyond his shoulder. "Can you hand me that box over there? We can deliver the bread once these final loaves are done, and I can give you a quick tour before we head to Rome, or Roma, as it's known here. That is, if you're up for another three-hour drive after that long ride in from Zurich."

"It was my plan to continue on to Rome tonight. I already have a room booked."

"Thank goodness, because it will be *impossible* to find one this close to Christmas."

"Nearly everything was taken. That's why the room is only for tonight and tomorrow night. I was thinking that we could see as much as we could tomorrow, and then maybe leave around noon on Christmas Eve. I can drop you back here and head back to Zurich." He paused for a moment before adding, "That is, unless you don't mind me hanging around until Christmas Day."

Her mouth opened, then closed. "I...I think I'd like that," she said.

Aiden couldn't stave off the smile that curled up the corners of his lips. "So would I."

Nyla cleared her throat and returned to packing the breads. "So, which hotel did you book in Rome?"

"I can't remember the name, but I know it's in the Termini Station District."

She looked up at him. "That's perfect. My friend Else lives not too far from there. I can stay with her." She tipped her head to the side and smiled. "I really am happy you invited me along. There's something truly miraculous about Rome at Christmas."

Aiden didn't doubt it, but he already had his Christmas miracle. Having her there with him was the only miracle he needed.

"Are you sure you didn't want to stay for the concert?" Aiden asked. He strolled alongside her, his hands stuffed in his pockets. They delivered the baked goods to the church, which was already filling up with both tourists and locals eager for the annual concert to begin, then took off for their walking tour of San Gimignano.

"Positive," Nyla said. "Don't get me wrong, I find watching a bunch of cute kids sing Christmas carols precious and all, but after about twenty minutes of standing in the cold my feet go numb. Besides, I want you to see the town."

The snow had finally stopped falling as they traversed

Via San Matteo, one of the town's main arteries, but flakes continued to shuttle down the eaves of the shop roofs that lined the popular tourist route.

Nyla pointed to the structure at the southern edge of the narrow street. "You see that stone tower up ahead? That's La Torre del Diavolo, the Tower of the Devil."

"Huh, didn't realize I'd get to see where the devil lives. I guess that's cool, though not what I had in mind when planning my Christmas vacation."

Nyla laughed. "Legend has it that the owner left for a trip, and when he returned, the tower had somehow grown taller. The townspeople attributed it to the devil, thus the name."

"I think the townspeople just wanted the owner to think he was losing his mind. They probably had those bricks tucked away somewhere and started adding to the tower the minute he left."

Nyla lolled her head to the side and released a tired sigh. "Your lack of appreciation for good folklore is such a disappointment."

"Sorry," he said, humor shading his voice. "I'll try to lock away my pesky scientific side so I can be more open to your folklore and fairy tales."

"It's for your own good. It will make this trip much more tolerable, especially when we get to Rome with all of its ancient legends."

"I can appreciate good history," he said. "I hadn't heard of San Gimignano before learning that you lived here, but I must admit I'm intrigued by these towers. The fact that they've survived this long and are still in such good shape is amazing," Aiden said, his eyes focused on one of the town's fourteen remaining medieval towers. "When you live in a country as young as the United

States, it's hard to comprehend structures that have been standing for several centuries."

"I know," Nyla said with a wistful sigh. "Even though I'm surrounded by it every day, it still takes my breath away."

Aiden looked over at her and, after a moment, blew out a resigned sigh. "You really do love it here, don't you?"

She nodded. "I do."

He dropped his head and huffed out a humorless laugh. "Shit."

"Don't be that way," Nyla said. "Tuscany has been good to me. It's been good *for* me. I thought moving to Paris and following one of my lifelong dreams would solve everything, but it didn't. I was still in such a dark place. There was something about San Gimignano that made me whole again."

Aiden stopped walking, causing her feet to halt midstroll. He took her hands in his and, with an earnestness in his voice that touched her soul, said, "As much as I hate that you had to leave in order to feel whole again, I'm happy you were able to find a place where you could be happy. Over the tens of thousands of times I've thought about you these past three years, the thing I've wished for most is that you were happy."

His words wrapped around her like a warm blanket, eliciting a measure of comfort that only Aiden had ever provided. It scared her as much as it consoled her. The feeling she experienced this very moment—the trust, the tenderness—it was the thing she feared most about being around Aiden again.

Three years ago, she'd fallen for him with amazing ease. As a result, her well-ordered life had been upended.

It was only by some miracle that Aiden's had not been destroyed, as well.

She would not be so stupid—so selfish—as to put them through that kind of turmoil again.

Two days.

She only had to get through two days. It would be a test of her will, but also a testament to how well she'd learned from her past mistakes.

They walked through the narrow arched passageway that led to the Piazza della Cisterna. Nyla gave Aiden a brief history of the triangular-shaped square.

"What's that?" he asked, pointing to the well in the center of the piazza.

"Probably one of the most visited sites in all of San Gimignano. For hundreds of years that well was where the town's residents got their water."

"It's a cistern. That's where the name Piazza della Cisterna must come from." He looked over at her. "Am I right?"

"I knew it wouldn't take long for that massive brain to catch on," she said with a laugh. She breathed deeply and pointed to the café just off to the right of the well. "Mmm...do you smell that? That place makes the best *ribollita* you will ever eat."

"I make it a point not to eat anything I can't pronounce," Aiden said.

She pinched his arm, even though she couldn't do much damage through his heavy suede coat. "There's more to life than Quarter Pounders with cheese," she said, remembering his ridiculous love of McDonald's. "*Ribollita* is a thick soup made with beans and topped with fresh red onions to give it a crunch. It's perfect on cold nights like tonight."

"I think I'll stick with the burgers and fries."

Nyla rolled her eyes, but she had to admit it was nice to see some things about him hadn't changed.

She pointed out several more structures as they walked through the narrow streets leading back to the bakery. They climbed the stairs behind it, which led to the small apartment she sublet from her boss's son.

Murano Leoncini had been living in San Francisco for the past two years. But he would be back in San Gimignano at the end of January, which meant she had an important decision to make.

"Well, this is home," Nyla said, shutting off thoughts of Murano's return and gesturing for Aiden to enter ahead of her.

He unwrapped his scarf from around his neck, took off his jacket, and draped them both over the arm of her living-room chair.

Nyla took in the size of his shoulders and marveled at how much he'd changed, at least physically, since the last time she'd seen him. His body resembled his brother's more athletic build, but he wasn't overly muscular as Cameron had been. Those nicely defined muscles looked very good on him, *too* good. So good that she was starting to question the wisdom of being confined in a car with him for three hours as they drove down to Rome.

He walked over to the scraggly three-foot Christmas tree she'd placed on a stand atop an end table. A crooked smile tilted his lips as he trailed a finger along the string of popcorn garland she'd made in a fit of nostalgia.

"Give me a few minutes to throw some clothes in a bag," Nyla said. "Can I get you something to drink while you wait?"

Aiden waved off the offer. Leaving the tree, he

plopped down on her sofa, leaned his head back and closed his eyes.

Nyla's breath hitched as memories assailed her. How many times had he assumed that pose after "dropping in" at her home in Kirkwood, exhausted from a day of challenging classes at Georgia Tech? She'd accepted his excuses about not wanting to face the traffic heading home to north Atlanta, and never questioned when an hour of hanging out soon led to two or three. And eventually overnight.

On those few occasions when he told his parents that he was bunking in a friend's dorm room, Nyla convinced herself that the little white lie wasn't all that bad. It wasn't as if they'd spent those nights doing anything untoward. They'd watched old movies, or played Scrabble until after midnight. When it was time for bed, she would sleep in her room and Aiden on the sofa. Nothing ever happened.

But she knew Aiden wanted it to. And as much as she'd tried to turn a blind eye to what was happening, she knew that *she* had wanted something more to happen, too.

She should have stopped it long before those feelings got so out of hand. But she had not wanted it to stop, because never in her life had she felt more alive, more true to herself, than she had when she was with Aiden. Even though their relationship had never become physical, what had started as just a friendship had blossomed into more.

That she had allowed her heart to become involved had made her into the thing she most loathed—a cheater. After suffering through the hurt of a philandering ex-lover, Nyla had thought it incomprehensible that she could ever do something remotely similar.

That's why she continued to feed herself the lies that what she and Aiden were doing wasn't cheating. There was nothing wrong with spending time with someone who shared her interests, especially when Cameron had shown a complete lack of enthusiasm for many of the "boring" things she enjoyed. Aiden had filled a void, and eventually he began to fill crevices in her heart she hadn't known were empty.

He'd made falling for him so damn easy.

Nyla's eyes fell shut. She would not go there again. She couldn't. She'd suffered enough guilt to last a lifetime; she would *not* put herself through that again.

She grabbed her weekender bag from the top shelf of the hall closet on the way to her room. As she snatched a couple of sets of bras and panties from her underwear drawer, she pulled up Else's number. She knew Else, a college professor originally from Phoenix, wouldn't have a problem with her bunking at her place for a few days, but Nyla would do her the courtesy of asking first. Her call went to voice mail, so she left a message, letting Else know that she would be darkening her doorstep in a few hours.

As she plucked a couple of sweater dresses and her calf-length boots from the closet, she tried to dismiss the anxiety creeping along her conscience.

"What are you doing?" Nyla asked the empty room.

On a list of bad ideas, this had to rank at the very top, right above jumping off a cliff. Which was how she felt with the way her emotions were all over the place. Had she not learned anything from the repercussions she'd suffered the first time she'd allowed herself to get close to him? Was she setting herself up for another fall?

"It's just a couple of days," Nyla reminded herself. She could handle a couple of days.

She reentered the living room and immediately re-thought that assertion.

Aiden stood with his back to her, observing the framed photographs she'd taken when she'd tried her hand at photography.

Nyla was struck by the quiet confidence he now ex-uded. It was evident in the way he carried himself, stand-ing strong with shoulders back and his head high. She'd caught glimpses of the young, sweet, slightly nerdy col-lege student she remembered so well, but there was no denying that he'd come into his own. Or that he was all man.

As his eyes roamed the black-and-white stills of the Eiffel Tower, the Arc de Triomphe and the tree-lined Champs-Élysées, Nyla's eyes roamed over *him*.

Her gaze immediately homed in on the way his soft brown corduroys cupped his backside. As her eyes trav-eled upward, she marveled at the way the wool sweater outlined the muscles in his back and shoulders. It was such a contrast to the slim, lanky body of a few years ago. His muscles weren't as big as Cameron's, but they were just as fine. Perfect, actually. She had never been a fan of huge muscles. Toned and trim was much sexier.

Nyla's head jerked back as she realized where her train of thought had led her. She had to stop doing this.

Aiden turned, catching her off guard. "Hey." He ges-tured to her bag. "You ready?"

"Uh, yes," she said. "I am."

His forehead dipped in a curious frown as he reached for her bag. "You okay?"

"Yes, of course," Nyla lied.

She wasn't okay. Not even a little bit. She didn't know how she would survive the next few days. The swift rush of pleasure she experienced every time she saw him, along with the anguish she suffered knowing that he would eventually share all that she loved about him with someone else, was bound to overwhelm her.

Envy toward the woman who would one day be a part of his world had been a constant struggle during those first few months after she left. It still was. Although, now that she thought about it, maybe knowing he was off-limits could actually help her get through these next few days.

"I've been meaning to ask how things are going with your girlfriend," Nyla said.

"Who?"

"The girl who was with you in your profile picture on Facebook for a while. She had that pretty light brown complexion and those green eyes."

"You mean Erica."

"I guess. Where did the two of you meet?"

"Work. She's in Human Resources. But we're not seeing each other anymore. We decided we worked better as friends and coworkers."

"Oh." Nyla staunchly ignored the sudden tingles that traveled across her skin. It shouldn't matter that he'd broken things off with his girlfriend. "So, is there *anyone* special in your life?" she asked.

Aiden paused for a moment, his eyes trained on her. "Yes," he answered.

She couldn't ignore the way her heart deflated at that

single word. "That's wonderful," she said, and tried to convince herself that she meant it.

She was happy for him. *Of course,* she was happy for him. Aiden was sweet, smart and funny; he deserved to have someone special in his life. And it was exactly what she needed to hear. Knowing that he was taken took the pressure off her. She wasn't about to become the other woman for anyone. She could relax now and just enjoy this time with him.

"Nyla," Aiden started. "That someone special—"

Her phone rang.

She held up a finger, grateful for the interruption. She was happy for him, but she wasn't interested in hearing about his latest girlfriend.

"One minute." She checked the phone, expecting to see Else's number. Instead it was Guido Leoncini's. "It's the bakery owner," she said. "I need to cover a few things with him before I leave."

She turned and spoke to Guido in Italian, letting him know the bakery was locked up but that he should go in tomorrow to make sure the embers in the oven had completely burned out.

She took pride in running Leoncini's, even though she'd known she would leave, even if Murano weren't returning. She had not put in so much time and effort into learning the craft of pastry making to spend the rest of her life in a small family bakery. Her dreams had always been so much bigger. She just wasn't sure she was ready to take the step she had been contemplating.

Nyla glanced at the tiny desk in the corner. The yellow legal pad next to her laptop listed several vacant storefronts in downtown Atlanta and a few in some of the wealthier suburbs where a high-end bakery would thrive. She'd slashed through the ones that had been leased over the past few weeks, but the one she'd had her eye on was still available.

All it would take was a phone call to the real-estate agent. She'd purposely refrained from accumulating too many possessions. A few boxes and her suitcase, and she could be on her way to Atlanta and the pastry shop she'd had her heart set on opening since her dad brought her to one to celebrate her tenth birthday.

Her chest tightened just at the thought of returning home, back to the family she'd missed like crazy over the past three years.

Back to the place where so many people knew of the humiliation she'd suffered.

Could she do it? Did she have a choice?

She couldn't stay hidden in Europe forever. And she didn't want to. As much as she loved Tuscany and the life she'd built for herself, she missed the life she'd left back in the States. Maybe it *was* time she returned.

Now was not the time to think about this. She'd vowed to put all that stuff aside and just enjoy herself these next couple of days. It was Christmas, after all.

She pocketed her cell phone and clapped her hands together. "Ready?" she asked.

"Nyla, about what we were talking about before your phone rang."

Yes. His new girlfriend.

If there was one thing she didn't want to think about more than those impending decisions she had to make regarding going back home, it was Aiden's new girlfriend.

She pointed to the digital clock on her DVD player and smiled a smile she wasn't really feeling. "It's already after six. We should probably get going."

Aiden started to speak, then stopped. He stared at her for several long moments before taking her bag and heading out the door.

Chapter 3

"Can we at least both agree that it makes more sense if I took over at the wheel? You've been driving all day."

"And you've been baking all day."

Nyla flipped her hands in the air. Two hours into their three-hour trek down to Rome and she was still trying to convince Aiden to let her take over driving duties.

"I've been driving in Italy longer than you have," she tried.

"Let's see. There's a road. It has lines on either side. As long as I stay between the lines, I think I'm good."

The look she sent him was sharp enough to cut through leather. Not that it mattered; with his eyes focused on the highway he wasn't looking at her anyway.

"Fine," Nyla said, settling back in her seat. "If you want to continue driving, you'll have to tell me the story behind that picture on Facebook."

He glanced over at her and laughed. "How exactly does that work? If I don't tell you the story, will the car magically stop moving?"

"Aiden," she said in a warning tone.

He let out a sigh. "Were you always this bossy?"

"Come on." Nyla pinched his arm. "I want to know how a picture of you stripped down to your skivvies ended up on Facebook."

"I lost a bet," he said. "I tried to get that stupid picture blocked, but no matter how many times I reported it, they never took it down. I had to threaten my friend Mike that I would post a video of him singing 'Dancing Queen' in drag on YouTube. He's in his last year of law school and is clerking for the Georgia Supreme Court. He definitely doesn't want links to that video showing up in the judges' in-boxes."

"Ouch. That's cutthroat," Nyla said with a laugh. "Knowing you, I should have guessed that the picture was the result of a bet, though I must admit I was sort of hoping you'd developed a bit of a wild side."

He glanced at her. "I may not make a habit of swimming in the Atlantic in my underwear, but I'm not the quiet guy I used to be, either. There's a little wild in me."

She studied him for a moment. "How much?"

"Just enough."

The effort it took to ignore the tingles those two words set off in her belly was exhausting. Yet she still spent the last hour of their drive contemplating what a little wild would look like in Aiden.

By the time they reached Else's, the snow was once again falling, covering Rome in a rare blanket of pillow-soft whiteness that made it seem even more romantic and magical. Nyla declared it the first Christmas miracle of the season when they were able to find street parking across from Else's building in the Trieste District.

Several of the balconies of the high-rise were trimmed with twinkling Christmas lights, but Else's, which she could see from street level, was bare. The window beyond, which led to her living room, was completely dark.

She tried Else's number again as she and Aiden crossed the street. She breathed a sigh of relief when her friend answered on the third ring.

"Thank goodness I finally got ahold of you," Nyla said. "I'm just outside your building. I hope you don't mind company for a couple of days."

Her steps halted as Else spoke.

"You're kidding me," Nyla said.

"What's wrong?" Aiden asked.

She held up her index finger, asking him to wait. "No, no. It's okay," Nyla spoke into the phone. "The trip down to Rome was very last minute. I came on the off chance that you'd be here. Enjoy Thailand."

"Thailand?" Aiden asked when she ended the call.

"Yes." Nyla blew out a sigh. "She was invited to spend Christmas there with a couple of fellow faculty members. She offered to call the landlord of the building, but she said there have been several break-ins in the area and they're hesitant about letting people into the building who were not previously on a visitors' list."

Nyla rubbed the bridge of her nose, trying to ease the headache that had suddenly formed between her eyes. She slipped her cell phone into her pocket before hunkering in her coat, pulling the hood over her head.

"As far as contingency plans go, what are your options?" Aiden asked.

She shook her head. "Finding an available hotel room

this close to Christmas will be impossible, and that's not considering how outrageous the cost will be even if I *do* find one."

In a low voice, he said, "You can always stay with me."

Nyla looked up at him from underneath the brim of her hood.

There was a time when spending a couple of nights in the same place with Aiden wouldn't have been a big deal. She'd done so not too long after she and Cameron first started dating. After a freak rainstorm made the roads too treacherous for her to drive home, Nyla had spent the night at his parents' house.

She and Aiden had stayed up way too late debating politics. He'd played the devil's advocate just to get a rise out of her. Nyla had held stubbornly to her positions for the very same reason. Talk of politics had soon turned to other things they disagreed on, like his affinity for fast food. Eventually, they began to discuss things they had in common.

That was the first time she'd started to see him as more than her boyfriend's younger brother.

She should have tried her luck with the rainstorm.

Nothing that would have happened on the slick roads that night could have been worse than what eventually resulted from the lapse in judgment she made when she allowed herself to fall for Aiden.

It was going to be hard enough being around him for the next two *days*. The thought of spending the next couple of *nights* with him made Nyla's breath catch in her throat and her skin warm, despite the snowflakes fluttering around them.

She was being ridiculous. This was Aiden. Kind, sweet, nerdy Aiden. Quiet, unassuming Aiden.

Grown and much-sexier-than-he-had-a-right-to-be Aiden.

No, she wasn't being ridiculous. She'd managed to fall for him back when he *was* quiet, nerdy and unassuming. The fact that he now had the physical qualities she attributed to her ideal man made these feelings of attraction coursing through her impossible to ignore.

"What about that eight-hundred-pound gorilla?" she asked. "European hotel rooms are notoriously small. It could get pretty cramped with the three of us in there."

"You're the one who has a problem with it. I'm ready to face the eight-hundred-pound gorilla head-on. Don't you think it would make the next couple of days less awkward?"

Nyla predicted it would do just the opposite. Resurrecting those past mistakes had trouble written all over it.

She shook her head. "No. Not yet."

She knew they would eventually have to confront it. Maybe.

It would be idyllic if they could spend the next two days as they had done back when they were just two friends enjoying time together. Aiden would go back to Zurich, she would return to her quaint apartment in San Gimignano and they would stay in touch via Facebook, this time with memories of the Christmas they shared in Rome.

But, as she knew all too well, the ideal rarely happened.

Sooner or later, she would have to confront her past mistakes. If not over the next few days, then when she left San Gimignano, which looked as if it would be even sooner than she'd anticipated.

Nyla hunched her shoulder. "I guess there isn't much choice. It's much too late to try to find a hotel room."

"Neither does it make sense for you to look for one," Aiden said. "I'm pretty sure the room has two beds if it makes you feel any better."

Just the mention of beds made her stomach flutter; she felt like a teenage virgin preparing to spend the night with her high-school sweetheart.

Nyla mentally rolled her eyes. She was neither a teenager nor a virgin, and at five years his senior she had already been out of high school before Aiden even entered. It was time for her to face this like the adult she was.

"Come on," she said, starting for the rental car. "It's already late and if you're going to see Rome in a day and a half, we'll have to get started early in the morning."

As they headed for the hotel, Nyla took in the charming lights and holiday decorations draped along the buildings. Because Italy's national colors were red, white and green, many of the businesses really played it up during Christmastime. She truly loved this city, with its rich history and many legends that Aiden was so fond of teasing her about.

Maybe when Murano kicked her out of her apartment next month, she could move in with Else and look for a *forno* here in Rome.

Get a grip.

The likelihood of finding an available storefront was minimal at best, and the probability that she would be able to afford it was zilch. Besides, those euros she'd managed to save over the past couple of years would stretch much further in the United States than they would in Europe.

The Hotel Villa delle Rose was within walking distance of Termini Station, the transportation hub that would take them just about anywhere they wanted to go in the city. They checked into the hotel and went up to the room, which thankfully *did* have two beds.

"Are you hungry?" Nyla asked. "It'll probably be a chore to find something opened this late, but I'm starving."

"Let me take a guess...no McDonald's?"

"You're in Italy, Aiden! There will be no Big Macs while you're here with me."

They found a small trattoria a couple of blocks down from the hotel. Just as they walked up to the door, a hand appeared from behind a curtain and turned the open sign to closed. Nyla thumped on the door until a balding man who was nearly as wide as he was tall appeared.

She explained their plight in Italian, describing their drive down from Siena in the cold and snow. After a few minutes of listening to her whine, the trattoria owner agreed to whip up a quick carbonara and pack it in take-out containers. Nyla grabbed two bottles of chinotto, the bittersweet citrus soda popular among Italians.

She knocked Aiden's hand out of the way when he tried to hand over his credit card.

"Hey!"

"You're paying for the hotel. The least I can do is pay for the meal."

"Are you forgetting that the only reason you're here is that I begged you to come? You shouldn't have to pay for anything."

Nyla put a hand up. She wasn't arguing with him.

It was after 10:00 p.m. by the time they arrived back to their room. She sat, cross-legged, in the middle of the bed, balancing the aluminum container in her lap. Aiden butted his back against the headboard, his feet crossed at the ankles out in front of him.

They were just two friends having dinner in the hotel room they would share for the next two nights. She could handle this.

God, please let me be able to handle this.

"Give me a list of what you want to see tomorrow," she said as she twirled fettuccini around her plastic fork. "Other than the Colosseum."

Aiden shrugged. "The normal sites, I guess. The Forum, the Vatican. According to the website, the Vatican will be open for touring up until Christmas Day."

"Most of the touristy spots should be," she said.

"Well, call me a typical tourist, but I'm excited to see all the places I've seen on TV and in the history books."

"I was the same way the first time I visited." She tapped her fork against her lips. "Come to think of it, I'm still that way. There's so much to see and do in this city, and to be here at Christmastime, and with *snow?* You are one lucky man, Aiden Williams."

His steady gaze caught her eyes and held them. "Tell me something I don't know."

It took some effort to tear her eyes away from his. Nyla pulled in a shaky breath.

"I, uh, I do have a couple of places that are off the beaten path that I think you'll enjoy," she said. "If we have time we should check them out."

"We should make them a priority," he said in that same low voice. "If you think I'll enjoy them, then I know I will, seeing as you know me as well as just about anyone."

Nyla tilted her head to the side, considering his words. "Why is that?"

He didn't answer, just continued to stare at her. She decided to press him on it.

"You once told me that you were always home studying because you didn't like opening up to people, but you always seemed to open up to me. Why?"

After several moments passed, he finally said, "You made it easy."

He set his food on the nightstand between the beds and folded his hands over his flat stomach.

"You never treated me like I was weird just because I preferred looking through a telescope instead of watching a basketball game or doing other things that 'regular guys' did. You *got* me. You understood me better than my own family did." He looked up at her and, with a grim smile, said, "You can probably do without my poor, neglected son monologue."

A sad smile formed on her lips. "It couldn't have been easy living in Cameron's huge shadow."

He shrugged. "It wasn't so bad."

Nyla wasn't fooled by his nonchalance. She'd observed early on how differently Aiden was treated from his older brother.

"I love Lynda and Russell, but I could tell from early on that they had crowned Cameron the golden boy. I'm smack in the middle of five kids, so I know about having to grab whatever attention you can, but with it being just you two boys, it's so obvious. Having them dote on him the way they do must be hard for you."

"I'm used to it," he said with another lift of his shoulders. "My earliest memories are of spending countless hours at Cameron's elementary-school basketball practices. The focus of the Williams family has always been about nurturing Cameron's talent and his career."

"Even though his career only lasted a few years," Nyla said.

By the time she and Cameron started dating, his NBA career had already been cut short by injury. He'd transitioned to the business side of things, working as a scout for Atlanta's professional basketball team, where she'd worked as a senior account executive in the corporate ticket sales department. Even though he was no longer on the court, Cameron's larger-than-life personality kept him in the spotlight.

The shadow he continued to cast was far and wide, leaving very little light to shine on all Aiden had achieved in college and graduate school. His tolerance of his family's disregard of his many accomplishments made him that much more extraordinary in Nyla's eyes.

"You really are special, you know that? Most people would be bitter, but you're not."

"Not *too* bitter. I have my moments," he said, a wry grin tipping up the corner of his lips. "I can't really complain, can I? Just look where I am." He gestured to their surroundings. "I'm spending the holidays in Rome. And I'm with you."

His penetrating gaze locked on her, making the confines of the small hotel room even more apparent. "Seeing Rome at Christmas is one thing, but having the chance to spend the holiday with you—anywhere—means even more. I know I've said it already, but I can't say it enough. Thank you for doing this, Nyla."

"You're welcome," Nyla said, her voice suddenly

huskier than it had been a minute ago. She averted her
eyes, concentrating on her dinner. She glanced up to find
that, thankfully, Aiden had gone back to his. He picked
up his drink, took a sip and started choking.

"Good God!" He held the bottle out and stared at it.
"What the hell *is* this?"

A peal of laughter tumbled out of Nyla's mouth. "It's
soda. I know it has a bit of a bite, but it's really popular here."

"A *bit* of a bite? It damn near snatched my lips off."
He set the bottle on her side of the nightstand. "You can
have the rest of that. I'll stick to water," he said, tipping back the half-full bottle of water he'd taken from
her apartment earlier. "Good call on dinner, though.
Whether it would make me give up Big Macs entirely
is debatable, but I can stand to eat a meal like this five
days a week."

"I told you," she said with another laugh. "Just wait
until tomorrow. Your taste buds are in for the experience of a lifetime."

His gaze dropped to her lips. "I hope that applies to
more than just my taste buds," he said, his voice low,
husky.

It was obvious they were no longer talking about
food. The air in Nyla's lungs constricted as she stared
at Aiden's mouth. He swept his tongue along his bottom lip, clearing a droplet of water. A tingle started in
her belly and moved lower.

"You'll have to wait and see," she returned in an
equally hushed tone.

The lightheartedness of a few moments ago evapo-
rated. In its place stood a heady dose of desire. It pulsed
around them, saturating the air, and bringing the real-

ity of their impending night together in this small hotel room into stark relief.

A silent warning rang through Nyla's head. This felt all too similar to what she'd experienced three years ago, when their playful banter soon escalated into something much more serious.

Yet, in the face of every consequence she'd suffered for falling for Aiden once before, the yearning to climb into bed with him and explore all the new dips and contours of his body was so strong Nyla could barely stand it. The devil on her shoulder urged her to give in to the impulse. Everyone thought they'd done more than they had anyway; couldn't she give in this one time?

What was she thinking?

Nyla jumped up from the bed. Avoiding Aiden's eyes, she said, "If you don't mind, I'll go first in the bathroom." She grabbed her toiletry bag from where she'd tossed it on the dresser.

"Nyla?" Aiden called. She looked back at him. "Ignoring this won't make it go away," he said.

She tried to tear her eyes away from the truth staring back at her, but she couldn't, because it *was* true. This feeling wasn't going away. It hadn't lessened one bit in the three long years they had been apart. She wasn't foolish enough to think that it would do so now that she was right here with him again.

But she only had to ignore it for two days. And she *would* ignore it. The high price she'd paid for disregarding her common sense and giving in to her feelings for Aiden had burned her once. She would not get burned again.

Without another word, she slipped into the bathroom.

* * *

Aiden stuffed the empty food cartons in the trash bin at the end of the narrow hallway and headed back to their room.

Their room.

His steps slowed as he came upon the door. He captured the handle, then released it, his hands falling to his sides, his limbs suddenly so heavy it felt as if the entire weight of the world was pulling him down.

He took a couple of steps back, until he reached the wall opposite the door. He stared across the hallway to the room he would share with Nyla, and thumped the back of his head against the wall.

How was he supposed to get through tonight? His eyes fell shut as a pain-filled groan climbed from his throat. His skin felt tight, his stomach a jumble of knots. Every fiber in his body hummed with electricity just at the thought of being in that room all night with Nyla.

Why did she have to be every single thing he could ever want in a woman? *Everything.*

And it had nothing to do with the fact that she was beyond gorgeous—which she most definitely was. He'd dated attractive women in the past. Even though he suspected that some of them had only shown interest in him because of his connection to Cameron, Aiden was pretty confident that a couple of them had been genuine. Yet not one of them had ever elicited the feelings within him that Nyla had.

Nyla's beauty radiated from the inside out. It was in that reassuring smile that came so readily, in her uncanny ability to sense when he needed to get something off his chest, or when he needed someone to silently be there, just so he knew he wasn't alone.

What he'd told her earlier was the truth. She *got* him.

When others in his family brushed off the rejection he'd received on a paper he'd submitted to an academic journal, Nyla provided a shoulder to lean on. Even though she'd only known him for a few months at the time, she somehow understood what was important to him better than people who had known him his entire life. That's just the kind of person she was: unique and special and giving.

And she was on the other side of that door.

"Just tell her how you feel," Aiden whispered.

But he didn't have to tell her. That was the thing that was driving him crazy. He would bet his last dime that Nyla knew exactly how he felt about her. She just wasn't ready to face it, just as she hadn't been able to face it three years ago.

She'd allowed others to shame her into thinking that she had taken advantage of him. Cameron, his parents, *her* parents, many of her friends; they had all put the blame at Nyla's feet. She had even convinced herself that she had somehow led him on, as if he wasn't mature enough to recognize that the attraction that had exploded that last night between them hadn't been building for months.

He never should have let her get away without owning up to the fact that she had been just as attracted to him as he had been to her. She'd wanted that kiss. She'd wanted even more than just that damn kiss.

Aiden started for the door, but once again stopped before opening it.

If he went in there demanding she acknowledge feelings she wasn't ready to admit to having, it could ruin these few short days he had with her.

"Dammit."

He couldn't bring it up again. Not yet.

But he would. Eventually, they were going to talk this through.

Shaking his head, he finally opened the door. Upon entering the room, he was met with the sound of the shower. His mind instantly conjured the image of Nyla standing naked underneath the spray of rushing water, her body glistening with rivulets of steamy moisture running down her skin. He nearly lost all feeling in his legs. Aiden fell back on the bed, covering his eyes with his forearm.

He would give up every single comic book in his Marvel collection—including the 1941 mint-condition Green Lantern—to be able to step inside that shower and have her wrap her arms around his neck. He wanted to feel her lovely, soft breasts pressed against his naked chest. He would give anything to wedge himself between her slick, soapy thighs and finally, *finally* discover what it felt like to make her his.

A groan tore out of his throat.

He could forget reenacting his favorite scenes from *Gladiator* at the Colosseum tomorrow. Pent-up lust would have him dead by morning.

"Hey, you okay?"

Aiden sprang upright. He hadn't even heard when she turned the shower off. She was dressed in calf-length pajama pants and a black-and-pink tank top with a glittery martini glass on it. She looked ridiculously good with her soft brown skin freshly washed. She smelled delicious, like peaches, as if she'd rubbed a bit of Georgia on her skin.

"Aiden?"

He shook his head. He had to snap out of this.

"I'm good." He grabbed his bag and headed to the bathroom, taking the quickest shower known to mankind. He wasn't wasting any of this short time he had with Nyla.

When he reentered the room she was already in her bed, under the covers. She had the bedside lamp on and was flipping through the magazine that was on the table.

"You read Italian, too?" Aiden asked, gesturing to the magazine.

"Enough to get by."

"You speak it like someone who's lived here your entire life."

"Working in Leoncini's, I had no choice. It's not as hard to pick up as you may think." She pointed to the window. "It looks as if the snow is letting up. That should make it easier to get around tomorrow."

Frowning, Aiden walked over to the window. "I was kind of hoping it would stick around for another couple of days. It would be my first white Christmas."

"I didn't think about that. Coming from Atlanta, you rarely get to see snow. I guess I've taken that for granted. It doesn't snow often in San Gimignano, but the winter I lived in Paris was just awful."

Aiden crossed his arms over his chest and leaned his shoulder against the cold windowpane. "What's your ideal Christmas?"

"Hmm, that's easy," Nyla said, setting the magazine aside. She scooted up in the bed and brought her knees to her chest. "Back when I was eight or nine, my family started spending the holidays in the Smoky Mountains. My dad would rent a cabin and we would drive out there as soon as Christmas break started.

"We would sit around the fireplace and have eggnog and rice crispy treats. My mom would read "Twas the Night Before Christmas' and we would decorate the tree with garlands made out of popcorn. It was the corniest, most *Leave It to Beaver* thing you've ever seen, but I truly did love it."

The light in her eyes dimmed. "I talked to my younger sister, Rae, just before you showed up at the bakery earlier today. They were heading out for the cabin. I've gotten used to not being around for birthdays or the big Fourth of July family picnic, but there's something about not being at the cabin with everyone at Christmas that just slays me."

"You miss them, don't you?" Aiden asked.

She nodded. "I do. My younger brother and his wife have had two girls in the last sixteen months, and my other sister-in-law is going to have a baby any day now."

Hearing the sadness in her voice triggered a deep ache in his chest. The thought that he had in some way contributed to the sorrow she was feeling caused him physical pain.

"Why haven't you gone back, Nyla? Is it really because of what happened between us? You've allowed *that* to keep you away all this time?"

"You say it as if it was just this thing that happened, Aiden. As if it was no big deal." She looked up at him, her deep brown eyes teeming with regret. "Everyone was there. My family, my coworkers, lifelong friends. Everyone I know witnessed that attorney coming to the church and telling me that Cameron didn't want to marry me because I was sleeping with his baby brother."

"But you weren't sleeping with me. It's Cameron's fault that he didn't give you a chance to explain. And are you seriously still giving him a pass, even after you found out that he was stepping out on you at the same time?"

She flinched. "One has nothing to do with the other."

"How can you say that? He cheated on you the entire time you were together, Nyla. He's cheated on every woman he's ever dated." The hurt that flashed across her face triggered a pang in his chest, but this was something that had bothered Aiden from the very beginning. "I still can't figure out why you were ever with him in the first place. It's common knowledge that Cameron has been a womanizer since birth."

"I knew your brother had flaws when I started dating him, Aiden. Maybe I was naive to think he would give up his old habits once we got engaged, but all of that is beside the point. It doesn't matter what Cameron was doing." She pointed to her chest. "This is about what *I* did. Was I eventually grateful that I didn't marry him after learning that he was still seeing other women? Of course I was. But that doesn't erase the fact that I was unfaithful to him, as well."

Aiden pitched his head back and groaned up at the ceiling. "You weren't unfaithful. It was one kiss, Nyla."

"It was more than just a kiss," she whispered. "We both know that. If I hadn't stopped us…"

An instant ache settled in his groin at the mention of that night. The memory of how close they had come to finally sleeping together was one he'd had to endure much too often these past three years.

It hadn't been just about sex. He wasn't the renowned ladies' man his brother had been, but getting sex had never been a problem. It had been all about Nyla, about being with her in the most elemental way. They had been connected on an emotional level for months leading up to that night. He'd needed that physical connection.

"Does this mean we're finally tackling the eight-hundred-pound gorilla?" Aiden asked.

She blew out a deep breath and dropped her forehead to her knees. "Please, Aiden. This is awkward enough as it is. Bringing that up will only complicate things."

"Maybe it would do the exact opposite. You ever consider that? We've been tiptoeing around this ever since I found you on Facebook, Nyla. Think of how much simpler things would be if we just got everything out in the open."

His skin tingled with expectancy as he waited for her response.

"You should try to get some sleep," she said. "You've had a long day and we have a lot to see tomorrow." She clicked off the bedside lamp and huddled back under the covers. She turned on her side, facing the opposite wall.

Aiden ran both hands down his face. He stared at her stiff form, highlighted by the moonlight streaming through the window.

Everything within him was clamoring for him to press her about this. The only reason he hadn't brought it up in the past few months was that she could have simply stopped responding to him on Facebook. But she was here now. They could finally hash everything out, face-to-face.

But he couldn't do it. Not yet. She would only clam up and go back to blaming herself.

Shaking his head, Aiden trudged over to his bed and slipped under the covers.

"Good night, Nyla," he whispered into the stillness.

After several weighty moments, she answered, "Good night, Aiden."

He turned onto his back and stared up at the ceiling, knowing sleep wasn't about to come his way, not with Nyla lying just a few feet away from him. After several minutes passed he heard a slight snore coming from her side of the room, and couldn't help the smile the sound brought to his lips.

What he wouldn't give to crawl into that bed with her. To wrap his arms around her, pull her against him, feel the rhythm of her breaths as she slept soundly. He wanted to wake her up in the middle of the night and make love to her, the way he'd dreamed of doing for years. He wanted to keep her in this hotel room for the next two days and show her just how much they belonged together.

Instead Aiden turned onto his side and stared at the few snowflakes still falling softly outside the window. It wasn't his ideal scenario, but at least he had this time with her right now. He would take what he could get.

Chapter 4

Aiden tried his best to maintain a stoic expression as he placed his knuckle underneath his chin and stared off into the distance.

"Would you stop it already?"

He looked over at Nyla, who'd plopped the hand that wasn't holding the camera onto her hip.

"What? You don't like my 'thoughtful' pose?" He gestured to the stone columns of the Temple of Antoninus and Faustina in the Roman Forum. "I'm channeling all the great minds that used to walk around this place. Can't you see me and my man Julius Caesar shooting the breeze over a couple of beers?"

Nyla just stared at him, her face the picture of weary impatience, though her grin ruined it. It was the first smile he'd managed to extract from her today.

After the chilly atmosphere that had encompassed

their hotel room this morning, even that small glimpse of a smile was enough to excite him. They'd tiptoed around each other, speaking in hushed monosyllables, the relaxed camaraderie from the night before nowhere to be found.

Aiden had been on the verge of apologizing for driving the uncomfortable wedge between them when Nyla spoke up, suggesting a moratorium on talk of anything that was too heavy. She wanted the day's focus to be on the magic of Rome at Christmastime.

If he'd had the choice, he would rather they spend the day hashing out everything that was standing in the way of them being together. But Aiden knew better than to push her. If he pushed her, she would run.

Instead he'd agreed to go along with this charade. He would traipse around Rome with her, ignoring the discussion they must have, pretending that his life's happiness wasn't hanging in the balance.

"Okay, okay," Aiden said, holding his hands up. "Maybe not a beer since I've never been a fan, but old Julius and I could talk over some iced tea."

"Would you please behave?" Nyla asked.

Deciding to give her a break, he posed for several more pictures, amused at her seriousness behind the camera.

"Exactly how many shots does that digital camera hold?" Aiden asked.

"About four thousand," Nyla called. She laughed when he dropped his head and groaned.

"Sorry, I guess I got a little carried away," she said. "I dabbled in photography for a while. It's been a long time since I had a human subject to shoot. I've mostly taken scenery."

"Did you take those framed photos on the wall at your apartment?"

She nodded. "Back when I was in Paris. That city is a photographer's paradise, professional or hobbyist."

"I can only imagine. It's on my list of must-sees before I return to the States."

Her eyes lit up. "Oh, you *must* visit Paris while you're here. It would be a shame not to."

Aiden's brow arched. "Are you volunteering to join me?"

The thought of venturing through the romantic streets of Paris with Nyla by his side, not as an old friend too afraid to admit her feelings for him, but as his woman, his *lover,* was the stuff of fantasies. What he wouldn't give to make that a reality.

He took several steps forward, bringing himself within inches of her. He captured her hand and ran his thumb across her inner wrist. "What do you say, Nyla? Are you willing to show me around the City of Lights?"

Her gaze dropped to his mouth, then quickly returned to his eyes. She let out a deep breath and tugged her hand from his hold. "We should probably go." She took a step back. "The lines to get into the Colosseum will be long."

"Not until you answer my question."

She shifted from one leg to the other, clearly uncomfortable. At the moment, he didn't care.

"We agreed we wouldn't do this," she said in a small voice.

Yes, they had, but for the first time in his life, Aiden was going back on his word. He was tired of her pretending that he was the only one who had been affected by the attraction between them.

"I have a modification to our earlier agreement," he

said. "I'll agree to put the conversation off while we're in Rome, but you have to agree that we discuss it before I leave for Zurich, Nyla. I don't want to go back to being just someone whose status you occasionally like on Facebook. I don't know what I mean to you anymore, but you mean too much to me to continue on the way we have been."

Her eyes slid closed. For the briefest second Aiden thought she would turn down his request, but then she said, "Okay." She looked up at him. "But we wait until after Christmas."

He nodded. "I'm holding you to that."

She released a weary laugh. "I wouldn't expect anything different."

They made their way to the Colosseum, which was as magnificent as Aiden had imagined. As they stood in the line that wound its way around the massive structure, Nyla pointed out the grass-covered stone ring about twenty yards from the entrance and explained that it was where the gladiators who survived their turn in the arena would wash after their fight.

When they entered the arena, Aiden just stood there for a moment and took it all in.

"This is amazing," he said. "I can't imagine this place filled with people cheering on a match to the death."

"It makes American football seem tame, doesn't it?"

"Like child's play," Aiden agreed.

They trailed behind a tour group with an English-speaking tour guide, who pointed out the many statues that remained intact after nearly two thousand years.

Once they exited the Colosseum, Nyla suggested he take a picture underneath the famed Arch of Constantine, located just steps away from the ancient arena. This time Aiden insisted he be allowed to pose like a warrior coming home from battle.

Her carefree laughter as he struck pose after menacing pose solidified his decision not to bring up the past again today. She was right. This was supposed to be a fun day of sightseeing. Every time he tried to insert the past, Nyla pulled further away. That wasn't why he'd brought her here. He didn't want her running away from him. He wanted the exact opposite.

"We're pretty much crisscrossing the city," Nyla said. "But I'd rather try to see the Vatican today instead of waiting until tomorrow. We'll come back to where we'll have dinner tonight."

Aiden gestured for her to lead the way. "After you, Madam Tour Guide."

Nyla hailed a cab, and ten minutes later, they were standing outside the fortresslike walls that surrounded Vatican City.

Aiden started for the line that wrapped around the wall, but stopped when Nyla tugged his wrist.

"Is there a problem?" he asked.

"Before we go inside, there's something else we *have* to do."

They crossed the street and stopped before a large plate-glass window. Behind the glass case inside were mountains—literally, they looked like tiny mountains— of ice cream.

"You're joking right? It's thirty-five degrees out here and you want me to eat ice cream?"

"Not ice cream, gelato. And I don't care how cold it is, you cannot come to Italy and not have gelato." She took him by the arm again and dragged him into the *gelateria*.

Aiden was baffled by the number of people waiting in line to buy gelato on such a cold day.

"I've had gelato before," he said with a shrug. "I don't get why people think it's so special."

"Just taste it," Nyla said, handing him his cone. His eyes grew wide at his first taste of the rich, creamy dessert. She grinned. "Told you."

"Yeah, so this is a lot better than ice cream," he conceded. He followed Nyla to the counter that faced the street and sat on a bar stool that afforded them a view of the line of people entering the Vatican.

"And this isn't even the best gelato I've had," she said. "It's pretty close, though."

She ran her tongue along the rim of the cone, lapping up the rivulets from the already melting dessert.

Aiden couldn't be sure, but it was a safe bet that he had never in his life gotten so hard so fast, at least not since he was twelve years old. He had to swerve the stool to the right just in case his sweater couldn't fully conceal the erection that had sprung up at the sight of her tongue stroking that gelato.

"Mmm..." Nyla murmured, licking her lips. "There shouldn't be something so sinfully good this close to the Vatican." She held the cone out to him. "Want a taste?"

It was an innocent enough gesture, but in his current state of mind Aiden couldn't help the barrage of erotic thoughts that suddenly crashed through him.

His eyes trained on Nyla, he leaned forward and took a taste of the sweet treat. "Mmm," he said. "The best thing I've tasted in a long time."

Her gaze dropped to his mouth. Her lips parted, then quickly closed as her eyes shot to his. Aiden held his cone out to her.

Nyla stared at it as if the gelato were forbidden fruit. "I've...uh...I've tried that flavor already," she said.

A grin tipped up the corner of Aiden's lips. "Try it again," he encouraged in a low voice.

She glanced at the gelato, then at him. Aiden saw her chest lift as she pulled in a steadying breath before she leaned over and licked in the same spot he had.

He swallowed back a moan, though just barely.

The situation in his pants reached nuclear meltdown proportions, a hot ache gripping him as he studied the drop of chocolate cream that clung to the bow of her bottom lip. It took every ounce of restraint in his body not to lean forward and lick it off.

"Is it as good as you remember?" he asked, his voice so husky he could barely hear it.

Nyla's gaze lowered once again to his lips. "Even better."

To hell with fighting this.

Aiden leaned forward, preparing to fulfill the fantasy that had been on his mind all day. But before he could connect his mouth to hers, Nyla reared back and twisted her stool toward the window.

She pointed across the street. "We'd better get going before that line gets any longer."

Aiden shut his eyes against the onslaught of lust that coursed through him. He nearly suggested they skip the tour; it seemed sacrilegious to enter into a holy place with such unholy thoughts flooding his mind.

The wait to get into the Vatican was longer than the one for the Colosseum, which was expected at this time of the year, but seeing the famed painted ceiling of the Sistine Chapel made it worth the wait.

They shuffled their way inside St. Peter's Basilica,

which Nyla explained was the length of two football fields. She pointed toward the massive tomb where St. Peter was buried. "Do you see that dove in the stained glass window past the altar? Its wingspan is seven feet."

"No way," Aiden said.

"Yes. And those letters up there," she said, pointing to the Latin writing that ran the entire length of the basilica. "They are six feet tall."

Aiden slowly shook his head. "Pictures do not do this justice. I can't even put it into words." He turned in a slow circle, completely awestruck. "A day and a half isn't enough. I'll have to come back here before I leave for the States."

"You must," she said. "There's no way we're going to get through all of Rome in one day." Nyla's brow arched. "Speaking of returning to Rome…" She reached into the shoulder bag she carried and pulled out a handful of coins. She took his hand and turned it, dropping them in his upturned palm. "You're going to need these for where we're going next."

Aiden joggled the coins. "An arcade?"

Her eyes lit with knowing humor, she took him by the arm and turned for the basilica's exit. "You'll see."

They hopped into another cab and crossed the Tiber River. When Nyla mentioned they were nearing the Mausoleum of Augustus, Aiden demanded they stop. He'd written a book report on the life of the first emperor of Rome back in grade school; he never imagined that he'd ever have the chance to see the burial place of the man who started the Roman Empire in person.

His eyes glued to the crumbling facade of the ancient tomb, Aiden rattled off facts that had stayed with him all this time. "Did you know he and Antony were friends before Cleopatra came into the picture?"

"Women." Nyla tsked. "Causing men strife for thousands of years."

"Tell me about it." Aiden snorted, then laughed when she playfully slapped him on the arm. "Augustus is the reason I've never eaten figs. After I read that his wife killed him with poisoned figs, I decided I could go through life never eating them."

Nyla's head flew back with her laugh.

They continued on foot, walking south on Via del Corso. Nyla spotted a scarf shop and scuttled ahead of him to see if it was open. He took the time to drink in how good she looked in the snug-fitting sweater dress and calf-high heeled boots. She'd paired it with a cream coat that reached the hem of the dress. She'd always been fashionable, even when she wasn't trying.

"They're closed," she said with a shrug.

"Maybe next time," Aiden said.

She nodded and smiled. A ridiculous thrill shot through him at how open she seemed to there even being a next time.

They continued on down the heavily traveled street. Even though he couldn't see where it was coming from, the gurgling rush of water and the chatter of what had to be dozens of people grew louder with every step they took. They turned left at another ancient building with stone columns, and a minute later, Trevi Fountain came into view.

Aiden's steps halted. "Wow."

"Amazing, right?"

He could hear the smile in Nyla's voice, but he couldn't take his eyes off the massive fountain.

"I've seen it in movies, but to see it in person…"
Aiden shook his head, amazed.

"This is one of the best sights in all of Rome. I can
sit here for hours and people-watch." She nudged his
shoulder. "My favorite reaction is the one you just had.
You have no idea how many people are stopped in their
tracks when they see it."

"Can you blame me? This is… It's incredible."

They took a seat on one of the steps surrounding the
marble structure. The only thing that could drag his attention away from the fountain was the smooth glimpse
of thigh that peeked out when Nyla crossed her legs.
It wasn't until she pulled the hem of the sweater dress
down over her knees that Aiden was able to pay attention to what she was saying. She filled him in on the
history of the aqueduct system that fed the fountain,
then started on the litany of movies it had appeared in.

"If Trevi Fountain was ever a category on *Jeopardy,*
you'd run the table on it," he teased.

Her admonishing frown was ruined by the amused
glint in her eyes. "I told you it's one of my favorite places
in Rome."

Aiden nodded toward a group of tourists facing away
from the fountain and tossing coins over their shoulders.
He slipped his hand into his pocket and came out with
the coins she'd given him earlier.

"I guess that's what these are for?"

Nyla nodded. She took him by the hand and tugged
until he stood. "Come on. No trip to Rome would be
complete without tossing a few coins into the Trevi."

Once at the metal bar that surrounded the base of the
fountain, Nyla captured his shoulders and twisted him
around until he faced her.

"Legend has it that you must toss three coins over your shoulder, like this." She motioned her arm across her chest and over her left shoulder. "The first is to secure a return trip to Rome, the second is to find your true love and the third leads to marriage."

"So, do you really believe that works?" Aiden asked.

He didn't know if the sudden redness on her cheeks was from the cold or embarrassment, but he liked it.

"I know it probably seems silly to someone as pragmatic as you are, but it's nice to imagine that it's true. I'll bet you think it's a waste of a few euros."

He slowly shook his head. "No, I don't."

His eyes still on her, he tossed each coin over his shoulder.

"Here's to returning to this very spot with the woman I love." After he tossed the last coin, he brought his fingers to her face and caressed her cheek. "And that when I return, she knows that she's the woman I love."

Her lips parted ever so slightly. Soft white puffs took shape with each breath that panted from her mouth.

"Not too many people know this, but there's a miniature fountain just to the left," she said. "Legend has it that if a couple drinks from it, they will be forever faithful to each other."

Aiden brushed his thumb across her lower lip. "I don't know about you, but I'm feeling pretty thirsty."

The tourists' chatter and gurgling rush of the water cascading over the stone fountain dissipated as he stared into Nyla's eyes. Time suspended, all thought vanished; at this moment, everything else ceased to matter.

His entire body humming with need, Aiden leaned forward and brushed his lips lightly upon hers. At the feel of her soft lips, every dark part of his soul burst into light. His only desire was to remain in this very spot, doing this very thing, for as long as possible.

He cupped Nyla's jaw in his palms, his fingertips tingling at the feel of her delicate skin. Aiden drew his tongue along her lips, willing them to open. After three long years, the need to experience her unique flavor was all he could think about.

He ran his tongue over the seam of her lips, steadily increasing the pressure with every swipe, until finally her lips parted. A groan of pleasure tore from his throat as he inhaled the sweet taste of her. He'd experienced it only once before, but he remembered every single thing about her kiss. The way her mouth relaxed, the warmth, the suppleness.

He thrust his tongue in and out, stroking the velvet softness, devouring the honeyed flavor. How had he survived without this? Why did he wait so long? It was impossible to imagine going even another day without kissing her like this again.

He held her head steady as he continued to stroke her warm mouth. He fought the urge to pull her flush against the hardness growing below his waist, but the need to connect his body to hers was more than he could withstand.

"Aiden." She spoke his name against his lips, sending an electric current racing through his veins.

"What is it?" he whispered, shoving his hand into the hair at the nape of her neck.

"We…we can't do this."

His chest nearly caved with the wave of disappointment that crashed through him. "Don't say that, Nyla."

She pushed against him, breaking the connection.

Then she took several steps back, straightening her dress.

Several people gathered around the fountain snickered and clapped, and Nyla's pretty brown cheeks turned as red as a beet.

Just great. Their first kiss in three years—their second kiss *ever*—and it happened in front of an audience of strangers.

Aiden took a step forward, but she stopped him, putting a hand up. "Don't, Aiden. Please don't make this any harder than it already is."

"Why are *you* making it so hard? Can't you feel what's happening here?"

"Yes, and it isn't right. I'm not doing this to someone else, Aiden. I've been the other woman before. I will not put someone else through that."

His head reared back. *What?*

"The other woman? What are you talking about?"

"You have a girlfriend."

"What? No, I don't."

"Yes, you do. Before we left my place yesterday, when I asked about the girl in your Facebook pictures, you said the two of you had broken up. When I asked if you have anyone special in your life, you said yes."

Aiden pitched his head back and pinched his eyes closed.

"Goodness, Nyla. Are you kidding me?" he said, his voice strained. He looked at her again and shook his head. "You never gave me the chance to finish answering you yesterday. If you had, I would have told you that *you're* the someone special that I'm *hoping* to have in my life. I don't have a girlfriend."

"Not even one you occasionally date?" she asked.

He shook his head. "I've tried to get over you, Nyla. I told myself that it would make life easier if I could just forget those months I spent with you three years ago ever happened, but there is nothing easy about forgetting you." He closed the distance between them. "I'm starting to think it's impossible."

"Don't," she said.

"It didn't matter how smart or beautiful or funny those other women were, not one of them could ever measure up to you."

She dropped her head. "God, Aiden," she whispered. "Why are you doing this to me?"

He captured her chin and lifted it until she met his gaze.

His heart pounded against the walls of his chest as he decided to put it out there, once and for all.

"Because I'm in love with you. It doesn't matter what you say, or what you do. I'm convinced that I'm destined to love you." He leaned forward and placed a gentle kiss on her forehead. "I want you to give us a chance."

She wrapped her arms around her middle and pulled her trembling lips between her teeth.

"I just don't know, Aiden. After what happened on my wedding—"

"Forget that one day," he said, cutting her off before she could bring it up again, as if that one day meant more than all the others they'd shared. He put his hands on her shoulders and stared into her eyes.

"Think about how you felt before your wedding day. Remember what it felt like to stroll around the Ancient Americas Exhibit at the Carlos Museum, or through the tulip meadows at the botanical gardens. Think about that first time you reached for my hand as we sat on the swing in my parents' backyard."

She tried to look away, but he wouldn't let her. Turning her face to his again, he said, "You felt it that night, Nyla, that very first time you reached for me. You knew then that there was more than just friendship between us. I know you did, because it was the first time I saw fear in your eyes. Because you knew what was happening between us."

"Of course I was afraid," she said. "You were my fiancé's younger brother."

"I was a man who cared enough to learn what it would take to make you happy. I was a man who deserved a chance." He tucked a finger underneath her chin and tipped her face up. "I still want that chance, Nyla, because even after three years apart there is nothing in this world I want more than to make you happy."

Her eyes fell shut.

Aiden had to fight the urge to pull her trembling lower lip between his teeth. He could practically see the war taking place within her.

This could all be so simple, if only she would let go of that guilt she still carried.

"Is it really that hard to give yourself permission to be happy?" Aiden whispered.

"I'm trying," she said.

"At the very least, I want you to admit that you loved me," he said. "Admit that what I felt wasn't one-sided."

She looked up at him, her soft brown eyes swimming with emotion. "I don't have to tell you how I felt about you, Aiden."

"I need to hear you say it."

She sucked in a deep breath, and said, "I loved you."

Her voice was so small he could barely hear it, but he did, and the pleasure her words set off in his head was as addictive as anything he'd ever felt.

"Thank you," he whispered against her hair.

He pulled back slightly and looked down at her. "I'm not going to push you, but can we please at least try to stop pretending that we're just these two friends who knew each other a few years ago, and just happen to keep in touch online from time to time? I can't go back to that. I need to know that there's at least a chance that we will finally be together."

After several weighty moments passed, finally she said, "Yes."

Aiden wasn't sure if he believed in Christmas miracles, but he was certain he'd just experienced his first one.

Chapter 5

Nyla rested her head on Aiden's shoulder as they swayed slowly to the delicate strumming of the serenading musicians on the Piazza Navona. For the first time in a long while—in three years to be exact—she felt light, free, as if a weight she didn't want to admit to carrying had suddenly been lifted.

Happiness.

That's what she was feeling right now.

If anyone had dared to suggest that she was anything but happy with the new life she'd built for herself, Nyla would have laughed it off. How could she not be happy? She'd left a job she never truly enjoyed to pursue her lifelong passion in one of the world's most amazing cities, then had moved to the rolling hills of Tuscany, with its gorgeous landscapes and rich history. She was living a dream.

But it wasn't *her* dream.

Her dream had never been to live so far away from her family and everyone she loved. No matter how adept she'd become at convincing herself that she was happy here in Europe, Aiden's dogged prodding had forced her to own up to the truth.

For the past three years, she had been living a lie.

She'd lived the lie for much longer than these past three years. Every time she'd told herself that she wasn't falling in love with him, that it had only been overcompensation for the hurt she felt whenever Cameron's lack of attention would disappoint her, it had all been a lie.

She *had* loved him. And though she still couldn't bring herself to voice the words, Nyla couldn't deny the truth nestled deep down in the well of her soul.

She *still* loved him. She had never stopped.

The musicians strummed one final, haunting note before taking their bow. She and Aiden, along with several other couples who had joined in dancing under the stars twinkling high above the popular square, tipped the musicians with several euros before reclaiming their seats in the outdoor dining area of one of the piazza's many restaurants. Aiden and Nyla both declined dessert, opting to grab something at one of the booths that lined the square.

"So, this is something special that they do just for the holidays?" he asked as they strolled past a booth selling handmade tree ornaments in red, green and white.

"The vendors selling paintings and postcards and the other touristy trinkets are always here, but these booths are known as the Christmas Market. This is just one of the things you get to experience being in Rome at this time of year that most tourists don't."

They came upon a booth with a collection of wooden puppets on one side and scraggly, witchlike dolls propped up on the other.

Aiden picked up one of the witches. "I can understand the Pinocchio dolls, but why would anyone want to give the Wicked Witch of the West as a Christmas gift?"

"That is the Befana," the vendor said in heavily accented English, holding another out to Nyla.

"Oh, yes," Nyla said. "Guido bought several of these for his grandchildren. It's another bit of Italian folklore," she explained. "She isn't a witch, despite the black cape and broom. The Befana delivers treats for the children just before the Feast of the Epiphany."

"It would creep me out if I unwrapped a present and found this," Aiden said, setting the doll back on the display shelf. "Makes me appreciate the Transformers and Teenage Mutant Ninja Turtles I got for Christmas even more."

Nyla shook her head in amusement as they continued on. They browsed several presepe stalls, with their hand-carved nativity pieces, and several other vendors selling delicate blown-glass ornaments.

"You never told me what your favorite Christmas tradition is," she said. Aiden looked over at her with a curious dip to his brow. "Last night, we were discussing our favorite Christmas traditions, but we never got around to yours."

"Ah, yes." Lightly swinging their clasped hands between them, he said, "My favorite tradition was opening presents on Christmas morning. I think my parents recognized that Cameron commanded so much of their attention throughout the year that they tried to make up for it at Christmas. I pretty much got anything I wanted.

I still regret not asking for something really cool, like a rocket simulator or something like that."

Nyla's shoulders shook with her laugh. "What was your very favorite gift?"

His mouth curved in a wistful smile. "A pair of used sneakers."

"*Used* sneakers?"

Aiden nodded. "A gift from Cameron. They were the sneakers he wore during the high-school basketball championship game his senior year. He was named MVP. I wanted those sneakers so badly, but I never said anything. Somehow he knew. He gave them to me for Christmas that year, and I wore them all throughout high school."

A deep ache pierced Nyla's chest. "I ruined your relationship with him, didn't I?"

"No, Nyla. Cameron and I were never all that close. I looked up to him at one time, but once he was drafted into the NBA and became a cliché, I just couldn't respect him." He shook his head. "I really don't know what you ever saw in him."

"I fell for the charm," she said. "Like so many other people, he won me over with that larger-than-life personality."

"You're just so different from all the other women he ever brought home."

"That's why I thought things would be different between us, that *he* would be different. I had no illusions about your brother, Aiden. I knew he was a player, and not just on the basketball court. Maybe I was naive, but I really thought that I could tame the great Cameron Williams."

Aiden snorted.

"I know. It seems *really* naive now that I think about it. Not just naive, I was stupid to think I could change him."

"Cameron was the stupid one. Not you. He'd always been a bit of an ass, but I blamed that on his coaches and all the people that used to hype him up. People began treating him like he was some basketball god before he even started high school. But once he was drafted into the NBA, it just grew to a ridiculous level. I pretty much gave up on having any type of meaningful relationship with him after that."

"I wonder if he realizes what he's missing out on," she said.

The moment the words left her mouth, Nyla was struck by how closely they applied to her own life. She had been missing out on the same thing.

Aiden hadn't missed the irony, either. "I won't point out the obvious," he drawled.

"It's not necessary," she said.

He rubbed his thumb along the sensitive spot on her inner wrist. "You don't have to miss out on it any longer, Nyla. Just say the word."

If only it were that simple.

Nyla entwined her fingers with his, giving his hand a squeeze, hoping he understood the words she couldn't yet bring herself to say.

Half an hour later, they sat on a stone bench on the Piazza del Popolo. The oval piazza was one of the highest points in Rome.

"You were right," Aiden said as he stared up at the clear sky. "Even with all the famous sights I've seen today, this is my absolute favorite part of the tour."

"I told you you'd enjoy it," Nyla said. His love for

astronomy was one thing he'd never hidden from anyone. Every time she'd come here on previous trips, she'd thought about how much Aiden would love it.

She huddled closer to him on the bench, her head tipped back as she, too, looked at the stars above them. "How perfect that with all the cloud cover we had today, the sky would be so clear tonight."

"I'd like to think you ordered it up just for me."

She laughed. "I've made a few connections over here in Italy, but I'm not *that* well connected."

"The way the city lights reflect off the snow, it makes it look as if everything is sprinkled with diamonds. And the stars." He tipped his head back again, looking at the crystal clear sky, peppered with twinkling stars high above Rome. "How often do you come out here?" he asked.

"Every time I visit. It's the best place in all of Rome, maybe in all of Italy, to look at the sky." She hesitated for a long moment, before admitting, "It took me a while to realize that I did it in order to keep a connection to you."

Aiden's gaze shot to her.

Nyla wrapped her hand around the crook of his arm, securing her hold on him as she snuggled even closer in the cold.

"I would often wonder—hope, even—that you were somewhere doing the exact same thing. I would picture you in your parents' backyard, looking through that old telescope with the duct tape around the barrel. Often, during those times when I was missing home so much that it hurt to even breathe, I would imagine you somewhere gazing at the same stars I was seeing. It was the only thing that would bring me peace."

"That's what's special about the stars," Aiden whispered. "Even thousands of miles away, there's always that connection." He lifted her chin and stared into her eyes. "I've lost count of how many times over the years I've stared up at the sky thinking about you, Nyla. Those nights we spent together, just like this one, gazing up at the stars. I loved that more than anything. That very first time you joined me, I think that's when I started to fall in love with you."

Nyla pulled in a deep breath. She looked away, focusing on the gleaming dome of St. Peter's Basilica.

"You're thinking about it, too, aren't you?" Aiden asked. "About the last time we looked at the stars together."

She kept her eyes straight ahead, but nodded.

It was a moment that had replayed in her mind more times than she could count over the past three years. It occurred on the night of her twenty-seventh birthday, when Cameron had planned a date at a fancy restaurant in downtown Atlanta. As usual, he'd asked her to meet him at his parents' because it was a shorter drive than having to cross the city and pick her up at her home in Kirkwood.

But Cameron never showed up. He'd called after being more than an hour late to tell her he'd been held up and wouldn't make it. Nyla had become used to him standing her up, but had thought he surely wouldn't let anything come before her birthday celebration.

But, of course, he had. Because, as she later discovered, Cameron had put just about *everything* before her.

Even though he had been under immense pressure preparing for finals, Aiden put his studies on the side for the night and joined her on the wooden swing in his parents' backyard. He'd lifted a bottle of champagne from his mother's collection, and they celebrated her birthday underneath the stars.

When she'd kissed him that night, it had felt right.

When he'd kissed her back, it had felt like heaven.

"It wasn't a mistake that time," Aiden said in a whisper-soft voice. "Just like it wasn't a mistake earlier today. When I kiss you, when we're connected that way, it's the only time that everything in the world seems right, Nyla."

A pained moan tore from her throat. "Why must you always say the right thing?"

"Why can't you ever accept it as truth?" She dipped her eyes, but Aiden wouldn't let her look away. He took her chin and gently turned her face toward him. "I love you, Nyla. And you love me. We fell in love when we shouldn't have, but it doesn't change the fact that it happened. It's been long enough, Nyla. Whether or not it was right shouldn't matter anymore."

"I know it shouldn't," she said. "But a part of me feels as if it still does."

He pushed out a frustrated breath. "I honestly don't understand why it's so hard for you to move past this."

Nyla stretched her legs out and crossed them at the ankles. She did the same with her arms, stretching her hands in front of her before plopping them down on her lap. Finally, she looked over at him.

"Did I ever tell you about the time I won second place in the school science fair back when I was in the sixth grade?" she started. "I probably didn't, because I was only proud of it for about an hour or so. Because just after lunch period, the principal announced the overall science fair winners on the school intercom. My sister

Charlene won the overall prize for the best science fair project in the entire school.

"Just when I thought I'd finally done something to make my parents proud, in swept Charlene. She was a year ahead of me, so I was constantly trying to step out of her shadow."

"But you told me your parents never played favorites or treated any of you differently," he said.

"They didn't, because I never gave them the chance," she said. "That day I came in second place at the science fair was the same day I decided I would never give my parents a reason not to be proud of me. And I lived up to it. I graduated at the top of my class at Spelman, and excelled in a job that I absolutely hated. It was worth it. All those long hours on the phone making deals—it was all worth it because my parents loved to brag about all of my top Account Executive of the Year Awards.

"You know what they didn't brag about to their friends? They didn't brag about my fiancé standing me up at the altar and accusing me of sleeping with his younger brother."

"Nyla—"

"The look of disappointment on my mother's face—I think that hurt me more than anything else. You can call me a coward, but it's the thought of seeing that look on their faces again that has kept me here, Aiden."

"Your parents have forgiven you, Nyla. You're the only one who can't let go of the fact that you weren't the perfect person you tried to make yourself into. When will you realize that you'll never be happy until you stop giving a damn about what other people think and start living for *you?*"

"That's easier said than done, especially when your mistakes have hurt so many people."

"It's easier than you think it is," he said. "All you have to do is decide that you're going to do it." He captured her hand and brought her fingers to his lips. "It's time to let it go, Nyla. We've both paid a high enough price for the hurt we caused three years ago. It's time you forgive yourself and accept that you deserve to be happy. Do you think you can finally find the courage to do that?"

Aiden did his best to appear calm and relaxed, but on the inside he was a ball of chaotic emotions.

This was it. There was nothing left to say.

If he had not convinced Nyla that they belonged together, he would just have to face the fact that they didn't. If she refused to accept his love, if she chose to remain in the past instead of looking toward the future they could have, then he would have to move on. He refused to live the rest of his life waiting for her to come to terms with that one mistake they'd made three years ago.

Seconds drifted into minutes as they sat silently underneath the stars, huddling together as the temperature continued to drop. After some time had passed, Nyla cleared her throat.

His heartbeats stopped as he waited for her to speak.

"It's getting late," she said in a small voice. "I think we should head back to the hotel before the snow starts again."

Aiden's eyelids slid shut. He had his answer.

The silence in the cab ride back to the hotel clawed at his skin. He wanted to rage, to force her to see that the mistake she was making this time was so much worse than what had happened back in Atlanta.

But what good would it do?

She admitted that she loved him. But apparently loving him wasn't enough to overcome the shame she'd allowed to paralyze her these past three years.

The only thing standing in the way of them being together was this ridiculous guilt she refused to let go of, and there was nothing more he could do to get her to see reason. His chest nearly caved in with the deep ache that settled there as reality set in.

It was time for him to move on.

Aiden held the door for her as she exited the cab, and gestured for her to walk ahead of him into the hotel. Once there, they stuck to separate sides of the tiny room, doing their best not to bump into each other. Nyla sat on the edge of the bed, her back to him. The room was so quiet that the sound of the zipper teeth pulling apart as she unzipped her boots echoed around them.

"You can use the bathroom first," she said, still facing away from him.

"No, you go ahead." He could barely get the words past the frustration clogging his throat.

Nyla pushed herself up from the bed and turned to face him. The pain in her eyes made Aiden want to pick up the chair next to him and crash it against the wall.

How in the hell could she deny that they belonged together? It was written all over her face.

Aiden clutched his fists at his sides. "Why are you doing this, Nyla? Don't you see that the only people you're hurting are the two of us? Everyone else has moved on. Why can't you just let me love you?"

"I wish I could," she said.

Aiden's eyelids slid shut. God, she was killing him.

"You're the only one who *can* do it, Nyla. You just have to decide that it's worth it. Stop fighting this."

"I've spent the past three years fighting my feelings for you," she said in a voice so filled with hurt that it caused him physical pain. "But I can't do it anymore."

His eyes flew open at her softly whispered admission.

She walked over to him, stopping when less than a foot separated them. "I don't want to fight this anymore, Aiden. I want to be happy. And you...*you* make me happy."

She brought her hands up and clutched his face between her palms, pulling his mouth to hers. Aiden wrapped his arms around her and crushed her to him.

The sensual gasp that escaped her lips set off a ripple of electric sparks down his spine. He walked them over to the bed and lowered her on top of it, covering the length of her body with his. His fingers traced along the hem of the sweater dress she still wore, sliding underneath so he could grip her lush, smooth thighs. He pulled her body to him, drowning in how good it felt to have her body flush against his.

How long had he dreamed about this, prayed for it? Nyla had become his ultimate fantasy from the moment he met her. But she soon became so much more than just a fantasy. She became the woman he loved.

And finally, *finally* she was going to be his in the truest sense.

Together they undressed, him helping her as she pulled the dress over her head, her doing the same as he took off his own sweater. Aiden stole a moment to just stare at the perfection that was her body. She lay beneath him in a satin bra that barely covered her nipples. His mouth watered at the sight of all that luscious skin stretched out so gloriously before him, just waiting for him to feast upon it.

He dipped his head and traced the scalloped edges of the silky fabric. He swirled his tongue around her erect nipple through the bra, laving the peak until Nyla cried out, her body shivering.

Eliciting that response from her only made Aiden want to do it again and again. Levering himself up on one elbow, he set out on a journey, using her body as his personal erotic playground.

He pulled down the cups of her bra, exposing her magnificent breasts to his lips. As he indulged in the silken softness, running the tip of his tongue along the base of her breasts before sucking one erect nipple between his lips, his fingers traveled down her gently curved belly. He flattened his hand over her belly button and tucked his fingers just underneath the edge of her satin underwear, and pulled the material off.

It became a personal test of will to see how long he could go without touching her, but when Nyla spread her thighs open, his will shattered. He plunged his hand between her legs, her wetness coating his fingers. He dipped one, then another into her incredibly snug, incredibly hot passage, then started to move in and out.

He sucked her nipple into his mouth as his thumb rubbed the bundle of nerves at her cleft, increasing the pressure on both until he felt Nyla's muscles tightened. Once again, a scream tore from her throat as she began to shake.

He wanted to bring her to orgasm one more time before connecting his body to hers, but Aiden couldn't hold out any longer. He shoved his pants and underwear down his legs and kicked them off, rolled on a condom, then moved between Nyla's open thighs. Taking himself in his hand, he guided his hardness into her incredible warmth.

The satisfied groan that tore from his throat was three years in the making.

Nothing he'd ever experienced could describe what it felt like to be surrounded by her hot, welcoming body. Aiden held himself still so he could take in the moment. He couldn't rush this. He'd wanted it for too long. Had dreamed about it, wished for it.

"I love you so much," he whispered into her ear as he rocked his hips slowly against her.

She wrapped her legs around his waist and clutched him to her. "More than words can say, Aiden. I love you so much more than words can say."

Her head thrust back, Nyla cradled his hips and helped to guide him as he pumped in and out of her, establishing a rhythm that matched their twin cries as they both panted with every thrust.

Aiden buried his head against the hollow between her neck and shoulder. He tried like hell to slow down, but with every lunge Nyla's body sucked him in deeper, squeezing him, cloaking him, saturating him with her wetness, until he could no longer fight the need to reach that paradise waiting just on the other side.

With one last, long, deep drive of his hips, pleasure exploded within his brain, swiftly reaching out to coat every fiber of his body.

Aiden collapsed on top of her but quickly twisted them around so that she lay on top. He'd never been more replete with satisfaction in all his life.

There was no denying it now. Christmas miracles really did happen.

Chapter 6

Despite the blanket of heavy clouds covering Rome, gentle streams of the dawn light filtered through the window. Nyla stared at the shadow the hotel room's lone chair cast against the wall. She wasn't sure how long she'd been awake, waiting for her conscience to ruin the peaceful silence. She thought surely it would happen, had convinced herself that if she ever gave into the long-held desire to make love with Aiden, she would burst into a ball of flame.

But things were different now. *She* was different now.

She was no longer Cameron's fiancée, preying on his younger brother. They were two adults in love, and they deserved this happiness that pulsed around them like a physical presence in the room.

Nyla stretched out on top of him, relishing how wonderful his hard body felt against her. She rested her cheek on his chest, the methodic beat of his heart steady and strong in her ear. She traced her fingertips over the soft dreadlocks that fanned out across his shoulder.

"Good morning," came Aiden's husky whisper.

Nyla looked up at him, smiling at the sight of the satisfied grin curving his lips.

"Good morning," she said. "Merry Christmas Eve."

"It's Christmas Eve already?"

"Yes, it is." She placed her hands on either side of him and tried to lever herself up, but Aiden clamped down on the small of her back, anchoring her to him. His strong fingers slid down to her naked behind and squeezed.

"Where do you think you're going?" he asked.

"It's your last day in Rome. There's still a lot to see before we leave at noon."

"The only thing I plan to see is how many more times I can make you scream out my name."

Before she knew what he was doing, he flipped her over and had her on her back. His impressive morning erection sent shivers skittering along her nerve endings as he rubbed it against her inner thigh. Nyla's eyes fell shut as she spread her legs wider and welcomed him inside.

"Open your eyes," Aiden whispered against her throat.

She did as he commanded, staring into his brown eyes as his hardness penetrated her. His long dreads cascaded down like a curtain around them, brushing against her sensitive skin.

"Faster," Nyla said with a throaty moan. She locked her legs over the back of his thighs and encouraged him to pump faster. Her inner muscles constricted just seconds before everything burst into white-hot light.

Aiden collapsed on top of her, their heavy breaths mingling.

"I'll see the Pantheon on the next trip," Aiden said. "I don't want us to go anywhere else but this bed until it's time to leave. And when we get back to San Gimignano, I don't want to go anywhere but your bed for the next *week*."

"It'll be hard for me to bake bread from bed," Nyla said with a laugh. "I'm not sure Leoncini's customers will like that."

"That's too bad for Leoncini's customers."

He kissed her shoulder and tightened his hold around her. His suggestion, though unfeasible, sounded like heaven to Nyla's ears. Spending an entire week wrapped up in Aiden's arms, making up for the three years they'd missed out on… Nyla couldn't imagine anything she'd want to do more.

"When do you leave Switzerland?" she asked.

"As early as mid-January. Unless something unexpected happens and the project gets delayed."

"If there aren't any delays, how soon after the project is completed do you have to return to the States?"

"I can take a couple of weeks off," he said. "If there's a good enough reason."

She smiled up at him. "How about a week in Paris with me playing tour guide?"

"That definitely sounds like a good reason," he said. "But you know what would be even better?" He kissed her bare shoulder. "If you came back to Atlanta with me."

"Aiden—"

"You told me that you'll have to leave your job soon anyway, Nyla."

"That doesn't mean I have to leave the entire country."

"Your dream is to open your own bakery. Come back home with me and see your dream through. There's nothing stopping you from making that happen."

"I'm not ready to make that decision just yet," she said.

"You do realize you can't stay here forever, don't you? You'll eventually have to come back home. There's too much waiting for you there."

Nyla nodded. Then she reached up and pulled his head down so she could lose herself once again in his kiss, partly because she couldn't get enough of kissing him, but also to close this subject. Thinking about the difficult decisions that lay before her was bound to ruin her Christmas Eve.

They remained in bed for another hour, and Nyla quickly discovered that Aiden knew about a lot more than just computers and astronomy. He knew exactly where to touch, as if he'd been giving her body pleasure all his life.

She finally convinced him to let her leave the bed around 9:00 a.m. so she could find some breakfast. When she returned to the room, she found a shirtless Aiden standing over his open bag, dressed only in a pair of black boxer briefs. He'd tied his hair back behind his head.

Nyla bit back a needy moan at the sight of his well-toned abs and broad shoulders.

He looked up and smiled. "Tell me you've got a Sausage and Egg McMuffin in that bag."

"Sorry, I only have a couple of *cornettos*," she said.

His mouth twisted in a frown. "Do I even want to know what that is?"

She laughed. "They're sort of like a croissant filled with cream." She held up the beverage tray. "They are a breakfast must, along with a hot cappuccino."

"It's not a Sausage and Egg McMuffin, but I guess it'll have to do." He walked over and hooked an arm around her waist, pulling her to him. He pressed a kiss to her lips. "Of course, I'd be just as happy to have *you* for breakfast."

"I'm not sure that would be a very filling breakfast."

"I beg to differ," he said, his head buried against her neck.

A sharp gasp escaped Nyla's lips as he sucked on a spot just below her ear. She tilted her head back. "If only I had known three years ago that you were going to be this insatiable."

"If I had known just what I was missing, I would have told Cameron about us a lot sooner."

Nyla stiffened. Her entire body grew tense as his words registered. She leaned back and peered at him. "What did you just say?"

Aiden's brow furrowed; then he shook his head. "Forget what I just said."

He aimed for her mouth again, but Nyla averted her face. She disengaged from his hold and took several steps back.

"What do you mean that you would have told him sooner? *You're* the one who told Cameron about us? That's how he found out, because you *told* him?"

Aiden dropped his hands to his sides. "That was three years ago, Nyla. Why does it matter how he found out?"

"It matters because *I* say it matters. Now answer me, Aiden. Did you tell him?"

The air around them grew taut with tension as seconds ticked by. Without answering, Aiden walked over to his bag and yanked out several garments. He tugged a shirt over his bare chest and stepped into a pair of pants, his jerky movements stiff with anger.

With every second that passed Nyla's patience withered, until it vanished completely.

"Aiden!" she called.

"I didn't tell him, okay?" He crossed his arms over his chest and looked over at the dresser before bringing his eyes back to hers. "But I made sure that he found the evidence."

Nyla's mouth fell open as a rush of air escaped her lips. "What…what evidence? Aiden, what did you do?"

A muscle in his jaw twitched and his expression grew more rigid.

"I left a string of emails we exchanged open on my computer," he started. He took a deliberate pause, and then continued. "Cameron had a habit of checking basketball stats on the computer whenever he came over to the house, so when he called to say that he would be dropping by, I left my computer open on the kitchen counter, because I knew he would look at it. And see the emails."

Nyla wrapped her arms around her stomach, trying to ward off the feeling of being kicked. With growing horror she recalled some of the emails she and Aiden had shared, some flirtatious, others downright sexual. She had stopped their exchanges when she realized that things were getting out of hand, had deleted them all from her computer. But apparently he hadn't.

Nyla looked at him now, unable to believe the role he'd played in all the heartache she'd suffered.

"How could you?" she whispered.

"How could I not? I wasn't going to just stand by and watch you make the biggest mistake of your life."

"That was not your decision to make!"

"Do you know how miserable you would be if you were married to Cameron right now?"

"Do you know how miserable I *have* been? For the last three years I've been cut off from my family, from everything I knew and loved."

"You chose that. You're the one who left."

"Because I was humiliated! And *you* did that to me."

"I couldn't let you go through with marrying him, Nyla. It's as if you were blind to the kind of person Cameron was, but I knew, and I just couldn't let you go through with that. I loved you too much to see you do something you would regret."

She shook her head. "Don't. Don't stand there and say you loved me. Because of what you did, I was made to look like a cheating whore in front of a church full of people whose respect I worked my entire life to get. *You* did that to me."

He took a step forward, but she held her hands up, warding him off.

"I have to get out of here," she said.

"Nyla, come on."

She grabbed her bag and began to stuff her clothing and toiletries in it. "I'm going back to Tuscany. I'll catch the train."

"Nyla, don't do this."

The pain in his voice matched her own. She looked over at him, her tumultuous emotions warring with each other. Just when she thought she could finally be happy again, that she could finally freely share the love she felt for him. To have him deal her a blow like this hurt her to the core.

Her limbs grew weary with the weight of the revelations that had come to light.

"Just how did you expect me to react, Aiden? Did you think I would be grateful to find out the one person I trusted the most is the one who betrayed me? And don't tell me you did it because you loved me," she said. "You did it because you were selfish."

"You're damn right I was selfish," he said. Nyla flinched at the bite in his tone.

He closed the distance between them, his voice softer, but no less angry.

"Did you ever once consider what it would be like for me to stand there and watch you marry Cameron, knowing that you were in love with me? Did that *ever* cross your mind, Nyla? Those family dinners when I had to sit there and pretend that you were nothing but a future sister-in-law? Your damn wedding rehearsal dinner, when I had to toast to you and my brother's happy life together, just minutes after you told me that the time we'd had together was over? You ever thought about how that made me feel, Nyla?" He shook his head. "Cameron had everything. His entire life, all he did was win. He wasn't winning you."

Nyla's head jerked back. "I wasn't something to be won," she said.

Aiden ran both hands down his face. "I didn't mean it that way." He reached for her, but she spun out of his reach.

"I think you did," she said. She grabbed her bag and walked out of the room.

She didn't make it past the door to the next room before Aiden's voice stopped her.

"Nyla, please don't leave," he called. "Not again. Not like this."

She didn't turn, but she couldn't continue walking, either. Her body shivered as Aiden's arm brushed against her when he walked past her and came to stand in front of her.

"I understand that you're upset. And I guess you have a right to be."

"You guess?"

He put his hands up. "Okay, you do. I can see how it seems as if I orchestrated what happened three years ago, but I never intended to have you humiliated.

"After you told me at the rehearsal dinner that we couldn't even hang out anymore once you and Cameron were married, that just did me in. Believe it or not, even though the wedding was only two days away, I still didn't think you would go through with it. I realized then that you would. That's when I decided to take matters into my own hands."

"Which you had no right to do."

"You weren't supposed to get hurt, Nyla." He shook his head. "When Cameron didn't say anything after he used my computer that night, I thought he just brushed it off as nothing serious. I decided then that I would just have to accept it. Knowing my brother, I should have known he'd take the most dramatic route."

Nyla's throat tightened as she struggled to swallow past the hurt clogging it.

"I'm still not sorry I did it," Aiden said. Her eyes flew

to his. "You wouldn't have been happy with him, Nyla. You deserve someone better than Cameron."

"You?" she asked. "Are you any better? You made decisions about my life without bothering to ask what I wanted. You took it upon yourself to define what would make me happy."

"Yes, I did, because I know you—the real you— better than Cameron ever could. I know you well enough to know that you would never have been happy with him. You admitted yourself that you're relieved you never married him."

"This has nothing to do with Cameron," she said. "It has to do with you, going behind my back." She shook her head. "I never would have thought the person I fell in love with three years ago could ever do something like this."

"Nyla—"

"I can't stay here in Rome with you," she said. "I need to go."

"It's Christmas Eve. Do you think you're going to get a train ticket back to Tuscany this close to the holiday? Come on." He held his hands out to her, pleading. "You came here because of me. At least let me bring you home."

She knew he was right. The chances of securing a last-minute train ticket back to Tuscany were slim at best.

Ignoring his outstretched hand, she said, "I'll be waiting in the lobby." She moved past him and continued down the hallway to the elevator.

Aiden felt as if he would crawl out of his skin as he waited for Nyla to open the door to the tiny apartment above the bakery. That she'd agreed to let him come up to use the restroom and get a cup of coffee before he continued on to Zurich was more than he'd expected.

"I'll put the coffee on," she said. "I have a travel mug that you can take with you."

Aiden pinched the bridge of his nose and let out a weary breath as he sat on the sofa.

He'd tried to get her to talk this out on the three-hour drive back from Rome, but her rote response was "I can't talk about it."

Dammit.

How had he let that admission about telling Cameron slip? He thought it was something he would take to his grave. Yet, in a way, Aiden was relieved that it was finally out.

He could never regret the outcome—he'd rather have Nyla mad at him for the rest of his life than to have her stuck in a miserable marriage with his womanizing brother. But Aiden had always felt a measure of guilt over the pain and humiliation she'd suffered. The more adult approach would have been for both of them to be up front with Cameron from the very beginning, when they'd first realized that the attraction between them was turning into something more serious. All of this could have been prevented.

Aiden ran his hands down his face. After the magic of yesterday and last night, he couldn't believe they were back here again.

He jumped up from the sofa and walked around the room. He stood before the framed black-and-white photos on the wall and was nearly done in by the remorse that overwhelmed him. It could have been the two of them, walking along the streets of Paris.

Aiden tore his eyes away from the photos.

He walked over to the window that overlooked the cobblestone street. He prayed that snow would start to fall again. Maybe if it did, he could buy himself some time. Although, if the past few hours were any indication, Nyla wouldn't care if he had to drive back to Switzerland in a blizzard.

He glanced down at the computer desk next to him. The words *Peachtree Street* scribbled on a yellow legal pad caught his eye. Aiden lifted the pad, his eyes roaming over the addresses listed, along with what looked like building dimensions.

Nyla picked that moment to walk back into the room. "The coffee is ready," she said.

He held up the legal pad. "What is this?" She stared at the pad in his hand, saying nothing. "What are these addresses, Nyla? Have you been looking into places in Atlanta?"

"That's not your concern."

The blood in his veins started to quicken. "You're moving back home, aren't you?" he asked, afraid to acknowledge the excitement thrumming through his blood, but unable to stop it. "You've been planning to move back."

"I was," she said. She folded her arms across her chest and straightened her shoulders. "But I'm not sure I can anymore. It would have been hard enough being back home, but after what I learned today…"

Panic constricted the air in his lungs.

"Nyla, don't." He rushed over to her and put his hands on her shoulders. "Don't let what happened today stop you from moving back home. Look, if you can't find a way to forgive me, that's something I'll just have to live with, but I can't live with the thought of you staying out here, isolated from your family, not pursuing this dream you've wanted for so long, because of what I did."

Her chin dropped to her chest and a soft cry reached out to grab Aiden by the throat. He put two fingers underneath her chin and lifted her face. Brilliant tears streamed down her cheeks.

"I'm sorry," he said. "But it's not as if I can go back in time and change what I did. It shouldn't have any bearing on your decision to move back home."

"Would you change it if you could?" she asked.

He pulled in a deep breath and shook his head. "No," he answered honestly. "I love you too much to let you be unhappy. And I would rather take that misery on my own shoulders for the rest of my life if it means you wouldn't be unhappy."

Her body shook with the sob she cried. "I don't want you to be unhappy, either, Aiden." She looked up at him, her tear-soaked eyes so hauntingly beautiful they stole his breath. "You were right," she said in a hoarse whisper. "We've suffered enough."

Aiden didn't dare to hope, but he had to ask. "Are you saying...?"

"I'm saying that I don't want to live without you. I want to go home, and when I get there, I want to be with you."

His knees went weak with the divine joy that coursed through his body. Aiden captured the back of her head and gently pulled her to him. He kissed her with everything he had inside him. He didn't want to let her go. Ever.

"God, I love you, Nyla."

"I love you, too," she whispered. "From the very beginning, you're the one I loved."

Later, Aiden lay on his back, tracing light circles along Nyla's damp, naked back. He'd never thought such bliss was even possible, but over the past few hours, Nyla had given new meaning to the word.

She tapped him on the arm. "Look at the clock." She looked up from where she lay on top of him and smiled. "It's Christmas." She pressed a kiss to his chest. "Merry Christmas, Aiden."

He cupped her jaw in his palm and ran the pad of his thumb back and forth across her cheek. "Merry Christmas, Nyla."

Epilogue

Nyla tightened the scarf around her neck as another blast of rare near-freezing temperatures made the air coming off the fountain even colder. The New Year's Eve tourists crowded around them, all wanting to get a picture in front of the historic site.

She looked over at Aiden with a skeptical frown. "Are you sure you want to drink this? Who knows what's in this water?"

"You're the one who said that if I threw three coins into Trevi Fountain I would return here with the woman I love. If the legend states that the couple who drinks from this fountain will remain faithful and in love forever, we're drinking from this fountain."

Her brow arched in amused curiosity. "So now you believe in the legend?"

A grin slipped across Aiden's lips. He tugged her forward and kissed her behind the ear. "I'm here with the woman I love, aren't I?" he whispered.

"Well, I guess that means we shouldn't argue with the legend."

She cupped her hands under the running water. Bringing her hands to her lips, Nyla sipped and held her hands out for Aiden to do the same.

He smacked his lips and made a satisfied *ahhh* sound.

"This makes it official," he said. "You're stuck with me."

Nyla wrapped her arms around him, linking them behind his head. "There's no place I'd rather be." She pressed her lips to his. "Whether it's in Atlanta, or Tuscany, or on the moon. As long as I'm with you, I'm exactly where I want to be."

* * * * *

For all the wonderful people out there who tango with me…page after page, from one story to the next. Thank you! And for all the wonderful people who are just now hearing the music. May I have this dance?

For my biggest fan—my mom.

CHRISTMAS TANGO

Opening Act

Chapter 1

A round of thunderous applause filled the Mildred E. Bastian Theater, and as Wendy Kincaid finished her closing speech, walked offstage and disappeared behind a heavy velvet curtain, she beamed with pride.

The cozy campus theater was filled to capacity, including the VIP sections rimming the back row and the balcony, and Wendy couldn't have been more pleased. This would make the first year that she wouldn't end up owing the St. Louis Community College rental fees on the back end because she had finally accomplished her goal and filled every seat. That alone was reason enough for celebration but definitely not the only one. The other reason that she was so amped was because this year's fall dance recital had been the best one yet.

She'd been on pins and needles all evening as one group after another had taken to the stage and dazzled the audience. Thank God there hadn't been any mishaps or injuries, only loud, enthusiastic applause. And, judging by the looks on the faces of various audience members every time she'd peeked out from behind the velvet curtain, the recital had done exactly what it set out to do—celebrate the art of dance, spectacularly.

The little ones had been the cutest, with little pink tutus circling their waists and matching pink bows tied around the buns at the crowns of their heads. They ranged in age from three to five years old and she didn't think there was one in the bunch who wasn't missing at least one tooth.

They'd gone on first because they tired easily and their attention spans weren't very long, and had made an absolute mess of their carefully choreographed and endlessly rehearsed ballet number. But they'd been so precious that Wendy could hardly begrudge them the fact that they forgot almost every single step that she and her assistant had taught them. It was enough that all fourteen of them had made it through the performance without any of them stopping to pick their nose or running to the front of the stage to greet a family member in the audience.

Her teens, bless their hormone-crazed little hearts, had gone on second and by the time they were done, she had to restrain herself from running out onstage and initiating a group hug. Not only would they have never forgiven her for embarrassing them if she had, but she would've also lost major cool points for outwardly showing so much affection.

They would've returned the hug, though, no doubt about that, because each and every one of them was well aware of how far they had all come—both artistically and personally—in the short time that they'd been together.

When she first opened the doors of the Wendy Kincaid Dance Studio five years ago, she'd been twenty-eight and filled with dreams of working with celebrity musicians, choreographing music videos and concert arrangements. But just like most of the dreams that she'd secretly harbored throughout her life, that idea hadn't exactly panned out. Instead of attracting the high-profile attention she'd been hoping for, the dilapidated, single-story schoolhouse that she spent most of her savings renovating had only attracted the attention of children from a nearby housing project. They had wandered in after school, sometimes alone and sometimes in small groups, asking questions and poking around in the studios, and then they brought their parents.

Unable to deny the desperate need for local recreational outlets that provided safe alternatives to what the little ones would find in the streets *or* the pile of bills that keeping the studio open was steadily creating, Wendy had begun enrolling small classes and keeping her offerings simple. But as word of her studio spread beyond the borders of downtown St. Louis, into the outlying suburban communities, her classes had grown larger and larger, until she had to hire both a full-time and a part-time assistant and create an official class schedule. Now her studio offered ballet, tap, ballroom and a variety of contemporary dance classes, as well as weekly Zumba, yoga and Jazzercise sessions.

Her youngest student was a cherubic three-year-old and her oldest was a sassy seventy-five, and she enjoyed working with all of them.

But she especially enjoyed working with her teen girls.

Not that it was easy, because it definitely wasn't. Teenagers, especially girls, were surly and temperamental, self-conscious and unpredictable. But they were also brutally honest when they didn't know you and were afraid to trust you. She'd used that honesty and lack of trust to goad them into letting their guard down and expressing themselves physically. Trust had come later and so had the mentoring that she unwittingly found herself engaging in. Under her guidance, her girls had soared beyond their neighborhoods and their personal tragedies and each had come into her own.

And in the process, so had she.

Money and fame, Wendy had discovered years ago, weren't what was important in life. Personal growth and positively impacting people's lives were. The art of dance was. That was why she had struggled to keep the studio open all these years and why she'd scraped, scrimped and saved until the term *creative accounting* had practically become her middle name, to make sure that it stayed that way.

She'd be lying if she said she didn't sometimes still think about what her life might've been like if she had actually followed her first dream, but whenever she did, it was never more than a fleeting thought. Well, maybe a little more than a fleeting thought, but still. She was happy and what she had to offer to the world made other people happy. Wasn't that all that really mattered?

What about making yourself happy?

The thought came out of nowhere, creating a wrinkle of irritation in the center of her forehead that she used tired fingers to massage away. She was happy. Wasn't she? That was what she'd told the talent scout from the Greeley Dance Company a couple of weeks ago, wasn't it? That she was happy running her own little dance studio and being her own boss? For the most part, she meant it, too.

Except, of course, that the Greeley Dance Company was world-renowned and a little voice in the back of her mind refused to let her forget it. The scout's persistence had almost worn her down right there on the spot, but she'd made one too many snap decisions that had turned into major regrets over the years to agree to anything except thinking about their offer. Oh, but it was tempting. Greeley was offering her the one thing that she'd given up hope of ever having—a professional choreography career with a world-renowned dance company— and she wanted that so badly that it was almost like a living, breathing thing.

But at this stage in her life, was it realistic to think that she could actually have it?

Before heading home for the night, she checked in with her assistants about closing up after the recital, and then collected her jacket and purse from the dressing room she'd used as a makeshift office.

Tomorrow was Saturday and she was the only one who had early-morning classes scheduled, which meant that she needed all the rest she could get between now and then. As it was, she was half-starved, exhausted and on the verge of trading her vintage Volkswagen Beetle for a double cheeseburger and twenty uninterrupted minutes of sleep.

Wendy was still thinking about the decision that she had yet to make when she drove off the theater's parking lot a little while later, stopped at a red light and dug her cell phone out of her purse. Besides her parents, there was one other person whose opinion on the subject mattered and after the phone rang twice on the other end, he answered.

"What's up, beautiful?"

Warmed by the sound of his deep, baritone voice, she smiled. It was so contradictory to his personality. Underneath that hot-sex-on-a-platter voice, he was really more like the Sherlock Holmes of finance and everyone knew that Sherlock never did anything without first thinking it to death and then running it by Watson. There wasn't a spontaneous bone in Frazier Abernathy's body, a fact that really hadn't bothered her until the offer from the Greeley Dance Company had appeared on the horizon. *Think about the offer,* he'd said. *Make sure it's really what you want to do. You have responsibilities here, you know.*

And, of course, he was right. He was always right. She did have responsibilities here, which was why she told Frazier that she'd turned Greeley down. It was easier to lie to him than to suffer through his endless lectures about weighing pros and cons. She didn't want to weigh pros and cons. For once, she just wanted to jump before looking both ways and see what happened. Was that too much to ask?

"I figured you were moping around because you were in meetings all evening," she said, pushing aside her thoughts and focusing on traffic. The Five Guys Burgers take-out sign flashing up ahead caught her attention and her stomach growled ferociously. She gave in to it and activated the turning signal. "So I thought I'd call and let you know that I'm coming over, and bringing double cheeseburgers and milk shakes with me. What do you want on your burger?"

Frazier Abernathy couldn't believe what he was seeing. Just to be sure that his eyes weren't playing tricks on him, he checked and then double-checked the figures that his computer had come up with. All of the totals looked correct, but computers couldn't always be trusted. Could they?

Telling himself that they couldn't and that there was at least a slight chance that there was a miscalculation somewhere on the page, he reached across his desk and dragged an electronic adding machine toward him. His fingers flew over the keys and the longer he punched in numbers, the deeper the frown on his face became. Finally, he gave up, tossed the spreadsheet aside and relaxed back in his chair.

When was that woman going to learn?

Probably never, he thought as he yanked the knot in his tie loose and blew out a strong breath. For as long as he and Wendy Kincaid had been best friends, which was something like twenty-five years now, she'd always been too concerned with whatever was going on up there in the clouds, where her head was most of the time, to be bothered with what was happening down here on earth, where everyone else's were.

Dumping the bulk of her savings into an old, broken-down schoolhouse was the worst decision she could've possibly made and Frazier hadn't wasted any time telling her that five years ago. As her financial adviser, he would've been remiss in his duties if he hadn't sufficiently warned her and, as her best friend, he cared enough about her not to want her to throw good money after bad. But that was exactly what she'd done and the spreadsheet on his desk proved it yet again.

The Wendy Kincaid Dance Studio was just barely holding on by a thread and, despite every piece of advice that he'd given her to the contrary, Wendy was still ridiculously absentminded when it came to keeping track of expenditures and terrible at following through with collecting what he felt were already absurdly low student tuition fees.

For the past four years, she'd barely turned a profit, narrowly missing sliding over into the red by *this much*. This year, the situation was even worse.

The only bright side was the fact that the studio had recently been granted nonprofit status by the government, which meant that it could now receive funding from grants and donations to help with the cost of upgrading the facilities, and recruiting and maintaining staff. Maybe somewhere along the way he could talk Wendy into hiring a bookkeeper, both for her own good and, as her financial adviser, his sanity.

Suddenly restless, Frazier got up from his desk and went to stand at the window in his twentieth-floor office. The panoramic view of the downtown St. Louis skyline was beautiful at night, especially now that the Arch had been refurbished and lighting had been added for effect, and work on the Jefferson National Expansion Memorial had been completed.

To the east of his office building was Kiener Plaza and on any given day or night he could look down on hundreds of people taking part in some sort of local outdoor event.

And to the west was the Old Courthouse, made famous by Dred and Harriet Scott, slaves who had set a precedent when they petitioned the court for freedom from slavery, and also by the slave auctions that were once held on the steps out front.

During the day, the French colonial and early-American architecture that dominated the downtown area was nice to study and appreciate, but it came alive at night, thanks to strategic lighting and a little bit of imagination. That was what he'd always liked about downtown St. Louis—the constant activity and the mix of old and new. And it was why, after being away from his home city for nearly a decade, it was the only area that he would consider living in when he decided to come back.

Whether or not he was staying, however, was still up in the air.

As if Frazier had conjured it, an image of Wendy rose in his mind and lingered there. He'd dated many women through the years and some of them he had cared for deeply. But he'd never really been in love, not even when he stood before a justice of the peace two days after high-school graduation and married Monica Miller, his high-school sweetheart.

Wait, that wasn't quite right.

The truth was that he'd never really been in love with a woman who *wasn't* Wendy Kincaid. His marriage had only lasted eleven months, but by then he'd already been quietly in love with Wendy for years.

On some level he'd probably always been in love with her, now that he was thinking about it. Besides the fact that she was smart and funny and outgoing, she was also the most exquisite-looking woman he had ever seen. Her milk-chocolate skin was like silk and she moved inside of it so gracefully that it was like watching water flow.

She'd been dancing since she was three and after

thirty years of dedication to her craft, her five-foot-ten-inch frame was lithe and almost boyish, which he supposed was par for the course. But as a slightly lopsided, devilish grin curved his lips, he thanked God that there were exceptions to every rule and in Wendy's case, the exceptions were her toned, powerful legs and her perfectly rounded, plump butt. When he was a teenager, he wondered what those legs would feel like in his hands, but now he was a man and he intended to find out what they felt like wrapped around his neck.

One day.

If anyone knew him from the inside out, it was Wendy. They'd been best friends forever and there were very few secrets between them. How he had managed to keep his feelings for her hidden for this long was anybody's guess, but based on everything he'd said and done over the past six months alone, he was 99 percent sure that, if his investment firm suddenly went south, he could definitely pursue a successful career in acting.

The other 1 percent was leaning toward feeling guilty about being so damn good at deceiving her, but feeling a little bit guilty was about as good as it was going to get. He'd learned a long time ago that good things didn't always come to those who waited. Sometimes they just waited and waited and waited and he wasn't that damn patient anymore.

His plans to move back to St. Louis from Chicago were already underway when Frazier had come to the conclusion that he'd waited long enough.

At thirty-five, and after years of first working on Wall Street and then for a prestigious brokerage house in Chicago, he was very well established in financial circles. His new brokerage firm, Abernathy Financial, was doing well enough that it was no longer a question of *if* he would hire an associate, but *when*.

They were finally both in the same city again, at the same time. If he didn't make his move soon, some other man would and that was simply not an option.

It couldn't be.

If not another man, then something else would get in the way, something like a damn job offer that could put the kind of gleam in her eye that he couldn't *and* plant them on opposite ends of the country. Again. That wasn't an option, either, at least not until everything was out in the open.

Turning away from the window, Frazier went back to his desk and the mound of paperwork waiting there for him. He spotted Wendy's spreadsheet on top of the pile and shook his head. Would she ever learn? Probably not. But they were perfect for each other. He just hoped she felt the same way when he finally told her the truth about who and what he was.

He was packing his briefcase when his cell phone rang. Knowing that it was Wendy, he pressed a button to put her on speakerphone and kept packing. "What's up, beautiful?" He listened to her talk about double cheeseburgers, heard his stomach growl in response and said, "Did you get a video of the recital yet?"

"Got it in my purse," she chirped. "It's an unedited, rough draft, but it'll serve the purpose."

"Meet me at my place," Frazier said. "We'll watch it while we eat."

Chapter 2

Saturdays at the studio were Wendy's busiest days. That was when most of the youth classes were in session and she taught over half of them herself. Not only was it physically taxing to transition throughout the day from ballet with teens to contemporary jazz with middle-aged adults to hip-hop fusion with college students and back to ballet again, this time with small children, but arranging and memorizing the choreography for each class was also challenging.

Usually, she enjoyed the hectic pace and the day flew by in a flurry of activity, but today she was a little off her game and she had been since before lunch. Thankfully, the day was almost done and relaxation was on the horizon.

She glanced out the window as she walked slowly down the length of the barre, critically eyeing the students lined up there. The intricately carved knob-handle wooden cane in her left hand tapped against the hardwood floor with every step she took.

Whenever she was forced to use it, her younger students teased her about getting old and her older students thought she was channeling a character from an '80s television show. But the truth was really somewhere in between. Fluffy white clouds were in the sky beyond the window, the sun was shining brightly, and the fall air was extra brisk today. But, according to the dull, persistent throbbing in and around her left knee, rain was on the way.

"First position," she called out, coming to a stop at the end of the line. She aimed the pointed end of her stick at the floor directly in front of a student's feet and tapped two times. The five-year-old girl promptly adjusted her heels so that they were correctly positioned. "Very good, Charlotte," she murmured to the girl. To the class as a whole, she said, "Second position."

There were thirteen students in her beginners' ballet class and she made sure to visit with each one of them as she slowly retraced her steps. In the floor-to-ceiling mirror on the wall in front of them, they watched her watch them and, one by one, met her eyes in the mirror when it was their turn.

"Excellent posture, Samantha," she remarked before moving on down the line.

Determined to ignore the nagging ache, Wendy took the adorable group of three- to five-year-olds through the five beginning positions of ballet over and over, alternately correcting posture and form, and imparting words of praise. She doubted the children noticed that she was leaning on her walking stick more and more as the minutes passed. But they would definitely notice if she suddenly started frowning at them, so she kept her face carefully neutral until it was either time to smile and praise or to tap her stick and correct.

Doctors had warned her years ago about putting too much pressure to perform on her left leg, for fear of aggravating the already injured joints, and Wendy had taken the advice just as seriously back then as she did today.

After years of physical therapy and strength training, her leg was in the best possible shape that it could be in, under the circumstances. A twelve-hour surgery had left her with a metal rod in her calf and scars that she'd have for the rest of her life, but she was grateful that she could still stand on her own two feet in the aftermath. She didn't mind having to lean on a walking stick every now and again. But she could've done without the superpower that she'd been left with—the ability to predict the weather, based on sporadic bouts of pain.

They were a constant reminder that every stupid decision she'd ever made in life had led her to the spot where she was standing right now. The stupidest of all was the decision to hop in a car with her cousin the night of her college graduation and tag along on a drag race through downtown St. Louis, she thought as she turned and prepared to make the trip down the line again. That one, more than any of the others, had shaped her life in ways that she'd never imagined, starting with completely ending her hopes of ever dancing on Broadway *and* ending with almost killing her cousin.

"Third position. Watch your posture, Melanie." Wendy couldn't help cracking a smile when Melanie flashed her a snaggletoothed grin. She winked before moving on to guide the next student's arms to the correct position.

"Fourth position. And…fifth position and hold. Very good," she said, stepping back to view the line as a whole and appreciating the effort she saw there. "Very good, ladies. Okay, that's it for today. I'll see you all next week, same time, same place. Class dismissed."

The noise level in the room went from zero to ten in just a few seconds, as students scattered in different directions to collect their belongings and file out of the room. Wendy waved at them until the last little person was out of sight and then, suddenly fatigued, she headed down the hallway in the opposite direction, toward the steps and her lower-level office.

"Wendy, wait up."

She looked back over her shoulder and saw a plump, neon-red-haired woman with black lipstick and black fingernails power-walking toward her. She stopped and waited for Rachel, her part-time receptionist, to catch up to her. "Hey, Rach, what's up?" Her gaze fell on the large envelope in Rachel's hand and turned wary. "Do I even want to know what that is?"

"I think you might," Rachel said, her Skechers skidding to a stop less than a foot away from Wendy. "A courier just delivered it for you. He wanted to give it to you personally, but you know I don't like to let strangers loose in the building. I promised him I'd put it directly in your hands, so here you are."

Wendy was reluctant to take it, but what choice did she have? Cautiously, she held it up to her ear and shook it to see if it rattled. When it didn't, she shrugged and ran a finger underneath the sealed flap, tearing it open neatly. "I have no idea what it could be, but thanks for bringing it to me."

"You bet," Rachel said, turning and power-walking back the way she'd come. "I'd better get to my desk before the students start answering my phone and spinning around in my chair," she called out to Wendy over her shoulder. "I hate it when they do that."

"Be nice," Wendy responded. Rachel's reply was a noncommittal flap of her hand just before she turned a corner and disappeared from sight.

In her office, Wendy propped her walking stick in the corner behind her desk, then dropped into her chair and upended the envelope on the desktop. A single five-by-seven card fell out.

She picked it up with one hand and dug around in a desk drawer with the other. When she found a bottle of ibuprofen, she popped it open with her thumb, shook out two, and washed them down with water from a bottle that she'd left on her desk yesterday or possibly the day before.

Then she read:

By now I know you're wondering who I am. Will you join me for an evening of dinner and conversation, and find out?
Wednesday at 8 p.m.
Tony's Place on the Landing.
Wear a red rose in your hair and I'll find you.
Meet you there?

At first, the idea of having a secret admirer scared the hell out of her. She'd seen too many television shows where women were stalked and terrorized, and that definitely wasn't an experience she wanted to gain firsthand knowledge of. She'd waited and waited for signs of danger, something tangible to pass on to the police, but they never materialized.

As far as she knew, there was no one lurking around her studio or following her home. There were no prank calls and nothing in her life was any more out of order than it always was. She couldn't quite explain it, but somehow, some way, she knew that she wasn't really the target of some sinister plot. Whoever her secret admirer was, he was very low-key and seemingly harmless, or at least as harmless as any secret admirer could be. If not, then she was just a sentimental fool.

Over the past six months, there were several deliveries to the studio, though none of the others had ever been delivered by special messenger.

Once, there was a postcard from the 1920s, with a picture of a prima ballerina *en pointe* on the front and a short note written by someone named Paolo to a woman named Annalise on the back.

It was old, and both the handwriting and the foreign postmarks on it were badly worn, but it was exactly the sort of thing that she would've stumbled upon at a yard sale or an antiques shop and purchased for herself, for no other reason than the fact that it was old-fashioned and incredibly romantic.

Another time, a vintage music box arrived. It was just like the one she'd had when she was a little girl, with rose-colored felt lining on the inside and a plastic ballerina that popped up when you opened the lid. If you wound it up, it struggled through "Love Is a Many Splendored Thing," while the little ballerina twirled 'round and 'round.

Most of the color and detail had worn off the little ballerina and it was pretty beat-up on the outside, but those signs of life made her love it even more.

And just last month she'd received a dog-eared Broadway playbill for *Les Misérables*. It was obvious that it had passed through many hands before landing in hers and she'd wondered about it. Had he gone to the play himself and then brought the playbill back for her?

She'd had it a week before she thought to open it and discover that it had been autographed by the entire cast and crew.

Now he was inviting her to dinner. He wanted to meet face-to-face, wanted her to know, finally, who he was. Was that a good thing or a bad thing? Was he interested in being friends or did he have something more sinister in mind?

Frazier would probably think she'd lost her mind if she showed him the invitation and told him that she was thinking of accepting.

She could picture him, his long legs pacing back and forth, and his glasses riding on the bridge of his nose as he glowered at her.

His hazel eyes would bore into hers every time he stopped pacing long enough to emphasize what he felt was a very important point and, every few minutes or so, he'd run his palm over his close-cut hair and then let his wide shoulders slouch in exasperation. He'd shake his head at her. Roll his eyes toward the ceiling. Go on and on and on, until she finally begged him to please just shut up. And then the argument would begin in earnest, because he hated it when she told him to shut up.

Just thinking about it exhausted Wendy. There was no way she could share this part of her life with Frazier.

If ever there was anything that had to be kept a secret from him, this was it.

How could she make him understand something that she didn't really understand herself?

He'd been her best friend for most of her life and she was crazy about him. Probably crazier about him than she should've been, but there it was. None of the men she'd ever dated had ever made her feel the way Frazier made her feel. He was gentle and kind, funny when he wanted to be, and so serious and intellectual sometimes that he made her head hurt.

She'd never understood his love of formulas and equations, his electronic date books and his annoying habit of always being five minutes early while she was always five minutes late.

He'd worn pocket protectors and carried an attaché case every day of junior high and high school, even though the other kids thought he was a little strange, and he was accepted to Stanford on early admission.

He would've been a nerd if it wasn't for the fact that he was the best varsity point guard in the entire state for two years straight and, once he got past his awkward and gangly junior-high days, he put the *F* in fine. Nothing about his caramel skin, dimpled chin and secretive smile was funny. But watching girls fall all over themselves to get next to him was. For a while, anyway.

She'd been in love with Frazier for more years than she cared to count and, unfortunately, every man she'd ever dated had been compared to him and found to be lacking something important.

So now here she was, thirty-three years old and still single, and with no prospects on the horizon. This secret admirer, whoever the hell he was, wasn't exactly a prospect but he managed to do something that, until now, only Frazier had been able to do—touch her. He hadn't just been sending her random tokens of affection, he'd sent her things that meant something to her, that made her feel like she was special. The way Frazier made her feel.

If this secret admirer of hers was anything like Frazier, anything at all, then she wanted to meet him. So, no, she wasn't going to tell Frazier about him, not until she found out if he was really as much like Frazier as she thought he might be...as she *hoped* he might be.

Chapter 3

"Wendy Elizabeth Kincaid, have you lost your mind?"

"No, Mom. I haven't lost my mind." Wendy glanced at the bedside speakerphone on her way over to the walk-in closet.

When her mother's number popped up on the caller ID a few minutes ago, she hadn't seen the harm in chatting with her while she finished getting dressed. Now she wished she'd let the call go to voice mail and called her mother back later tonight. Her nerves were frazzled enough as it was.

Selena Kincaid was annoyed, very annoyed, if the shrill tone of her voice was any indication. It was exactly the reaction Wendy was expecting, which was why she'd waited until the last possible minute to mention the possibility of a blind date to her mother. "It's just something I'm thinking about. I haven't made any decisions yet."

After a few seconds of internal debate, she chose a pair of jewel-dusted black pumps from a shelf inside the closet, stepped into them and then walked them over to the floor-length mirror across the room to check out her reflection.

The little black dress that she'd decided to wear tonight was probably a little too dressy for a blind date, but she wanted to at least look good on the outside, even if she was a bundle of nerves on the inside. It was a sleeveless, fitted little thing with a slightly flared, handkerchief hem that skimmed the tops of her knees and a plunging V neckline that eliminated the possibility of wearing a bra underneath. It was the one thing she'd bought for herself during her trip to New Mexico last year and, until tonight, she hadn't had the nerve to wear it.

Right now, though, her self-confidence was in short supply and the dress was just what she needed to kick it into overdrive.

"Well, aren't you afraid of what could happen if you decide to go through with it?" Selena wanted to know. "I mean, what if this person is a serial killer who preys on desperate women?"

Wendy paused in the midst of fastening a diamond pendant around her neck and rolled her eyes to the ceiling. Why did she even bother trying to have these kinds of conversations with her mother? They never ended well, mainly because Selena was from the old school. Anything other than being courted Rhett Butler–style by a man was simply unacceptable. Bringing up the subject had been a long shot at best, but at least now she could say she'd tried.

"Tell you what, Mom," Wendy said as she put on matching diamond studs. "If I decide to go—and that's a big *if*—I'll hire a bodyguard to go with me. Would that make you feel more comfortable?"

"I would feel more comfortable if you'd put the whole thing out of your mind. This isn't a joking matter, Wendy."

"I know it's not, Mom. I'm sorry." She heard a muffled voice in the background and sent up a silent thank-you for the much-needed distraction, then seized the opportunity before it could get away. "Is that Daddy?"

"Yes, that's him." Selena's voice went from shrill to long-suffering. "He's been grumbling about dinner not being ready for the past half hour, so I guess I'd better go and finish up before he passes out. Do you want me to put him on before I go?"

Wendy looked up from double-checking the contents of her beaded clutch and smiled, even though neither of her parents could see her. She always enjoyed chatting with her daddy and if she wasn't already on the verge of running late, she would've been happy to talk his ears off. But she *was* running late and she didn't want to risk it. "Tell him I love him and I'll call him tomorrow morning, okay, Mom? I'm kind of in the middle of something right now and I want to get it done and over with while it's fresh on my mind."

"Will do, sweetie, and don't worry. I won't bother upsetting your father with this blind date nonsense. But we aren't done talking about it, Wendy Elizabeth," Selena warned. "We are nowhere *near* done talking about it. Do you hear me?"

Wendy fastened a delicate gold bracelet around her wrist and spritzed on her favorite cologne. "Yes, Mom, I hear you."

"I love you."

"Love you, too. Bye, Mom."

After disconnecting the call, Wendy took one last twirl in front of the mirror. Satisfied that she was as ready as she'd ever be, she picked up her clutch and wrap from the foot of her bed, and headed out.

She pulled up in front of Tony's Place a few minutes before eight and, after turning her beloved Beetle over to a white-jacketed valet, entered the supper club's dimly lit reception area. It took a moment for her eyes to adjust and when they did, she looked around the spacious area curiously, noting the teal-blue walls, glossy hardwood floor and recessed lighting.

Oil paintings in ornate frames adorned the walls and plush seating arrangements invited guests to sit back and relax while they waited to be seated in the main dining room. There was a short line at the coat check counter and a formally dressed hostess manned the reservations desk.

Unsure of what her next move should be, Wendy approached the reservations desk. She had pulled her hair up into a sleek chignon and tucked a red rose at the side of the loose bun, but so far no one had approached her. There were several men in the room, but each one of them appeared to be part of a couple, even though they were giving her sideways looks that lingered a little too long. Maybe the hostess could give her some direction or, if nothing else, tell her where she could get a stiff drink to calm her jittery nerves.

"Wendy."

She glanced up and froze. "Frazier?" Relieved to see a friendly face, she smiled and moved closer to him. "What are you doing here? You didn't tell me you had a date tonight."

"Hey," he said, spreading his arms and smiling down at her. "I don't tell you everything, you know."

"Yes, Frazier, you do, so stop it." She leaned sideways to see around him and then straightened with a cocked brow. "Where is she? Do I get to meet her?"

It didn't occur to her to move away when he reached out and touched her hair. But she did step away when she saw the red rose between his fingers. He took it to his nose and inhaled its aroma, including the Dior cologne that she'd accidentally spritzed on it before sticking it in her hair.

"Dior," he murmured, catching her eyes again. "Your signature scent."

She looked from his face to the rose and back again. "Y-you bought me my very first bottle years ago, for my—" He was wearing a black suit—expertly tailored, as usual—but in place of a crisp shirt, power tie and polished wing tips, he wore a black crewneck sweater and trendy suede loafers. Gray.

"Birthday," he cut in smoothly. "I bought it for you for your birthday because I thought it was very feminine and very sexy. Just like you. You look wonderful, by the way."

"Frazier, what…" It seemed like the thing to ask— *what*.

"I'm glad you came, Wendy," he murmured. "Frankly, I wasn't sure if you would."

"I'm, uh, a little…" She fanned herself delicately, absently, her gaze darting around the crowded room as if she was waiting for her cue to run, and then rested the hand on her chest.

"I'm a little confused, Frazier. I'm supposed to be meeting someone here and…"

But suddenly, she knew.

It all made sense now. The perfect gifts, the feeling that her secret admirer somehow knew her, all of it. She understood it now. But all the lying that he'd been doing and for all this time—she didn't understand that and she didn't think she ever would. Her eyes drifted closed for a moment and then opened on his face.

She sighed. "It was you, wasn't it?"

He looked thoughtful, slightly regretful. "Wendy..."

"Why wouldn't you just tell me what you were thinking, Frazier? Why would you play a cruel trick like this on me?"

"I thought—"

"You thought—" She heard herself, the hysterical notes in her voice and the jarring volume, and snapped her mouth shut so she could regroup. People were staring and she hated scenes. She looked around nervously and cleared her throat, spoke her next words softly and carefully. "You thought catching me off guard and embarrassing me, tricking me was the right thing to do? Oh, my God, you never really knew me at all, did you?"

He reached for her and she flinched, jumping away from his touch so violently that she bumped into a man standing near her and made him spill the drink in his hand. Tears stood in her eyes when she turned around and saw him wiping at the stain that she caused. "I— I'm so sorry. I didn't mean to—" She saw Frazier in her peripheral vision, reaching for her. "No, Frazier! Don't touch me."

"Why don't we go somewhere and talk," Frazier suggested as he retracted his hand. "Somewhere we can be alone."

"Talk about what? How you've been lying to me for months? Laughing at me behind my back?"

"It wasn't like that," he hissed. "It's never been like that between us and you know it."

If she had ever been more embarrassed in her entire life, she couldn't recall when. People were staring at them and a few were whispering behind their hands but, after sucking in a deep breath and letting it out in one long *whoosh,* she decided that she didn't really care what they were thinking and saying.

The one person whose thoughts and words she did care about was standing in front of her, and she didn't know where to begin making sense of what was happening between them. Whatever it was, the last thing she wanted was an audience while she tried to figure it out.

"You know what? I have to go."

"Wendy."

"No, Frazier. Talk is what we should've done in the first place, before you decided to do all this. It's too late for that now. I'm leaving." She put up a hand to stop him when he would've followed her to the door. "No. Please don't. Please…"

Running in four-inch heels, Wendy discovered a few seconds later, was much easier than she thought it would be.

He called her. She didn't answer, so he left a message. And then he called her again. After the tenth call with no answer, Frazier stopped calling and started worrying. What if she was hurt? What if she'd been in an accident? What the hell had he been thinking, surprising her like that?

He took a shower and thought about it. Okay, so obviously Wendy didn't feel the same way he did. Now what? Judging by the look on her face when she figured out what was happening, he owed her one hell of an apology, but damn if he knew where to begin giving it. Should he apologize for being in love with her? For wanting to be with her?

He stepped out of the shower, slung a towel around his hips, and answered his own questions with a resounding *no*. Hell, no.

He was worried, though. Wendy wasn't the world's greatest driver under the best circumstances. Add in the fact that she was crying and upset, and visions of ten-car pileups suddenly started dancing around in his head. Of all the possible scenarios that he'd entertained when he decided to go through with his plan, this was definitely not one of them.

Neither was warming up leftovers in the microwave and eating dinner alone in front of the television, he thought as he sat down on the couch with a plate of leftover meat loaf and sautéed green beans, a cold beer and the remote control. But that was exactly what he was doing.

He found a *CSI* marathon on cable and sat back, wondering where the hell Wendy was and if she planned to ever speak to him again.

Frazier didn't know he'd fallen asleep until the sound of the television switching off woke him up. He bolted up from his sprawl on one end of the couch into a sitting position, looking around wildly and thinking about the revolver that was in a lockbox at the top of his bedroom closet.

When he saw Wendy standing with her back to the big screen and her finger on the power button, a relieved breath shot out of his mouth, with a quick expletive right behind it.

He cleared his throat. "You realize that now I'm going to have to reprogram the damn remote, don't you?"

"I was looking at the phone every time you called," Wendy told him. Their gazes locked and she sucked in a deep breath. "A part of me wanted to answer, but another part of me was afraid to."

Ready to have it out and get it over with, he scrubbed a hand across his face. "Look, Wendy, I'm sorry if I—"

"Ask me why I was afraid," she cut in softly.

He froze, peering at her through his fingers. "What?"

"Ask me why I was afraid, Frazier."

He ran a hand around his neck and watched her watch him. Earlier, he had only glanced at her dress, long enough to notice that she looked great in it, so now he helped himself to a more leisurely inspection. It fit her like a glove, showing just enough leg to make her legs look like they went on forever and her waist no more than a whisper. The deep V between her breasts revealed smooth, dark skin that he suddenly wanted to taste, and the imprint of her nipples through the material made his mouth water. Underneath the towel around his waist, his penis stirred. "Okay," he said, staring at her. "Why were you afraid?"

"I was afraid because just the other day I was thinking about you and wanting him to be you. Then tonight, before I left to meet him, I thought about you again and hoped it was you. And then when I got to the restaurant and it *was* you, I didn't know what to do. I've had feelings for you for years, Frazier, and now to suddenly find out that you have feelings for me, too? What was I supposed to do with that?" He understood that it was a rhetorical question and didn't offer a response. "You picked the absolute worst time and place to do something like that and, for a while, I was really angry with you. I was driving around, fantasizing about the many ways that I could kill you, and the next thing I knew, I was just fantasizing about you."

So aroused that he could hardly think straight, Frazier cracked a smile. "Do you want me to ask you about the details of your fantasy?"

"My panties got wet—that's the most important detail—because I couldn't stop thinking about what making love to you would be like." Her words were punctuated by the sharp breath he sucked in, but she'd said too much to stop now. "So I turned my car around and came here to find out." She reached behind her and eased the zipper down, and, as soon as it was low enough, shrugged out of her dress until the top half fell down around her waist.

The sight of her naked breasts was such a jolt to his system that his hips bucked in response and he felt his groin flood with heat. When he slowly started rising, the towel slid away and his eyes narrowed on his target.

Wendy walked over to where he sat on the couch and stared down at him with a question in her eyes.

"You came all the way over here to use me for sex? That's..." He trailed off as the rest of the zipper was lowered and she stepped out of the dress completely.

The tiny jewel in her navel caught his eye because it was sparkly and the pink stone matched her thong, and he leaned forward to flick his tongue across it. "Are you sure this is what you want, Wendy?"

Intrigued, he hooked a finger in the strap of her thong, eased the lace aside, and tipped his head to lovingly gaze at the tip of her clitoris peeking from between her womanly mound. He hoped she enjoyed receiving kisses there as much as he was going to enjoy giving them to her.

"What I want, Frazier, is to finally meet my secret admirer, so why don't you hurry up and introduce yourself to me?"

Before she could prepare herself, he sank down to his knees and parted Wendy's clean-shaven lips with nothing but his stiff, extended tongue.

She gasped and her knees buckled, but he caught her, one hand gripping a butt cheek and the other gently guiding her leg over his shoulder. A groan rumbled deep in his throat when she gripped the back of his head and began rocking her hips in time with his tongue's rhythm. Her nub was a juicy little pearl, made for worship, and he tongue-kissed it lavishly, stroking it from all angles as his head rotated 'round and 'round between her thighs, and her high-pitched sighs filled the air.

"Yeeeees," she crooned, moving against his tongue and a throaty moan curling out of her mouth. Her right hand joined the left one on his head, rubbing it gently. "Yes, Frazier, just like that. Don't stop. Oh, God, I'm coming." Her stomach caved in at the same time that her thighs started trembling. Her moans turned into short, sharp bursts that went on and on, even after he had freed her and slid back onto the couch.

He was waiting for her when she straddled his lap. His cock was standing straight up and, drenched from the inside out, she sat herself down on it in one smooth motion. His head rocked back on his neck and his eyes went to half-mast as he felt her stretching to accommodate him.

* * *

Oh, my God was all Wendy could think. Frazier's flesh was impossibly hard and sizzling hot inside of her.

And incredibly huge.

She had taken him in as far as her body would allow and she still didn't have all of him. She felt his veins throbbing against her walls, setting off delicious little shock waves that took over her system, paralyzing her with pleasure.

He was slowly rotating his hips, stretching her around him and unwittingly challenging the muscles in her thighs to keep her steady. They lost the battle when his hips began bucking up and down, easing his hard, pulsing cock in and out of her in a steady rhythm. Pushing a little bit deeper into her with each stroke until she was as accustomed to his size as she could get without giving in to the explosion on the horizon.

She didn't think she'd ever felt anything so rapturous in her life. Her head lolled on her neck, her mouth fell open and her eyes drifted closed. A fluttery gasp slipped out of her mouth.

She sobbed when his mouth closed over her nipple and his tongue began lapping at it slowly. Heat swept through her from head to toe as his hands slid up her thighs, took a detour around to her butt cheeks and filled themselves. He guided their mutual strokes, bouncing her up and down on his thick length while he feasted on her breasts, one after the other, over and over.

She couldn't stop her hands from roaming everywhere they could reach, whispering over and across his head one second and reaching behind her to grip his thighs the next. The sounds coming out of her mouth sounded foreign to her own ears, like primal cries for mercy. Mingled with the deep bursts of sound coming out of Frazier's mouth, it was music to her ears.

He ran a hand up through her hair and destroyed her chignon. Cupped the back of her head, pulled her face down to his and fed her his tongue. He kissed her masterfully, stretching her mouth wide for his tongue and helping himself to hers greedily. He tongued Wendy so deeply that she had to go still and focus all her attention on meeting the demands of his mouth.

He went still, too, and guided the kiss to a gentle place, a place where his long fingers massaged her scalp, the pace of their tongues slowed and they sighed into each other's mouths.

Her second orgasm rolled over her from the pads of her feet to her scalp, tingling everywhere that it spread, making her walls pulse rhythmically, and stealing her breath. She broke the kiss only because she was drowning and she wanted every ounce of her consciousness to experience it.

"Shit," Frazier hissed a few seconds later, just before dissolving into a trance of intense vibrations.

He got chilly in the early-morning hours and woke up in search of the covers. Wendy was lying less than a foot away, lying on her stomach, staring at him when he opened his eyes.

They had stumbled into his bedroom a couple of hours before and collapsed naked on top of the bed. His eyes roamed over the smooth line of her back and butt in lazy appreciation, then drifted back to hers and stayed there.

"I don't know how this can work between us," she whispered, searching his eyes.

"I don't know how it can't work," he whispered back. He'd never been more in love with her than he was at that moment. "I'm in love with you, Wendy, and I have been for a long time."

She gasped. "Really? I'm in love with you, too."

He gave her a lopsided smile and then mimicked her high-pitched, breathless tone when he said, "Really?"

She laughed. "Yes."

"So what are we going to do?"

"I was hoping you knew." She uncurled an arm from underneath her head and reached out to play with the trail of dark hair snaking down his abdomen. His body instantly reacted to her touch. "It feels a little strange."

"Yeah, it does." He sucked in a sharp breath as he watched her long, delicate fingers slowly wrap around his thickness. Just like that, he was fully erect. "So we take it slow."

"Yes, but do I get to keep this?" Wendy asked, squeezing him gently.

"For as long as you want, but you have to take the rest of me with it," he murmured as he slid across the bed and stretched out on top of her. His chest hugged her back and his erection lay between her butt cheeks. He pressed soft kisses to the side of her face and wet, openmouthed ones to the ball of her shoulder.

She shifted, granting him access to her treasure, and he wasted no time accepting. "For as long as you want," he whispered again, into her ear as he slowly filled her.

Intermission

Chapter 4

The next two weeks passed in a blur of activity. The last serious relationship that Wendy had been involved in was over two years ago and even then it was more like a cross between keeping-options-open and semiserious. She'd forgotten how time-consuming relationships could be. If she wasn't at the studio teaching classes, then she was with Frazier and, when they were together, the last thing on her mind was her never-ending to-do list.

Not that she was falling behind in her work, because that was hardly the case. Thanks to two very capable assistants and a receptionist who was worth her weight in gold, the Wendy Kincaid Dance Studio ran like a well-oiled machine.

Most of the time, anyway.

Just last weekend, when she needed someone to cover her Saturday classes so that she and Frazier could go away for a romantic three-day weekend, as always, the ladies had her back. She'd been on pins and needles the entire time, wondering if the studio was still standing and if the ladies were okay, but her cell phone hadn't rung once. Unless, of course, Wendy counted the time Patricia, her part-time assistant, called to get the name and contact information for the Inn at Glenstrae, the B&B where Wendy and Frazier were staying, for her sister and brother-in-law. But Wendy didn't count that.

If anything, she could afford to take more time off if she wanted to, which, while very unlikely, was still nice to know. She loved her work too much to be away from it *or* her studio for too long. Dancing was the one drug she had ever tried and the only one she'd ever been addicted to. Two weeks of only coming and going to the studio during business hours was starting to take its toll. She hadn't had a minute to herself in all that time and it was a strange feeling to suffer from withdrawal pangs. It was either dance or go crazy, and dance was the only logical choice.

Sunday was the one day of the week that the studio was closed and Wendy could dance in complete privacy. After changing and warming up at the barre, she slipped a mixtape CD into the boom box and went to the middle of the hardwood floor. There, she took a deep breath and got in position. A moment later she was combining elements of contemporary, ballet and hip-hop dance to the rhythm of a hip-hop-infused jazz song, and losing herself in the music.

It felt great, like coming home to a warm welcome after being away on a long journey. She moved effortlessly from one song to the next, being careful to balance the weight she put on her left knee whenever her feet left the floor, and smiling when she felt perspiration beading on her scalp and forehead.

An hour into it, her muscles were screaming with joy and her mind was clearer than it had been in days. She needed to think and this was when, where and how she did it best.

She loved spending time with Frazier and discovering the differences between *best friend* Frazier and *the greatest sex she'd ever had* Frazier, who was sexy and exciting. But it would be a toss-up if she ever had to choose between him and her first love—dance. With every day that passed, though, it looked like that was ultimately what she was going to have to do.

The scout from the Greeley Dance Company was still interested in recruiting her as a choreographer and she wouldn't be able to put off giving him an answer for much longer.

In the brief silence between songs, her cell phone rang but answering it didn't even cross her mind. The way her life was working these days, it was either Frazier on the other end or the scout, and she wasn't ready to deal with either one just yet.

The next song began and she took her cue instead.

It snowed four inches on Thanksgiving Day. Just enough, Wendy thought as her Beetle crawled along with the bumper-to-bumper traffic on I-40, to cover the landscape with a blanket of blinding whiteness, but not quite enough to justify staying inside to avoid it.

Not that she could've gotten away with that anyway, because her mother never would've stood for her missing the family dinner, not even for a foot of snow. Holidays in the Kincaid house were serious business—formal affairs that normally began promptly at 3:00 p.m. and hardly ever a minute later, and her presence was just as required as the turkey's was.

She breathed a sigh of relief when she finally reached the exit she needed and got off the interstate. Within minutes, she was turning into her parents' West County subdivision and parking her Beetle in the driveway behind her father's Lincoln MKX. Armed with a bottle of her mother's favorite white wine and a fall floral bouquet, she carefully navigated the slushy walk from the driveway to the front porch in four-inch heels.

Her mother was waiting just inside the open door for her. "Thank God you made it in one piece," Selena said, stepping out onto the porch to meet her daughter. She took the wine and flowers and ushered Wendy inside the house, closing the door as soon as they were safely across the threshold. "I was worried about that horrible little car of yours making the drive out here in this weather. How are the roads?"

Wendy shrugged out of her coat and hung it in the foyer closet. "Not too bad," she said as she walked into her mother's open arms for a hug. "I only slid on the ice once. Hi, Mom."

"I don't understand why you won't just let your father and me buy you something safer and more reliable."

"I would, but then one of you would always be telling me how to drive the thing." They eased apart and Wendy met her mother's concerned expression with an amused one. "I'd be sixteen all over again and that was not a good year for me. I never want to repeat it."

Selena tsked the way she always did when Wendy was being hardheaded. "I don't recall enjoying that year all that much, either," she drawled as she led the way to the kitchen. "Come and say hello to your father before he comes looking for you. Then I'd like you to please finish setting the table for dinner. Oh, and take out my Waterford vase for the flowers. We'll use them as the centerpiece."

"Yes, ma'am," Wendy said, wondering if her mother would be open to popping the cork in the wine sooner rather than later.

After gathering supplies from the sideboard in the dining room, Wendy went to work setting the table. She had just finished arranging three place settings when her mother backed into the room through the swinging door off the kitchen. The flowers had already been cut and arranged in the Waterford vase and now Selena experimented with different places to set them on the tabletop. Eyeing the spread critically, she said, "This looks very nice, Wendy. I'm going to set the flowers in the very center of the table and throw myself on your mercy, because it slipped my mind until just now to mention that we need two more settings for dinner tonight."

"Two more?" Wendy was confused. She set the table every year and she couldn't remember the last time she'd arranged more than the usual three place settings. "Who else is coming this year?"

"Lily and Frazier didn't take their holiday trip to Chicago this year, so I invited them here. They should be arriving any minute now. It's almost three." Selena replied as she swung back through the door and disappeared into the kitchen.

She didn't notice that Wendy had gone stiff with shock.

When Wendy and Frazier parted ways this morning, she'd been looking forward to spending some time alone with her parents. And then, since he and his mother weren't supposed to get back from Chicago until very late tonight, some alone time with herself. She couldn't help feeling a little resentful about watching it slip right through her fingers. He hadn't mentioned anything about a change of plans this morning over breakfast and she wondered why.

They had agreed not to tell their parents about their relationship just yet. It was true that Wendy had agreed a little more strongly than Frazier had, but still. They had *both* agreed. What was he doing?

The doorbell rang just as Wendy was placing the last water glass on the table. A minute later, she heard her mother's and Lily's excited voices in the hallway and then Frazier's deep voice saying something that must've been funny because both women burst out laughing immediately afterward. She rolled her eyes to the ceiling.

As soon as her father's good-natured chuckle reached her ears, Wendy knew she couldn't hide any longer. Jacob Kincaid was always the last one to make an appearance and if he had already done so, then it was past time for her to show her face.

She took a deep breath, smoothed her navy blue sweater dress down over her hips and stepped out into the hallway at the exact moment that her father asked, "Where is Wendy?"

"Here I am, Daddy." She went to Lily first because she was the safest choice. She clasped the woman's hands and met her halfway for a heartfelt hug. She'd always liked Frazier's mother and over the years, not only had Lily and her parents grown close, but so had she and Lily. "I'm so glad you could come, Mrs. Abernathy. I see Mama's already taken care of your coat, so can I get you a glass of wine or a mug of hot apple cider?"

"Apple cider sounds wonderful, Wendy. Thank you," Lily said, smiling. "I wish I'd thought to pick up something more festive, instead of letting Frazier talk me into bringing a bottle of wine."

"Wine is always a good choice." Especially since she was probably going to need as much of it as possible to get through the evening. She could feel Frazier's penetrating gaze boring into the side of her face, waiting for her to acknowledge him, to acknowledge *them,* and it was unsettling.

Aware that Frazier's mother and both of her parents were watching, Wendy turned to Frazier with what she hoped was a friendly smile. "Hi," she said, wondering if he could tell that she was pissed. *What are you doing here? I told you I didn't think we were ready to make any announcements. Please, please, please don't do what I think you're here to do, Frazier.*

"Hi, yourself," Frazier murmured, holding her eyes for a beat longer than necessary. Still smiling, she shook herself out of the trance that his gaze was threatening to put her in, reached for the bottle of wine he offered, and took off in the direction of the kitchen. "I'll just go and open this."

"I'll help you," Frazier said, falling in step right behind her.

"Oh, Wendy, go ahead and bring out wine for everyone, would you?" Selena called after them.

"Yes, ma'am," Wendy chirped. *Dammit.*

She rounded on Frazier the second the door swung shut behind them in the kitchen. "What are you doing here, Frazier? I thought you were taking your mother to Chicago."

"I was, but she got into an argument with my aunt Nancy last night. Something about an old photo of my grandmother that they both think the other has." He flapped an impatient hand and leaned a hip against the countertop, studying her thoughtfully. "Anyway, I didn't find out that she wasn't going until after I was already in my car, on my way to pick her up this morning. And I didn't find out that we were coming here until I had already picked her up to take her out to dinner this afternoon." A teasing smile curved his lips when she shot him a suspicious look. "Scout's honor."

"This isn't funny, Frazier." Irritated, Wendy snatched a corkscrew from a drawer and slammed the drawer shut with her hip. She rolled her eyes at Frazier on her way over to the refrigerator. "I wasn't expecting this, so excuse me if I'm still a little surprised."

"Liar."

"What?"

"You're not surprised, Wendy," Frazier continued calmly. "You're angry. This isn't the first time my mother has been here for dinner, so what's the problem today?"

She traded the wine Lily brought for a bottle that was already chilling in the refrigerator and took it over to the island in the center of the room. "It's just that I wasn't expecting you, that's all."

"Oh, so it's me who isn't welcome here," he speculated.

Wendy looked up from uncorking the bottle and shot him a quelling look over her shoulder. "Of course you're welcome here, Frazier. Don't be ridiculous."

"I was under the impression that your parents liked me."

"My parents love you. You know that." After a few seconds of maneuvering, the cork slid out of the bottle smoothly. She set it aside and braced her hands on the edge of the counter. "That's not what I meant. It just… feels like we're together every second of the day sometimes. I guess I'm still getting used to it. And I wasn't planning to tell my parents about us until after I was used to it."

"You mean, despite the fact that we're actually *not* together every second of the day?" His eyebrows met in the middle of his forehead. "What is this really about, Wendy? And who said anything about telling your parents?"

A wave of relief washed over her. If either of their parents knew that they were intimately involved now, they'd have the wedding planned and all ten of the requested grandchildren named before the evening was over with. The thought of being hit over the head with all that made her feel like she couldn't breathe. But now that she knew he wasn't planning to go there, she felt herself calming down and breathing more easily. "I thought that was what you were going to do." Steadier now, she opened a door on the side of the island and took out a serving tray.

Frazier sighed tiredly. "I know you did, Wendy." He pushed off from the counter and walked over to her slowly, his hands deep in his pants pockets and a laid-back expression on his face. "Do you need help with the wine?"

God, he was gorgeous. In a matter of minutes, she'd gone from being irritated at him, to being happy to see him, to being ridiculously aroused. On a bad day, he could've doubled for the actor Laz Alonzo and on a good one, he was as close to a visual orgasm as a woman could get. Even when she was upset with him, she wanted him inside of her. "Um...no," she said, staring at his lips. "No, I don't. Thanks."

"Okay, well, I think I hear voices in the dining room, so I'm going to go in and join whoever's there, let you have your space."

Not quite sure she liked the tone of his voice, Wendy watched him swing through the door that led to the dining room and pressed a hand to her belly to settle the butterflies there.

Composed again, she arranged the wine bottle and five glasses on a tray and backed through the door into the dining room. The first face she saw was Lily's.

"Wendy, your mother was just telling me about the job you have lined up in Chicago this spring. You must be so excited."

Wendy opened her mouth to clarify that the job in question—the one she hadn't yet decided on—was in Las Vegas, not Chicago. But Selena spoke up before she could.

"Lily has some excellent suggestions for the kinds of clothes you'll need to pack," her mother said. "Oh, and she can tell you about all the sights to see, too."

She could see Frazier in her peripheral vision, staring at her, but she wasn't about to look at him. "I've been to Chicago before, Mom, remember? You have, too."

"I know, sweetie, but it's always nice to get a fresh perspective right before a trip."

"You're going to Chicago, too?" Wendy's father asked, looking confused. He reached up and scratched his bald head as if that might help him keep the facts straight. "I thought the job was in Las Vegas. When did it change to Chicago?"

"It didn't, Daddy. The job is in Las Vegas."

"Well, then, what does Chicago have to do with it and when are we going to eat? I'm starving."

"Nothing, Daddy." She dropped a hand on his shoulder and squeezed lovingly. "Chicago has nothing to do with Las Vegas. Why don't I start bringing out the food?"

"How about pouring us each a glass of wine before you do, Wendy?" Selena suggested, sending Wendy a meaningful look over everyone's heads. Swallowing a sigh, Wendy poured a glass and passed it to her father, since he was sitting closest to her. "While you're doing that, you can tell Lily all about the job."

"There's really nothing to tell," Wendy hedged as she passed a glass of wine down to Lily and gestured for her to pass it over to her mother. "There's a youth dance corps in Las Vegas that's recently gained a lot of national attention. They need a choreographer to work with a group of new recruits this spring and they've asked me to take the position."

"Oh, that's wonderful," Lily said, beaming. She looked genuinely happy for Wendy. "Do you think you'll like living in Las Vegas?"

"I wouldn't necessarily have to relocate to Las Vegas, not permanently, anyway. At the most, I'd be there for a year, maybe less. I don't have all the details yet, because I haven't given them a firm response. Right now the offer is still on the table and I'm still thinking about it, but I do appreciate your support, Mrs. Abernathy."

She wasn't exactly lying to her parents and Mrs. Abernathy, but she was being evasive. For some reason, it seemed like the thing to do just then. There was enough tension between her and Frazier as it was and talking about the possibility of her moving to another state certainly wouldn't help matters any. She wished her mother would, for once, pay attention to the nonverbal cues that she was sending her and drop the subject.

Of course there was something to tell. How could there not be? The Greeley Dance Company was world-renowned. With branches in London, New York and, most recently, Las Vegas, they recruited dance students from all over the world and toured extensively. They were as comfortable performing on Broadway as they were in quaint community theaters, and they managed to do both superbly.

Wendy was already a freshman in high school when Greeley was first established, so she hadn't grown up with dreams of dancing with the company. But before the accident, they had definitely been on her short list of coveted placements.

The youth program that Greeley wanted her to work with was new, only about two years old, but it was already making important waves in the dance community because of its work with underprivileged youth. Thanks to Greeley, talented young dancers who might not have otherwise been given the opportunity to train professionally were now training under master dancers and performing for audiences all over the country. If she took the position, she'd be working directly with a group of high school students from Las Vegas, training and preparing them for a summer tour that would begin in Las Vegas and take them all the way to New Zealand before it was over.

And if she took the position, she'd need to be in

Las Vegas and ready to get to work in less than three weeks' time.

Wendy poured one last glass of wine and forced herself to meet Frazier's eyes as she passed it to him. If he noticed that her hand was trembling, he didn't say anything. "I forgot the apple cider, Mrs. Abernathy. I'll bring it out to you and then I'll start bringing out the food. Can you wait a couple more minutes, Daddy?"

He slanted a dubious look in her direction. "Do I have a choice?"

"I'm afraid not, but I promise I'll be quick. Does anyone need anything, other than food, before I—"

Frazier's calm, accusing voice cut her off. "You told me you turned down the job."

She met his gaze and looked away quickly. "No, I didn't. Not yet. I'll, uh, be right back."

Frazier was seething.

He couldn't remember the last time he felt so invisible. All through dinner, Wendy had avoided eye contact with him and only responded to his attempts to engage her in socially polite conversation with one-word responses. She'd only glanced at him a handful of times in two hours and now that dinner was over and they were, once again, alone together in the kitchen, she wouldn't even give him that.

Their parents were two rooms away, having after-dinner coffee and dessert by the fireplace. To get away from him, she volunteered to put away the leftovers and start on the dishes. And because he'd been on a slow simmer all evening, he had offered to help. Now she was giving him the invisible-silent treatment, hoping he'd go away, and full of attitude because he wouldn't.

Like he gave a shit.

Frazier had always known that he was one of the "good guys." Growing up, he'd always held doors for women, stood when a woman entered a room, and looked away when another man would've ogled. It wasn't hard to respect women and as he'd grown older, he discovered that the extra perks afforded to "good guys" were well worth the wait.

He'd been with more than his share of women, but a good guy never kissed and told, and he'd never tried to be anything other than just that.

When he was a kid, he hadn't minded being the butt of nerd jokes…up to a certain point. When he was a teenager, the nerd jokes dried up around the time that he suddenly and very mysteriously became irresistible to girls. And, as a man, he was happy to be the nerd who earned a six-figure salary and was very close to never having to work another day in his life if he didn't want to…and he was still mysteriously irresistible to women.

He almost laughed out loud at the thought. There was no damn mystery to what he did, to who he was. He respected women…people. Period. And when you gave respect, it was only natural that you demanded it in return.

Up to a certain point, he'd let the jokes roll off his shoulders, mainly because they were good-natured and he did have a sense of humor, but he had never allowed himself to be willfully and intentionally disrespected. Experiencing it now was strange and, as he watched Wendy load up the refrigerator with plastic storage containers filled with leftovers, he decided that it was as unacceptable now as it was back then.

Wendy knew that better than anyone.

Thirty minutes of strained silence had passed when

he glanced at his watch and straightened from leaning in the kitchen doorway. Earlier, he'd offered to help her with KP duty and been summarily dismissed, so he wasn't about to offer again.

Instead, he closed the distance between them in a couple of steps and leaned a hip against the countertop next to where she stood at the sink. It was getting late and his mother would be ready to leave in a little while, so if he was going to tell her to go to hell, now was probably a good time.

"I think you mistake my kindness for weakness," he said thoughtfully.

Her hands went still in the sudsy water. "Frazier, please."

"Oh, no, you're not the only one who gets to speak." He studied her profile—her smooth dark skin, the delicate line of her neck—and told himself not to reach out and touch her. "Earlier, you accused me of smothering you—"

"That's not what I said."

"That's what you meant, though. You said you didn't realize that we'd be together all the time, as if I'm the sole reason we spend so much time together. As if I'm smothering you. Don't insult my intelligence by trying to backpedal now, all right?"

"Frazier, if you came in here to start a fight with me, I am so not in the mood right now." She dropped a soapy plate into the double sink harder than necessary, then started scrubbing another one. "Can we please do this later?"

"I don't think so, Wendy, because I don't think there will be a later."

Now she did look at him. It was the first time in half an hour. "What?"

He tipped his head to one side, stared into her gorgeous brown eyes and answered her question with a question of his own. "This new dynamic between us isn't working, is it?"

That rattled her. He could see it in the way her shoulders stiffened and hear it in the way her breath caught in her throat. When she finally released it, it was long and shaky. "Are you breaking up with me? Is that what this is?"

"You'd like that, wouldn't you? It would make your decision so much easier, wouldn't it?"

"Frazier, I—I don't know what you want from me. I mean, right now, I don't even know what *I* want from me."

"Is that why you lied to me about the job in Vegas?"

"I didn't exactly lie—"

His sigh was long-suffering. "Wendy…"

"Well, I didn't. But if I had told you that I was keeping my options open, you would've just tried to talk me out of going because of this new thing we're doing and I probably would've listened."

"That's bullshit and you know it. I have never tried to talk you out of doing anything you wanted to do. Ever. Come up with another lie, because that one doesn't apply here."

Her shoulders sagged in frustration as she walked over to the breakfast nook across the room and pulled a chair away from the cherrywood table there. She dropped into it heavily and looked up at him wearily. "Frazier, we've been seeing each other for what, a month now? Do you realize that you bring up the subject of us getting married at least twice a week? You know how many kids you want and what schools you want them to go to. You probably have their names picked out, too. You have your future all mapped out and, suddenly, because we're exploring what it feels like to be together, you've got *my* future all mapped out, too. And I have a feeling that it doesn't include me moving across the country."

"So my crime is wanting to marry you?" He tried to keep from laughing out loud, but he couldn't help himself. A deep, sarcastic chuckle shot out of his mouth before he could stop it. "My crime is wanting to make a life with you and—"

"I never said I wanted marriage," Wendy blurted out.

In the silence that followed her declaration, he could see that her words had caught her by surprise. If so, then one out of the two of them wasn't bad. For his part, she had just confirmed what he'd already suspected. "You're right. You never said that…" He trailed off, considering her. "As a matter of fact, you never said much of anything, except, of course, when you wanted sex. Perhaps I should've been paying more attention to what you *weren't* saying and, if so, that was my mistake."

"Frazier…" His name was a soft plea on her lips. She was hurt and trying not to show it.

"I won't waste my time being with someone who just wants a good fuck, Wendy." For a moment, he let his own hurt show. Then he checked it and gave her a lopsided smile instead. "Even if she is my best friend."

"What are you saying?"

"I'm saying you're off the hook. I think I liked you much better when we were friends."

She stared at him for the longest time. Then she was up and crossing the kitchen in his direction. Anticipating her, he slipped his hands from his pants pockets and used them to steady her when she pressed up against him, slid her hands up his chest and then palmed his face. "That's not what I want."

"What *do* you want, Wendy?"

Silence. Then a whisper. "Frazier...I just... I need some time to figure things out."

"So take it," he told her, though it cost him dearly. "Take all the time you need."

"So we're breaking up because I don't want to marry you right now?"

"No, Wendy. We're breaking up because I want more from you than just sex."

"That's not fair."

He rested his forehead against hers and sucked the breath from her mouth into his. "Fair to whom?"

"Frazier." There it was again. His name. This time, though, it was his mother who said it.

Lily's caramel brown cheeks were bright red when he turned to look at her. She and Wendy's parents were crowded in the kitchen doorway and it was a toss-up as to which one of them was more scandalized. "I-It's getting late and the temperature outside has dropped, so there's no telling what the roads might be like. We should probably go."

"I was just thinking the same thing," Frazier said as he stepped back from Wendy and clasped her hands in his. They stared at each other for a beat and then he brought one of her hands to his mouth and pressed a kiss into her palm. She looked just as scandalized as their parents, so he said, "I guess our secret is out."

Chapter 5

Wendy taught ballet classes every week, but teaching and dancing, though intricately intertwined, were two different animals. While teaching required her to dissect the mechanics of the dance, dancing allowed her to connect with them on a physical, almost spiritual plane. Dancing required her to move within the music and movement was what she needed right now. When all else failed, it was what kept her mind clear and focused...and blank. *En pointe,* nothing else mattered, nothing except the combination of muscle and skill, of technique. Balance was everything. There was no room left for thought or feeling.

She chose the first movement of Mozart's *Eine Kleine Nachtmusik* to put her through her warm-up paces. Then, when she was damp with perspiration and her muscles were so loose that they flowed like liquid, she slipped another CD into the boom box. The music on it—five arrangements in all—were twisted fusions of R&B/hip-hop and classical music that couldn't be found in any retail store. She'd had the tracks created especially for her own use and the choreography that she had paired with each track was part of the reason the Greeley Dance Company wanted her to train its students. What better way to engage inner-city youth in the art of ballet than to show them how it could be used to make hip-hop come alive? And who better to show their students exactly how to merge the two than Wendy?

She certainly wasn't the first dancer to come up with the concept of a hybrid dance genre, but she was definitely one of the best choreographers to create movement within it, even with a less-than-perfect leg.

En pointe she waited for the first track to begin and then, when it did, she let it lead her into oblivion. There, she didn't think about the fact that she hadn't seen or spoken to Frazier in almost two weeks, because every time she did, the shock of missing him punched her in the gut harder than any fist ever could. It made her want to curl up into a ball and do something that she hadn't allowed herself to do in earnest since the day she learned she would never dance on Broadway—cry.

More than anything, she missed his friendship. He was such a huge part of her life that his absence left a giant, yawning void that she didn't know what to do with. Dancing helped, but after the music stopped, he reclaimed his place in her thoughts, took control of her ability to focus and then the cycle began all over again.

It stopped just then, a five-second break between songs, and the studio was completely silent. The sound-proof walls blocked sound from outside and tended to amplify sounds from within. That's why she heard it as clearly as she did—a soft breath expelled into the room. Not close, but close enough. To Wendy, it seemed as if she could feel the heat of that breath on her damp skin.

She squeezed her eyes shut for a moment, wondering if she might be hallucinating and praying that she wasn't. Then she turned toward the doorway, the direction from which the sound had come, and saw him standing there. A hot gush of honey soaked her panties when their eyes met and he started walking in her direction.

Watching him come toward her, she slowly sank down into a seat and removed her pointe shoes.

Frazier had been standing there for at least ten minutes, watching Wendy dance as if her life depended on it and wondering if it really did.

Arousal had whispered across his skin every time a leg sliced through the air or an arm swept across an air current. The glow of perspiration on her skin was an aphrodisiac. The music was an interesting mix of beats, bass and orchestra, and her body swayed, twirled and vibrated to it in perfect sync. She looked like she was in a utopian bubble, one that he couldn't help wanting to infiltrate.

The past two weeks had been hell for him. Not seeing her, not speaking to her every day left gaping holes in his daily routine that he didn't have a clue how to fill. He'd been busy enough during business hours—hiring and training a receptionist, and acclimating himself to the presence of both another broker and a college intern in the office—that putting her out of his mind had been partially doable. But only partially, because nighttime inevitably arrived and the images in his mind of her and of them together electrified him.

When she saw him and he started walking toward her, his plan was only to talk to her, to see for himself that she was okay.

From his mother, who'd heard it straight from Wendy's mother, he knew that she was packed and ready to leave for Nevada in a few days. Her assistants were dividing up her classes and continuing with their own classes in her absence, with Wendy's mother volunteering to supervise the administrative duties. As far as the studio was concerned, she'd covered all her bases. But how long she'd be gone was anybody's guess and, at this point, whether or not she was planning to return was, too.

His plan was to say goodbye to her and somehow leave things between them on a positive note. Too many years of close friendship depended on it. But then, she was back on her feet, in his face and looking up at him like the whole world was about to end and he was the only person who could stop it. And he forgot about everything except her wet, open mouth.

She took his tongue like a trouper, reaching up to wrap a hand around the back of his neck to bring him close and keep him there, and parting her lips as wide as they would allow. Her body came up against his and his hands went straight to her butt and held on. They squeezed and kneaded, while his tongue plundered her mouth hungrily. Each stroke of his tongue against hers drew a soft, sexy whimper from her and each whimper made him harder and harder.

Music was blasting in the background, echoing off the walls around them, and he heard it clearly for a minute

or two. Then it faded to black and all he heard was the
sound of mounting anticipation. Heavy breathing and
sighs and moans lit the air. Hands explored, squeezed
and gripped.

In one quick motion, he tugged her leotard straps
down the length of her arms until her breasts sprang
free and then he promptly tongued one of her puckered
nipples deep into his mouth. He sucked and lapped at
her nipples hungrily, one at a time, over and over, until
she was palming the back of his head with one hand
and cupping her breasts and feeding him with the other.

When tasting her flesh was no longer enough, he let
her walk him backward to the nearest wall and press his
back against it while she went to work on his belt. His
shaft was between them seconds later, a bead of pre-
cum glistening on its tip.

He wanted to watch her watch his body's reaction
to her, wanted to see every expression that crossed his
gorgeous face, but she had other ideas.

Before he could prepare himself, Wendy slid down to
her knees before him and wrapped her soft lips around
his flesh. She sucked on the head of his cock silkily,
causing his breath to back up in his throat on contact. His
eyes went to half-mast and a soft hiss whistled through
his clenched teeth. Now it was his turn to palm the back
of her head, to play in her hair until the messy bun at the
top of her head was in wild disarray.

The sight of her lips sliding back and forth on him,
her tongue drawing erotic designs on his flesh, made his
blood pump through his veins and sharp jolts of pleasure shoot down his spine. He fought the urge to come,
even though his hips were rocking back and forth, mak-

ing love to Wendy's mouth, and pushing him closer and closer to the edge.

The music stopped and its absence was jarring, leaving only his hoarse groans and her breathless sighs to fill the room. His voice sounded strange even to his own ears, like a drowning man fighting for air but losing the battle willingly. He felt himself swelling dangerously and withdrew from her mouth before the rush of sensation pooling in his gut got the best of him. He needed to be inside of her now.

"Ah…aahhh…yes, yes, yes…"

The glass against her back was chilly but Wendy was sizzling with heat. Unintelligible sounds were all she was capable of making, all she could wrap her mind around. Her tone was guttural, her knuckles were damn near white from gripping the barre behind her so tightly, and her toes were deliciously curled in on themselves. She had never felt so delicate, so weightless in her entire life…or so damn turned on.

Frazier's large, powerful hands held her butt suspended in midair, at the perfect angle for his long, forceful strokes. She bounced up and down on his thick length, coating him with her honey over and over again as her walls pulsed around him. The intense look on his face as he stared at her breasts only added to the jolts of electricity shooting up and down her spine. In spite of the condom between their flesh, it was as if she could feel every engorged vein in his penis. Fingers of ecstasy traveled up and down her legs, until they were trembling and her hips were spasming in his hands.

The orgasm, when it finally took mercy on her and rolled over her from head to toe, was so fierce that she lost her grip on the barre. She might've slid down to the floor and taken him with her if he hadn't shifted his stance at exactly the right moment.

When it was over and they were both preoccupied with putting themselves back together again, she looked up from straightening her leotard and caught him staring at her. She blushed under the intensity of his gaze. "What?"

"Nothing," Frazier said, adjusting the knot in his tie as he closed the distance between them. When they were close enough to kiss, he dipped his head and did just that, dropping a juicy gift on her upturned lips. "I love you," he said softly.

The tears in her eyes sneaked up on Wendy before she could hold them back. "I love you, too."

He took her hand, threaded their fingers together and brought it to his mouth for a kiss. "Good luck in Las Vegas, Wendy."

She stood there staring at the empty doorway for a long time after he was gone, wondering why, if she'd been expecting him to ask her to stay and she'd been prepared to tell him no, she was so disappointed because he hadn't.

Six Weeks Later

This year, Christmas and New Year's Day were miserable affairs for Wendy. She loved that her parents had flown to Las Vegas to be with her for the holidays, but she hadn't been able to spend as much time with them as she would've liked. With auditions just wrapping up, upcoming performances to choreograph new routines for and practice schedules to create, she barely had time to get a full night's sleep, let alone take extra time off for leisure.

Her schedule was exceedingly demanding, much more so than she'd been expecting, but the work was as satisfying as she'd hoped it would be and that helped make her fatigue worth it. As an added bonus, the warmer weather seemed to be agreeing with her leg, too, because she hadn't had a flare-up in over three weeks, which was always a good thing.

Just about the only issue she had with being in Las Vegas, aside from the tiny apartment that Greeley had rented for her stay, was that Frazier hadn't yet come for a visit.

Since their last interlude at the studio, they spoke over the phone at least twice a week, but their conversations were noticeably strained when they never used to be and way shorter than they'd ever been. She had invited him to visit at least twice now and both times he'd only given her vague maybes in response.

Her feelings were bruised and her confidence in whatever the future held for the two of them was shaken, but she refused to regret crossing the line into intimacy with him.

She hadn't been a virgin since college, but when Frazier was inside of her, he made her feel like everything she experienced was new and unique. Every touch set her skin on fire and her pulse racing. Every kiss was so deep that she thought she might drown in it, that she wanted to drown in it. His lovemaking was the best she'd ever experienced and she'd been in love with him for so long that there was no way in hell what they'd done was wrong. It couldn't be. She wouldn't let it be.

So, okay, she thought, their friendship had taken a

few hits along the way. She'd fix it and them, when she got back home.

"Georgia," Wendy said, snapping out of her reverie quickly. "You're lagging on the second swing. I need you to pick it up a bit." She glanced at the circle of students spread out around her in the dance studio, randomly picked a male student and motioned for him to join her in the center of the circle. "Like this. Watch my legwork." The male student got in position and so did she. "Five, six, seven, eight…"

It was all the twirling, she thought as they finished the short combination and she spun to a complete stop. That and the fact that she'd only eaten half a cup of yogurt for breakfast this morning and had worked through lunch. Rooms tended to spin when you didn't eat properly…or couldn't remember the last time you'd eaten at all, for that matter. She stood still with her eyes closed until the feeling of vertigo passed.

"Miss Wendy, are you okay?" a female student asked.

She opened her eyes on a teenage girl's concerned face and smiled. "Yes, I'm fine, thank you. I haven't had lunch yet and I'm starting to run on fumes, that's all." She cleared her throat and clapped her hands, looking around the room. "Okay, where were we?"

She didn't get around to eating lunch until it was at least an hour past dinnertime and by then, she was completely wiped out.

Later, instead of staying late at the dance school to work on her choreography, as she usually did, as soon as all of her students were gone, she left anything having to do with work at the school and went home, too.

For the time being, Wendy's home base was a one-bedroom garden apartment in a quiet, nicely landscaped complex that was within walking distance of the school.

Usually, she found the short walk to and from work refreshing, but today she would've given anything for a bike or, better yet, a car. It was only a little after eight o'clock in the evening, but she was dying to crawl into bed and stay there until morning. The idea of a hot shower just before falling asleep was so enticing that it almost brought tears to her eyes. As tired as she was, she practically ran the last half block to her apartment complex.

The next day, after Wendy lost her equilibrium and had to grab the wall to keep from dissolving into a heap on the floor, the same female student who'd asked her if she was okay yesterday, asked again today. Only this time she added, "Dang, Miss Wendy, my sister's in college in Atlanta and she came home just last week because she was having the same problem as you. She's not a dancer, though."

"Oh?" Wendy wiped the perspiration from her forehead with the towel that was dangling around her neck. "Is she burning the candle at both ends, too?"

"No, she's pregnant."

Chapter 6

"Have you been listening to anything I've been saying?"

The tone, more so than the question itself, was what caught Frazier's attention. It wasn't necessarily irritation that he'd heard in it, but he couldn't completely rule out impatience. Either way, it was a definite hint that he wasn't being a very good host.

Unfortunately, the question was a valid one and he could appreciate that the woman sitting a couple of feet away from him on his living-room couch had the guts to ask it. Another woman might have pretended not to notice that he was distracted and kept talking anyway, a concession that he would've immediately picked up on and been a little put off by.

But not Simone Patterson.

She was an NYU-educated attorney, in town only for

the next couple of months while she and another partner in her New York law firm acted as cocounsel on a high-profile, politically charged embezzlement case. He'd been introduced to her at a charity fund-raiser a week ago and tonight was the first time that their schedules had both been clear at the same time, so they'd gotten together for a late dinner.

After-dinner drinks back at his apartment were her idea, but he hadn't exactly protested when she'd brought the subject up, so he supposed the outcome was just as much his fault as hers. Simone was interesting and funny and sexy as hell, but, no, he hadn't been listening to a word she'd said.

His smile was guilty and apologetic at the same time. "I'm sorry," he said as he refilled their wineglasses. "I did wander off for a moment, but I'm back now."

She took her glass with her when she sat back and crossed her legs, sipping slowly and eyeing him curiously. "So…who is she?"

A sip of wine almost went down the wrong way. It took him a moment of clearing his throat to get himself together enough to answer the question. "Excuse me?"

"Oh, come on now, Frazier." When she smiled, the small gap between her even, white teeth flashed at him. "You've been wandering off all evening. I'm almost used to it by now, but the attorney in me can't help but be curious. Was it a bad breakup or something?"

"Uh, no," he said, chuckling. There was no way in hell he was about to tell Simone about the particulars of his relationship with Wendy. "Nothing like that."

"So there is no woman?"

"Oh, there's a woman, all right. But there was also a breakup and it's over, so…"

"So you'd rather not talk about it."

"Something like that, yes." He reached for his own wineglass and sipped. "I would, however, like to talk a little more about you."

"Okay. What would you like to know?"

He already knew that she was a successful criminal attorney, a full partner in a very well-known law firm, and she had only just celebrated her fortieth birthday last month. She'd never been married and she didn't have any children. She liked to cook, though she didn't get to do it very often, and she was the middle child in a family of seven. All of that, he'd learned over dinner.

What he couldn't quite figure out, though, was why she was still single. And he'd been wondering about that all evening.

Simone was a walking, talking wet dream, with her Coke bottle figure, seductive brown eyes and smooth, shapely legs. She was petite and voluptuous, and just as capable of holding her own conversationally as she was at crossing her legs and making a man's mouth water.

She was nothing like Wendy and that in itself should've been enough to hold his attention, but it wasn't. He couldn't imagine, though, that there was a shortage of men in New York who wouldn't have an issue with staying focused on her.

"Why aren't you married?" His gaze wandered to her ample cleavage for a second before returning to hers. "Or at the very least involved with someone?"

"What makes you think I want to get married or be tied down in a relationship?" Simone shrugged indifferently. "It's not every woman's dream, you know."

Appreciating her more and more, he decided to keep it light. "It's not?"

A warm, rich laugh curled out of her mouth as she shook her head at him. "Of course it's not. I know it's hard to believe, Frazier, but some of us women like things as uncomplicated and stress-free as possible."

"Ah." They stared at each other. The gauntlet had been thrown down.

"Take me, for instance," Simone went on. "I travel a lot and I do miss sleeping in my own bed sometimes, but I also enjoy the change of scenery. So it'll probably be a while yet before I decide I've had enough and cut back. Maybe I'll be ready for a relationship then, and maybe I won't. Right now, though, uncomplicated and stress-free works for me."

"Yeah, but how exactly does that work? Do you just travel back and forth across the country, leaving a trail of broken hearts in your wake or…"

"Are you asking me if I'm a serial dater, Frazier?"

She was a straight shooter and he liked that. He liked that a lot. "Are you?" He watched her intense gaze drop down to his lips and narrow speculatively. Her tongue darted out and wet her top lip and arousal tried to whisper in his ear.

"Not that it's any of your business, but I've been celibate by choice for the past two years. I said I was into uncomplicated and stress-free, not reckless and irresponsible." She finished her wine and set her empty glass down on the coffee table. "But you could probably get it." His eyebrows shot up and she giggled. "Don't act surprised, Frazier. I've been sending you signals all night. You've just been pretending not to get them."

"Not pretending," Frazier put in, holding up one long finger. "Just contemplating and evaluating."

Her cell phone beeped and, instead of taking it out of

her purse, she glanced at her watch. "That's my taxi and it's right on time. Now I know I'm not in Kansas anymore because I'd still be waiting if I were." She stood, then picked up her purse from the coffee table and tucked it underneath her arm. "I, uh, guess I'll leave you to your contemplating and evaluating...for now."

Frazier rolled to his feet and towered over her five-foot-three frame. "That sounded like a threat," he joked. "Should I be afraid?"

"No, that was more like a promise. Walk me downstairs?"

"Of course, just let me grab my keys from the other room." With a hand on the small of Simone's back, he ushered her out of the living room and into the foyer. "I'll be right back." On his way into his bedroom, his landline phone rang. The closest extension was in the kitchen, which was close to the door. "Would you mind getting that for me?" he called out as he disappeared into his bedroom.

A minute later, when he joined Simone in the foyer, she was shrugging into her coat.

"They hung up," she told him. "But before they did, I could've sworn I heard heavy breathing."

He caught the teasing glint in her eyes and chuckled. "You're cute," he said as he helped her into her coat.

"So are you, Frazier. So are you."

They were out in the hallway, waiting for an elevator, when Simone said, "So, this relationship of yours—it's really over?" The elevator arrived and they stepped inside. Frazier pressed a button for the lobby and slid his hands deep into his pants pockets.

"I think so, yes."

In another week, two months would've passed since

Wendy had left for Las Vegas. They spoke over the phone a couple times a week, but never about anything of importance and certainly never about where things stood between them. He knew that things were going great with the youth program, that she liked the weather in Las Vegas and that her tiny apartment was making her feel claustrophobic. But he didn't know what she was thinking or feeling.

Did she miss him? Miss them? They had always been able to talk about anything and now they barely talked at all and, if there was one thing he regretted about crossing the line with her, it was that. He missed having her as a lover, but he missed her friendship even more.

At some point, he hoped they could regain at least some of what they'd shared before he screwed up everything, but with her in Las Vegas and him in St. Louis, that point couldn't be now.

Wendy needed something that he was incapable of giving her, something that, until now, she'd been searching for, for years. As much as he'd wanted her to stay in St. Louis with him, she would've grown to resent him if he had asked that of her and that wasn't what he wanted for either of them. He wanted her to be happy, even if it was without him. And, sooner or later, he was going to have to try to be happy, too.

Simone's sultry voice crept into his thoughts. "Well, in that case, maybe we'll see each other again soon."

There it was again, an open invitation. If he wanted to, he could bring her back upstairs with him and they'd probably be in bed, all over each other, in fifteen minutes flat. He'd be lying if he said there wasn't an attraction between them, that her sexiness didn't arouse him on a couple of different levels. But he'd also be lying in all the ways that counted if he took one woman to bed while he was craving another one. He was a man. He could appreciate an attractive woman and Simone was definitely an attractive woman.

But she wasn't Wendy.

"Maybe we will," Frazier said, catching her eyes and returning her smile. He clasped her hand, released it and then watched her walk out of the building to meet her waiting taxi. As he rode the elevator back up to his floor, he wondered where Wendy was right now and what she was doing.

Pregnant?

Seriously?

It had to have happened the first time she and Frazier were intimate. It was the first and only time that they hadn't used protection. But it only took one time, didn't it? Now that she was thinking about it, spotting wasn't quite the same as having a full-fledged cycle, but she'd been so caught up in work that she hadn't thought to question the difference.

Until now.

Idiot!

Wendy was beyond incredulous. She was also scared and confused…and angrier than she had ever been in her entire life. If she really was pregnant, she didn't know what the hell she was going to do. The timing couldn't have been any worse if she had planned it that way and, besides that, she was nowhere near ready to be anyone's parent at this stage in her life. And, really, did she even like children?

She stopped pacing a tread into the bathroom floor long enough for her shoulders to sag with guilt. What was she thinking? Of course, she liked children. Why wouldn't she? That didn't mean she wanted one, though. Maybe she'd thought about being a mother when she was a little girl, but now? Not so much.

After everything she'd been through in the aftermath of the accident, she finally had a shot at achieving some of her professional goals and this had to happen? God, if it weren't for bad luck, she swore she'd have none at all.

She thought about diapers and formula and lack of sleep and the responsibility of it all and a rush of fear punched her in the gut, buckling her knees and forcing her into a seat on the edge of the bathtub.

She'd never had a pregnancy scare before and it was a strange feeling to find herself in the middle of one at thirty-three years old. Theoretically, it shouldn't have been the end of the world. Actually, far from it. She was an adult, she was capable of supporting herself reasonably well, and she wasn't exactly getting any younger. Even as a single parent, a child could do a lot worse than ending up with her as its mother.

But it *was* the end of the world.

Wendy didn't quite know why it was the end of the world or exactly how, but the ball of anxiety sitting like lead in the pit of her stomach made the feeling very real.

Suddenly she was confused about everything—who she was, what she was doing, where she was going, how she was supposed to get there…everything.

There was a sliver of a chance that she was getting herself all worked up over nothing, but the thought wasn't especially comforting at the moment, not when she still had hours of waiting ahead of her before she'd know anything definite. Tomorrow morning couldn't get here fast enough and she was too upset to even think about trying to get some sleep between now and then.

Steeling herself to get through the rest of the night in one piece, Wendy dragged herself up from the edge of the bathtub and splashed cold water on her face at the sink. If she was pregnant, she'd have to deal with the consequences. But she couldn't even begin to think about what those consequences might be until she knew for sure that life as she knew it was really over.

When Wendy finally did crawl into bed, her thoughts were back in St. Louis, with Frazier. She tried calling his cell phone, but it went straight to voice mail, so she dialed his home phone. After two rings, a woman answered…and Wendy lost her voice.

"Move…move…move!" Wendy's walking stick tapped the floor rhythmically as she circled around the perimeter of the room, studying her students' movement and technique. "Here's your count…one-two-three, one-two-three! Kick…kick…kick! Good! Now, shuffle to the left, Group A! Keep up, Kimberly!"

She couldn't have asked for a more talented group of teenagers to work with and they were coming along quite nicely, but something was missing, something that she couldn't quite put her finger on.

"Group B, you should be moving to the front now! Faster! Nice job, Carlos! Here's your count…two-four-six, two-four-six!" The stick kept tapping and she kept circling the room, but her mind was a million miles away.

After leaving the women's clinic she'd gone to this morning, she had climbed into the back of a taxi and, instead of coming straight to work, asked the driver to take her on a scenic tour of the city.

They had driven past museums, through parks and residential communities and then along the Vegas Strip before the taxi had finally pulled up in front of the school and let her out. And she barely remembered any of it.

Her students were already in class, warming up, when she arrived and only a few of them seemed to notice that she was late. Or that she was even there, for that matter.

At home, her students would've pounced on her as soon as she walked into the room, demanding to know where she'd been and why they hadn't known beforehand that she was going to be late. It would've turned into a whole big thing and half the class time would've been gone before they got around to the reason they were all there.

Here, though, her presence wasn't so much necessary as it was complementary. The students she worked with in Las Vegas didn't need her to be their confidant or their counselor, they didn't laugh at her walking stick and they certainly didn't care about her reasons for being late. They just needed her to help them learn how to dance.

"Okay," Wendy called out when only five minutes of class time remained. "We'll stop here today. Tomorrow we pick back up with pointe work, so remember to bring your pointe shoes, all right?" She paused to accommodate the round of muffled agreement that rose up in the air. "Good work, everyone. Be safe out there and I'll see you tomorrow."

She waited until all of her students were gone to release the long, shaky breath that she'd been holding in all day. Walking on legs that suddenly felt like they were made of rubber, she went into the small office at the back of the classroom and closed the door behind her.

For the first time since early that morning, she was completely alone with her thoughts and the quiet wasn't entirely welcome. It was the very thing she'd been avoiding all day and now she couldn't escape it.

As if somehow connected to her thoughts, Wendy's cell phone rang. She reached across the desk for it reluctantly and pressed a button to take the call when she saw that it was her mother calling.

"Hi, Mom," she said, tucking the phone between her head and shoulder, and dropping into the chair behind the desk heavily. "How are you?"

"Never mind about me," Selena said. "I don't like the sound of your voice, Wendy. I think a better question would be, how are you? Is everything all right?"

Wendy didn't know what it was about her mother's concerned voice that brought everything back to the surface. Earlier, she'd used the time she spent riding around the city in a taxi to get her mind right and, until now, she thought she'd done a pretty good job of it.

Coming to terms with the results of her pregnancy test was harder than she'd thought it would be, but by the end of her two-hour-long tour, she was confident that she'd done it. Now she didn't know what to think or to feel.

According to the doctor she'd seen that morning, her iron levels were low and she was moderately dehydrated, but she wasn't pregnant.

She had sat in the examination room for several minutes after the doctor was gone, waiting for the news to settle in and happiness to take over. But it hadn't. Instead, the news made her incredibly sad and she'd been feeling sick about it all day.

"Wendy, are you still there?"

She sucked in a shaky breath and squeezed her eyes shut against the tears welling up there. "Yes, Mom, I'm still here. I'm so glad you called."

"So am I, baby. Now answer my question, please. Are you all right?"

Wendy opened her mouth to say something reassuring to her mother, something about how much she was enjoying her new job and the weather in Las Vegas, but a sob came out instead. She pressed her fingers to her lips to keep more sobs from slipping out. "No, Mom, I'm not all right," she finally managed to get out. "Everything is a m-mess and its all m-my f-fault."

"Okay," Selena said cautiously, stretching the word out over three syllables. "Is this about Frazier? Because if it is—"

"Oh, my God, you cannot think that this is a good time to lecture me, can you?" She found a tissue and blew her nose noisily. "I can't take a lecture right now, Mom."

"No, sweetie," her mother crooned softly. "I don't think this is a good time to give you a lecture. Okay? Calm down. Tell me what I can do to help you pull yourself together. Whatever it is, you know I'll do it."

"That's just it, Mom. Everything is coming together for me right now. My own dance studio is practically running itself and here I am in Las Vegas, working with the Greeley Dance Company. Do you have any idea how huge that is?"

There was a hint of impatience in Selena's voice when she asked, "Then what's the problem, Wendy? If it's so huge, why are you crying? If you're upset because Fra-

zier has moved on and started dating…well…honey…
what did you expect? He probably wants to give *his*
mother grandchildren while he still can. *I,* on the other
hand, should be so lucky."

This was news. Bad news. "What? Why is he dating
someone else?"

"I don't know, Wendy. I suppose you'll have to ask
him yourself."

She should've seen that little zinger coming. Her
mother had never kept her feelings about Wendy's and
Frazier's friendship secret. Left up to her, they would've
been married years ago and working on their third child
by now. "You're not on my side at all, are you, Mom?"

"Of course, I'm on your side. I'm your mother, I love
you. I just think your problem is—" Wendy's long-
suffering sigh was loud and heartfelt, but Selena was
undeterred. "No, really, Wendy, hear me out now. I think
your problem is that you're confused about what you really want."

"I refuse to choose between dancing and Frazier." Just
thinking about it made Wendy well up all over again.
"I love them both."

Now it was Selena's turn to sigh long and hard. "Then
why do you have to choose one or the other? You love
dancing and you always have. You love Frazier and,
believe it or not, you always have. The two of you have
been dating since the day you met, you just didn't know
it. But, trust me, everyone else did. I'm glad you both
waited until you were adults to finally consummate the
relationship, because as much as I want grandchildren,
I'm happy you didn't give them to me while you were
still in school. But, honey, do you know what you were
doing all the time you were pseudodating Frazier? You

were dancing, too. You've done both all these years, so why the hell can't you figure out how to do both now? Why in the world do you have to choose one or the other? Why can't you have both? Other women do it all the time. What makes you so special that you can't?"

After a lifetime of lectures and screaming matches, Wendy understood that her mother's questions weren't just mostly rhetorical, they were entirely rhetorical. She'd learned a long time ago not to interrupt Selena Kincaid when she was on a roll, so she didn't even think about going there this time. With Selena, if you stuck your neck out, she had no qualms about chopping it off.

"You know, sweetie, when your father and I met, I was a third-year lawyer and, even though I was still considered a newbie, I was already on my way to making associate partner. Then I fell in love with your father and I decided that I wanted to marry him just as much as I wanted to be partner. So…you know what I did? Don't answer that because I know you already do know what I did. If I hadn't done it, you wouldn't be here, would you? But I'm going to tell you again right now, because I don't think you were truly old enough to appreciate it back then. Something tells me that you'll appreciate it fully now, though. I got married, sweetie, and then I had you. Yes, I had to rearrange some things and I missed out on a lot of sleep, but that was mostly because you hardly slept the first three years of your life and I insisted on attending every one of those awful softball games your father used to play. I didn't choose one or the other, because I didn't have to. I wanted them both, so I figured out a way to have both and still make partner. Honey, you just have to ask yourself if you want it badly enough." Several seconds of silence passed before Selena added, "Well, do you?"

Did she want it badly enough? Wendy honestly didn't know. But what she did know was that, while the position with the Greeley Dance Company would look great on her résumé, there was no telling when she'd actually get around to updating the damn thing. She worked for herself and it wasn't as if she was going to interview herself.

And, even though she liked the idea of working with students who had a natural affinity for dance because they were ready, willing and able to be molded, she couldn't quite get over their elitist attitudes.

She liked Las Vegas well enough, but she missed her temperamental, street-smart kids, and she especially missed introducing them to their very first experience with the language of movement.

Then there was Frazier…

As if sensing her train of thought, her mother's insistent voice broke into her thoughts to probe one last time. "Well, do you?"

She tried to muffle the sob that slipped out of her mouth, but Selena heard it, anyway.

"Oh, sweetie," she cooed. "Don't cry."

The endearing tone, coming from her mother, touched Wendy's heart in a way that only her mother's words could, but if it was meant to comfort, it had the opposite effect. The second her mother beseeched her not to cry, that's exactly what she did. She laid her head on the desktop and cried until she was empty.

Then she burst out crying all over again, for the baby that she hadn't even known she wanted, until the moment she learned that she wasn't pregnant.

The Finale

Chapter 7

There was a short knock on Frazier's office door, and then it swung open and a stylish woman in her mid-fifties strode in. All business during work hours, Marilyn Bowman, his new receptionist, came to a stop in front of his desk and handed him the day's mail and two client files that he had asked for less than two minutes ago. He set the bundle to the side and turned back to his computer screen. "Thank you, Marilyn," he said, glancing up at her briefly.

His fingers had been flying across the keyboard for at least sixty seconds when he glanced up again and noticed that she was still standing there. "I'm sorry, Marilyn. I didn't know you were still here. Was there something else?"

"Yes. This just came by special messenger for you."

He waited until she was gone to break the envelope's seal and slide the white card out.

> *You are cordially invited to attend*
> *Wendy Elizabeth Kincaid's*
> *one-woman production of...*
> *TWO TO TANGO.*
> *One night only at the*
> *Wendy Kincaid Dance Studio*
> *Suite C on the lower level.*
> *Wednesday at 8 p.m.*
> *Let yourself in, take a seat anywhere you like,*
> *and I'll find you.*
> *See you there?*

What in the world? Intrigued, Frazier sat back in his chair and considered the invitation.

He hadn't even known that Wendy was back in town, let alone that she was putting on a dance recital. A one-woman show, the invitation said, and he was cordially invited. He was half-tempted to call her right now, but he decided against it. They hadn't spoken in weeks, but Wednesday was just a couple of days away. He'd find out what was going on soon enough.

Suite C was one of three small auditoriums on the lower level of Wendy's dance studio. They were cozy rooms, just big enough to seat around fifty people in rows of seating that fanned out into a wide arc and faced a performance platform at one end of the room. Usually, Wendy used them to host in-house recitals for small groups of students but tonight she was using Suite C to host an in-house recital for herself. And, Frazier discovered, when he let himself into the studio and she locked the door behind him, he was the entire audience.

He picked up the lone program booklet that was sitting on a wooden table by the auditorium door and scanned it as he walked inside. The photo of Wendy *en pointe* printed on the front cover caught his attention, mainly because she looked beautiful and serene, but also because he had taken the photo himself years ago.

He chose a seat down front, center stage in the dimly lit theater and loosened his tie. He'd come straight from work and he was exhausted, but he wouldn't have missed her show for the world. Tonight was about more than just watching her perform. It was about simply watching her…seeing her with his own eyes and finding out for himself that she was happy.

He sat back in his seat when the lights dimmed even more and the room was a shade away from being completely dark. A spotlight switched on, illuminating the performance platform, and there was Wendy. In profile, dressed in a soft pink leotard and ballet skirt, matching tights and pointe shoes, with her head thrown back and her arms extended toward the sky, she stood perfectly still until the music began—Mozart.

Ballet was her specialty and she was very skilled at it. Her movements were feminine and graceful, mesmerizing and weightless. His gaze followed her every move, until the concerto ended and, once again, she was completely still. She held her position for a few seconds, allowed him to clap for that long, and then she relaxed, faced the audience and laced her fingers together in front of her.

"Welcome, Frazier. Thank you for coming tonight and I hope you enjoy the show," Wendy said through a wireless headset microphone. Her voice floated in the air around him, courtesy of the speakers mounted in all four corners of the ceiling. "What you've seen was the prelude to the opening act, a reminder of when we first met. I was a little girl and ballet was my world. Then I met you and my world got a little bigger. Sit back, relax and let me show you how much bigger." The spotlight switched off and the room went almost completely dark again.

He smiled even though she couldn't see him and wondered what the hell she was up to.

When the spotlight switched on again a couple of minutes later, she had exchanged the pink outfit for a white leotard and a flowing, multicolored, ankle-length skirt. Soft-soled, leather dance shoes replaced her pointe shoes. This time, she was seated on the floor. "Whenever I had problems that I needed to talk through with someone or secrets to share or I just needed a shoulder to cry on, you were always there for me, Frazier. I don't think I could've made it through high school *or my mother* without you. But the funny thing about being your friend back then was that I was always so confused about my feelings for you." She giggled softly, coyly. "We always said we'd never keep secrets from each other but I did keep one secret from you. I was the one who sent you all those anonymous love poems back in high school. I used to slip them in your locker after school so you'd find them first thing the next morning and I could watch you read them."

Frazier's eyebrows shot up and shock sat on his face for a moment. He remembered those poems clearly, and the fact that he'd never found out who sent them...until now. He felt his face flush with heat and was glad for the cover of darkness.

She stood and positioned herself. The music, when it started, was slow and bluesy, rich in wailing saxophone and sweeping piano notes. Wendy's body flowed with the rhythm of it, bending and twirling fluidly in a song of movement that stole his breath and aroused him beyond belief. As the song came to an end and she relaxed into a loose-limbed stance, facing her audience, she said, "That's when I first admitted to myself that I was in love with you."

The spotlight switched off and Frazier released the breath he was holding in one long whistle of pent-up frustration. Two months' worth. He sat completely still in his seat, waiting to see what she would do next and wondering if whatever it was could possibly make him love her any more than he already did.

A hard-core instrumental rap beat blared through the speakers next and, after a few seconds, his head bobbed in time to it. Her soft voice curled around him in the darkness. "I was on top of the world in college. I was at the top of my game, in the best shape I had ever been in and probably will ever be in. I saw myself becoming a superstar and dancing on Broadway, but then a horrible accident stole that life from me and I had to build another kind of life for myself. I was angry and hurt and cynical about life...feeling something like this."

The spotlight switched on and she was in the center of it, dancing. Now she was wearing a billowing white T-shirt that was knotted at her waist over her leotard, a studded red baseball cap on her head, and red leather dance shoes on her feet. Her movements were efficient and perfectly timed, angry and vibrating with intense emotion. Her feet hit the floor simultaneously with the bass and the expression on her face was stoic throughout the entire hip-hop number.

She danced her heart out until the track drew to a close, glistening with perspiration and favoring her right leg toward the very end. When it was over, her chest was rising and falling with rapid breaths that tapped against her microphone forcefully. When her breathing had calmed down, she spoke again.

"You helped me rebuild my life, Frazier, and I have never been able to imagine a time when you wouldn't be in it. These past two months, being away from you and pretending like what we shared didn't matter, like being with you didn't matter, have been the worst two months of my life. I was so busy chasing the life that I thought I should have that I wasn't paying attention to the fact that the life I have right now is pretty damn great just the way it is. I finally figured out the reason I was so unhappy in Las Vegas and it was because I wasn't here…with you. I guess you could say I had an epiphany, Frazier."

Darkness took over again, but her voice kept him company.

"You've always known that I love dancing. It's who I am, what I was born to do. And you've seen me do a lot of dancing—ballet, contemporary, hip-hop, all kinds. But I don't think you've ever seen me dance the Tango. I've never really cared for it because it requires one person to lead and the other to follow, and I've never been good at following." She giggled seductively. "I think you've always known that, too."

The air around him shifted and he knew immediately that she was standing behind him. Her name sprang to the tip of his tongue, but he held it in and sat still, waiting. If they were about to make any new moves together, then she was going to have to be the one to initiate the dance.

"I always thought I didn't like the Tango because it meant that I would have to give the best parts of myself over to another person, even if it was only for a few moments. But I know now that it wasn't the giving over part that I was unsure about. It was the fact that I hadn't yet found the right partner to lead." Her hands landed on his shoulders softly, sliding down onto his chest just as she hung her head over his shoulder and whispered in his ear. "Until now."

"Wendy," he said, turning his head and feeling her soft lips near the corner of his mouth. Whatever else he'd been about to say flew right out of his mind.

"We've been circling around each other for years. Now I think it's time for us to choose partners for the dance of a lifetime and I choose you. Tango with me, Frazier."

"I thought you'd never ask," Frazier replied as he turned his head a little more and met her open mouth with his tongue.

Encore! Encore!

Chapter 8

Christmas Day
Ten Months Later
Las Vegas, Nevada

The applause was deafening and, as Wendy finished her closing speech and walked offstage, she beamed with pride.

The Greeley Dance Company's Christmas recital had been a raging success and, if the standing ovation that she'd just received was any indication, her choreography was a big part of the reason why. Her students had danced beautifully, giving as much to their onstage performances as she had given to them during countless hours of instruction and rehearsals. Now that it was all over, the nostalgic emotions that had been swirling around inside of her all day were threatening to bubble to the surface and spill over.

This was the third recital that she'd been a part of, but it was the first one that she alone had choreographed from start to finish. It was sort of like her official coming out with Greeley and she'd done it spectacularly. If she could've jumped up and clicked her heels together, she would've. Instead, she settled for a dainty fist pump and a quick little victory shuffle.

Blinking back happy tears, Wendy quickly made her way through a maze of backstage corridors to her dressing room.

A cast party had been planned for right after the recital and she wanted to grab a few minutes of alone time before it started. She couldn't wait to get out of the floor-length, royal-blue sequined dress and the strappy, four-inch heels that had been in cahoots to silently torture her all evening.

Luckily, the cast hadn't yet begun drifting backstage and the stagehands were too busy dealing with the close of the recital to notice her, so her getaway was clean. And thank God for that because she was exhausted. The next time anyone set eyes on her, she thought as she walked into her dressing room, collapsed back against the door and closed her eyes, she would be wearing a pair of leggings, her favorite ballet flats and a freshly scrubbed face.

As far as appearances went, she planned to put one in at the cast party and make her excuses as quickly as possible. Greeley's founders, as well as a whole host of sponsors and patrons would be there; therefore skipping it altogether would be rude. But she had a plane to catch later that night, so after she shook a few hands and posed for a few pictures, she was out of there.

As much as she was going to miss working with her students at Greeley, she missed being home in St. Louis with Frazier even more. They were still a few months away from their first wedding anniversary, but she already knew that she wanted to share a million more anniversaries with him.

They had only just moved into the home they'd finally stopped debating about purchasing. Frazier's investment firm had grown so much that he was now splitting his time between two branches and her dance studio was holding its own. She was so ready to be home again, sharing her life with the love of hers, that longing for it brought fresh tears to her eyes.

After a quick shower, Wendy slipped into black leggings and a matching cashmere tunic, then sank down into an overstuffed chair to begin the arduous task of putting on her shoes. By the time she was done, which was at least four minutes later, she was slightly winded and even more eager to get home.

She'd only been away from Frazier for three days, but she missed his helping her with things like zippers, socks and shoes with an outrageousness that bordered on obsession. Three days felt more like three years and, as if that wasn't bad enough, today was Christmas and they were apart. They had agreed that he would travel with his mother to Chicago, since Wendy had to be in Las Vegas for the recital, but still.

As if sensing her thoughts, a dull thud reverberated through Wendy's midsection.

Relaxing back into the chair's cushions, she wrapped her arms around the area and cradled the beach-ball-size source. Apparently, she wasn't the only one missing Frazier. The wee one currently hiding out in her tummy wasn't scheduled to make an appearance for another three months, but he or she was already making a statement.

A light knock sounded at the door and then a woman's voice called out, "The cast party starts in ten minutes, Miss Wendy."

"On my way," Wendy called back and slowly pushed herself up and out of the chair. She waddled over to the dressing table, quickly smoothed her hair into a bun at the top of her head and dabbed on lip gloss. One hour, she promised herself. One hour of making the rounds and munching on hors d'oeuvres, and not a second longer. After that, she was going to treat herself to some real food and then head straight for the airport.

She picked up her cell phone from the dressing table, checked for any missed calls and then shot off a text to Frazier.

I love you.

She was imagining him sitting in some stuffy parlor in Chicago, listening to his mother's and his aunts' lively chatter and wishing for a cold beer, when she opened her dressing room door and froze.

"I love you, too, baby," Frazier said, grinning devilishly.

Shocked, Wendy launched herself at him, wrapping her arms around his neck as he pulled her up and against him in a grip that accommodated the baby bump between them, but was still so sure and masculine that she almost swooned.

The kiss he laid on her was deep and possessive, capable of sending a rush of pleasure straight to her core.

After reveling in it for several seconds, she pulled back from his lips and stared up at him.

"Babe, what are you doing here? I thought you were in Chicago." He set her on her feet and she instantly leaned into him again, pulling his face down for another kiss.

"I caught a flight back here a couple of hours ago. You didn't really think I'd miss your last recital of the season, did you?"

His words, combined with his infectious smile, warmed her from the inside out. "You saw it?"

"Yep. All the way from the balcony, I saw it." He dropped a kiss on her upturned lips and then on her forehead. "It was wonderful, baby. Perfect. I'm proud of you."

There they were again, the tears that lately Wendy couldn't seem to control. Seeing them made Frazier chuckle and Wendy blush. "Aww, baby, don't cry. It's Christmas Day and I'm holding the best gift I've ever gotten." He swiped at her tears with the pads of his thumbs and then drew her into a gentle hug. "Merry Christmas, beautiful."

God, she loved him.

Wendy buried her nose in Frazier's neck, held on to him for dear life, and whispered, "Merry Christmas, Frazier."

* * * * *

For my brother-in-law Earl F. Milloy—the World Traveler—you are now in the best place of all… At Home with the Lord! Rest well, Good Brother! We will love you always and forever!

Velvet

TIED UP IN TINSEL

Chapter 1

Brooklyn Samuels nestled into the plush leather seat of the chartered jet. Her heart raced as the Falcon 2000 soared closer to its destination. Brooklyn was en route to New York from Los Angeles for a weekend of festivities surrounding her best friend's post-Christmas wedding. The impending nuptials were not responsible for her nervousness. She couldn't have been happier for Pepper and Michael, who had been college sweethearts. The source of her angst was Landis Keates, the former star of their university's football team. The four of them—Brooklyn, Landis, Pepper and Michael—had attended college together, but Brooklyn hadn't seen Landis since she'd made her drastic transformation.

She was no longer Brooke Lynn Samuels, the shy, overweight coed who was invisible to the hunky linebacker. In college, Brooke had lacked confidence and social graces; aside from her dormmate Pepper who had taken Brooklyn under her wing, she'd had very few friends. Brooke had never partaken in any of the school activities; her only outlet had been music. Although she had been a premed student, she'd never had any intentions of becoming a doctor, which had been her parents' dream. Brooke had tied her sights set on stardom. And to achieve her goal of becoming a professional singer, Brooke had hired a vocal coach and studied with him when she wasn't in class or cramming for an exam. By the time she'd graduated, she'd not only had a bachelor's degree but enough confidence in her singing ability to head to New York. She had been Broadway bound.

Living in New York had been an exhilarating experience for Brooklyn. Although she shared a cramped one-bedroom apartment with three other people, her spirits were high. Being in a city filled with people from all walks of life helped her to fit in comfortably with the masses. She was pursuing her dream and was no longer that shy college girl. Her focus had been on landing an agent, which she did. With her considerable singing talent, she'd had no problem finding representation.

Her agent had set her up on auditions, and Brooke rushed through the crowded streets of Manhattan on a regular basis. Brooke had walked as a means of transportation and was oblivious to the miles she had trekked, which led to her gradual weight loss. The pounds had melted away until she was a svelte size six. Although Brooke never had a problem with wearing a larger size, she'd been ecstatic with her new figure. Brooke had then decided that she needed a complete makeover, starting with her name. She'd reasoned that her birth name didn't seem glitzy enough for a singer, so she'd combined her first and middle names and legally became Brooklyn, forgoing a last name like some entertainers did. She'd then lightened her jet-black hair to auburn with honey-blond streaks and traded her baggy wardrobe for form-fitting, sexy clothes. She'd looked and felt like a star.

Following her drastic transformation, Brooklyn had begun booking gigs regularly. After years of singing in the chorus, she finally landed a lead role in a musical, which led to more leads, which led to a deal with a major recording label.

Brooklyn's overnight success had taken twelve long, hard years, and now she was a megawatt star, touring the country, selling out concerts and gracing the covers of magazines.

Throughout the years, Brooklyn remained close to Pepper, never forgetting the close friendship they'd shared when she was an unpopular nobody.

During their college days, Brooklyn and Pepper had bonded like sisters. Pepper had confessed one afternoon that she had no real interest in having a career. She had only gone to college to find a husband. Although Brooklyn had thought Pepper's way of thinking was antiquated, she hadn't judged her friend. Brooklyn had told Pepper that getting married was the furthest thing from her mind. Besides, the only guy that Brooklyn would ever consider marrying—Landis—had never even given her a second glance. Pepper had tried to set Brooklyn and Landis up on a double date with her and Michael, but it had never happened.

When Pepper announced that she was getting married and asked Brooklyn to be the maid of honor, Brooklyn cleared her schedule and also offered to sing at her friend's wedding.

Michael, Pepper's fiancé, and Landis were also buddies in college, and when Pepper told Brooklyn that Landis was going to be the best man, Brooklyn suddenly felt like that shy, overweight coed from years ago. Landis hadn't given her a second look in college and had no clue that he was her secret crush. Brooklyn was curious to know whether or not Landis knew her new identity. Before heading to New York, she had called Pepper to find out.

"Hey, girl, I can't wait to see you in the flesh. Your picture was amazing on the cover of *Essence,*" Pepper had said.

"Thanks. I can't wait to see you, either. You have to come straight to my hotel suite once I arrive. I'll order room service and champagne so we can spend a few hours catching up."

"I would love nothing more, but don't you remember that I've planned a gathering for the wedding party?"

"I've been so busy that I forgot all about it, but I'll be there for sure."

"Instead of checking into a hotel, why don't you stay with us?"

"Sounds like a plan. Congratulations again on your new penthouse."

"Thanks. Now that Michael's the managing director of the investment firm, we can afford our dream place in the city."

"I can't wait to see you. So…will Landis be at the party?"

"He most certainly will. He's a part of the wedding party, and so are you. I can't believe that you're going to sing at my wedding!" Pepper exclaimed.

"It's nothing, really. I'm just singing one song," Brooklyn said modestly.

"And that one song will be amazing. You're one of the hottest singers around with platinum-selling CDs, who just so happens to be my best friend. I still can't believe that you've cleared your calendar for my wedding. Oh, and I've scheduled a rehearsal with the church's pianist so you guys can go over the song."

"Thanks, and, Pepper, it's my pleasure to be a part of your big day. So…does Landis know about my transformation from Brooke Lynn Samuels into Brooklyn?"

"Nope. I had Michael tell Landis that our wedding is going to be quaint with family and old college friends, which is true. I made him promise not to tell Landis. Besides, I thought you would want to see the expression on Landis's face when he sees how fabulous you look. The moment he lays eyes on you, he's going to know you're Brooklyn. You're world-renowned now, so he'll recognize you instantly."

"Yeah, but he won't know that I'm Brooke Lynn from college. If I had gone to our ten-year college reunion, we would've seen each other and he would know that I was that overweight girl in his statistics class. I haven't seen him since college. I'm sure he doesn't have a clue about my transformation. To be honest, the thought of seeing Landis makes me nervous."

"Why? He's still the man of your dreams and maybe now you guys will finally connect. Being in the same industry, I'm surprised you two haven't bumped into each other over the years," Pepper said.

"I did see him once at a Grammys after-party, but I didn't get a chance to speak to him. After all of these years, I wouldn't even know how to approach him."

"Don't worry. I have the perfect ice-breaking game planned for the gathering."

"Really? What type of game?"

"You'll see when you get here. Look, I have to run. I'm meeting Michael at the dance studio for our tango lesson. Have a safe trip. Love you."

"Love you, too. Bye."

As Brooklyn replayed that conversation in her head, she couldn't help but wonder what type of game Pepper had planned.

"Would you care for anything else before we land?" the flight attendant asked.

"No, thank you. Maybe John would like something," Brooklyn said, turning around and looking in the direction of her burly bodyguard.

"Okay, I'll check with him."

"Ms. Samuels, we'll be landing shortly," the pilot announced over the intercom.

Anticipation gripped Brooklyn again as the plane made its descent into New York. Within a matter of hours, she would be face-to-face with Landis, and the thought of being in his presence made her stomach flutter. She was nervous and sexually aroused at the same time.

Chapter 2

The Keates Agency was located in a centuries-old three-level gray stone that overlooked Gramercy Park, a quaint private oasis on the east side of Manhattan. Landis stood at the window of his office and peered out at the park, which resembled a life-size snow globe with snow covering the manicured evergreens and tree branches. Gazing at the pristine park usually had a calming effect on him, but not today. He was too wound up.

Landis and his team were working vigorously trying to land an important contract and were having a difficult time pinning down the potential client. The star's manager had reservations about signing with Landis's boutique agency. In order to prove that his company was up to par with the larger, seasoned agencies, Landis had made an unorthodox move—he'd gone out on a limb and pitched Brooklyn for an endorsement deal

with a major cosmetics company, even though she wasn't
his client yet. Her manager had been so impressed by
Landis's business savvy that he was ready to sign on
the dotted line.

There was one last hurdle to jump, and that was meeting with Brooklyn personally. Landis had seen her at
a party once and had admired her from afar. She was
beautiful in every sense of the word. Looking at her
smooth skin, long, flowing hair and toned body had
made Landis want more than just a business connection.
He hadn't been in a relationship in a while and found
himself wondering what dating Brooklyn would be like.
He had wondered if she was as sensuous as the soft romantic ballads she sang. His mind had drifted far away
from business, and before he had a chance to introduce
himself, she had left the event.

Landis had been told by Brooklyn's manager that the
final decision was hers. There had to be synergy between Brooklyn and her potential new marketing team.
Landis knew that once he met with Brooklyn, he would
win her over with his charming personality and business
acumen. Landis had worked hard over the past couple
of months and was anxious for a formal introduction,
but the meeting with Brooklyn was on hold. Her manager informed Landis that Brooklyn had taken a personal holiday.

Landis moved away from the window and sat at his
antique mahogany desk. He made a few calls, trying
to get his mind off of the impending deal with Brooklyn, but his focus kept returning to the superstar. If his
agency secured the contract with such a major talent, it
would expand his business exponentially. He picked up
the phone and dialed Brooklyn's manager.

"Hey, Malcolm, it's Landis Keates. How are you?"

"Good, Landis. What can I do for you?"

"I know Brooklyn is taking some time off, but I'd like to set up a conference call. I was hoping to put this deal to bed before the end of the year."

"That's not going to happen. Brooklyn was adamant about not being disturbed."

Landis sighed. This wasn't the news he wanted to hear, but he would just have to wait until after New Year.

"Okay. Thanks anyway."

"No problem."

As soon as Landis finished his conversation with Malcolm, his cell phone rang. He picked the phone off the desk and looked at the caller ID before answering.

"Hey, Mike. Man, what's up?" Landis said, greeting his best friend.

"You didn't forget about the party tonight, did you?"

Landis paused for a moment. "What party?"

"Oh, man, don't tell me you've made other plans. Pepper is going to blow a gasket if you don't show up! Didn't you get the invitation?"

"I've been so busy lately that I haven't checked my personal mail. What is your fiancée planning?"

"Pepper has put together a small gathering for the wedding party at the penthouse. Although Pepper and I are close to all of you, some of you guys haven't seen each other since college."

Landis wasn't in the partying mood. His mind was on the impending deal with Brooklyn, but until she came back from her personal holiday, there was nothing he could do. "I'll be there."

The afternoon wound down to early evening. Darkness had settled over the city by the time Landis left his office. He flipped the collar to his coat up around his neck to ward off the winter chill. Snow muffled Landis's footsteps as he walked the short distance to his condo. Along the way, he dashed into Dean & DeLuca to buy a hostess gift to take to the party. The gourmet retailer was decorated with gingerbread houses, candy-cane Christmas trees and fruit baskets. With his purchase in hand, he made his way home to change.

Landis wasn't in the mood to socialize; his mind was still on business. However, he knew that over the course of the next few days, little to nothing would get done. The holidays were in full swing and people were immersed in the traditions of the season—traveling to be with family, gift shopping, holiday dinners and office parties. Landis showered and traded his blue pin-striped Brooks Brothers suit for a pair of black gabardine slacks, a black-on-black-plaid Burberry shirt and a gray cashmere overcoat.

In front of his building, he hailed a taxi and headed uptown for the gathering of his old college friends. Reminiscing with them would be the perfect distraction to get his mind off the impending deal with Brooklyn. On the taxi ride over to the party, Landis made a promise to himself to relax, have a good time and forget about business.

Chapter 3

Brooklyn had taken Pepper up on her invitation and
canceled her reservations at the W hotel in Union Square.
After she had settled in at their penthouse, Brooklyn
exchanged her jogging suit for a slinky, red Tom Ford
cocktail dress, and matching red stilettos. Her long hair
was swept up in a sexy French twist, and her ears were
adorned with teardrop-shaped diamond earrings. She
went into the living room, where Pepper was putting
the finishing touches on the Christmas tree.

"Wow!" Brooklyn admired the decorations and marveled, "You sure outdid yourself."

In front of the floor-to-ceiling window was a six-
foot-tall blue spruce decorated with silver, red and green
ornaments. White lights were draped around the massive Christmas tree, and there were beautifully wrapped
presents of various sizes underneath. Rolls of evergreen

garland with bright crimson bows adorned the fireplace, and sitting atop the mantel was a miniature village complete with a general store, railroad tracks, snow-covered trees and tiny people strolling through the town.

"Thanks. It took me an entire day to decorate. I'm glad you approve."

Brooklyn walked closer to the tree. "You have everything on the tree except tinsel."

"I have tinsel. It's just not for the tree," Pepper said with a sly grin.

Brooklyn turned around and saw the mischievous expression on her friend's face. "Pepper, what are you up to?"

Pepper was always full of lighthearted pranks and games. Once in college, she painted their room in the school's colors for homecoming and had painted it back to its original drab gray the next day without being caught by the dorm monitor.

"Remember that game I was telling you about?" Pepper asked.

"That game to break the ice between your guests?"

"Yep. That's the one. It's called Tied Up in Tinsel, and…"

Brooklyn wrinkled her nose. "Tied up in tinsel? What's the premise?"

"Two people, say, for example, you and Landis, will have one index finger each tied together with a long string of tinsel. You have to go through the entire evening together without breaking the tinsel. Doesn't that sound like fun?"

"It sounds like a game that I'm sure to lose. You know how clumsy I am. Remember back in college I was always bumping into the bed frame and would have huge bruises on my legs?"

"Of course I remember. You were the only person I knew that would fall *up* the stairs," Pepper said, and then let out a hearty laugh. "Don't tell me you're still all thumbs."

"I'm fine when I'm onstage performing. Now, I only trip over myself when I get nervous. And being around Landis after all these years is sure to have my nerves on edge. I'm sure I'll break the tinsel within the first sixty seconds of the game."

"No, you won't. What you need is a glass of bubbly to calm your nerves."

Pepper led Brooklyn to a cozy lounge adjacent to the living room. The room was painted a metallic gray with navy velvet drapes. A lacquered wood cabinet covered one wall, and an oversize charcoal-colored sofa filled the space. Pepper went over to the wall cabinet where a silver champagne bucket sat on the lowest shelf. She poured two flutes of champagne and handed one to Brooklyn.

"Here's to the holidays!"

"Here's to you and Michael and your wedding!"

The friends clinked glasses, took a sip and then sat on the sofa.

"I'm so glad we finally have a chance to sit down and catch up. So…how's your love life?" Pepper asked.

"Nonexistent."

"Why is that?"

"I spend half the year touring, and the other half in the studio. I just don't have time to focus on dating."

"Brooklyn, I know you love singing and performing, but there's more to life than working. You need balance."

"I agree, but I haven't met the right guy yet."

"I have a feeling that after tonight, you'll be singing a different tune."

"Why is tonight so special?"

"Two words…Landis Keates."

Brooklyn took a sip of her champagne and exhaled. "I don't want to get my hopes up. For all I know, he has a girlfriend."

"No, he doesn't. I already checked. He's a free agent, and so are you. Landis and Michael have remained close over the years, and I've been around Landis long enough to know that he's a good guy. You two are perfect for each other."

Brooklyn was nervous about seeing Landis after all of these years and revealing her true identity. Although she had transformed into a beauty on the outside, sometimes she still felt like that unpopular, overweight teen.

"We shall see," Brooklyn responded, sounding apprehensive.

"Yes, sooner rather than later. The guests should be arriving soon." Pepper rose from the sofa. "Let me check on the caterers. I'll be right back."

When Pepper left the room, Brooklyn poured herself another glass of champagne. As she sipped her drink, she heard a pair of male voices. Brooklyn moved closer to the doorway.

"Here, I bought you guys a fruit basket."

"Thanks, Landis."

"Man, your fiancée sure knows how to decorate."

A knot instantly formed in Brooklyn's throat as she recognized Landis's sexy baritone voice. He had a distinctive Barry White–type quality to his tone. In college, they'd had a statistics class together. Her ears would perk up whenever he spoke and she would listen intently to his smooth, sensuous voice. Years later, the effect was still the same. Brooklyn could feel herself becoming aroused as she stood in the doorway listening to him now.

"She sure does. She's made our home into a winter wonderland. Pepper is so creative. That's one of the reasons I love her so," Michael replied.

"I admire you guys. You're lucky to have each other. You have no idea how many horrific dates I've had over the years."

"Aw, it can't be that bad. You're a single, successful man in a city full of beautiful women. What's the problem?" Michael asked.

"The last woman I dated thought she was the man. Jesse was a trader on Wall Street."

"Wow, she even had a man's name," Michael commented.

"Yeah, she sure did. Anyway, she barked orders at me as if I worked for her. Jesse was mean as a snake. The woman before her was pretty as a picture, but had no substance. All she talked about was her Pomeranian-poodle. She treated that dog like he was a kid. She even brought him with her on our dates, saying that he couldn't be home alone."

"Man, that's rough, rough," Michael said, barking like a dog.

Brooklyn put her hand to her mouth and chuckled.

"Ha, ha. Not so funny. What do you have to drink around here?"

"Let's go to the lounge and have some champagne. Pepper and I put a few bottles on ice in the lounge earlier this afternoon," Michael said.

Brooklyn's skin tingled and her throat slowly began

to dry just like it had done at the Grammy after-party. She had wanted to speak with Landis that night but her mouth felt like it was full of cotton balls. Even though she was no longer a shy college student, Landis Keates still made her nervous. She hadn't even laid eyes on Landis and yet her mouth was getting drier by the second. Brooklyn took two huge gulps of champagne, hoping the cool liquid would dissolve the imaginary cotton in her mouth.

She heard their footsteps coming closer and quickly tiptoed back to the sofa, sat down and casually crossed her legs as if she had been sitting there the entire time. Her heart raced with the anticipation of coming face-to-face with Landis.

Within a few seconds, he was standing in the doorway. Landis was a vision in all black. Brooklyn's gaze roamed the length of his six-foot-tall frame. His shirt hugged his broad shoulders, and his midsection had remained taut even after all these years. He had been a star football player in college and still resembled an athlete. Brooklyn exhaled and recrossed her legs. Landis was staring directly at her, and his gaze was sending an erotic warmth throughout her body.

Chapter 4

Landis couldn't believe his eyes. Sitting on the sofa in the dimly lit room was none other than Brooklyn, looking like a vision in red. Landis was captivated by her aura. She exuded sensuality in a mature dignified way. Her dress exposed just a hint of cleavage. Landis stood there and took in her lovely shape. Even though she was sitting, he could see that her breasts didn't look fake like some celebrities. They had a natural shape to them, and Landis couldn't help but envision her in the buff. Her beauty was captivating, rendering him momentarily speechless.

"Hey, man, you remember Brooke from college, don't you?" Michael asked.

Landis locked eyes with Brooklyn as he quickly searched his memory trying to remember a classmate named Brooke. The only person he could recall was the chubby, quiet girl in his statistics class.

No, it can't be the same person!

"Michael!" Pepper exclaimed entering the lounge. "You let the cat out of the bag!" Pepper gave her fiancé a shove on the shoulder.

"What?" Michael asked, looking dumbfounded.

"Brooklyn wanted to tell him herself," Pepper replied.

"I don't see what the big deal is," Michael said, looking from Landis to Brooklyn. "We all went to school together."

Oh shit! That is her! Landis thought. He went over to Brooklyn and extended his hand. "Uhh, I didn't know... uhh..." Landis's words were all jumbled; he was caught totally off guard.

"Hey there. Long time no see."

"Hello, Landis." Brooklyn smiled and shook his hand.

Landis held her hand in his for a few seconds. Her hand was as soft and smooth as velvet. He couldn't help but wonder if the rest of her skin felt the same way. He released her hand but kept his gaze locked on her.

"Let's toast before everyone else gets here," Pepper said, pouring champagne. Once everyone had a flute of bubbly, Pepper held her glass high and said, "Here's to old friends."

Landis peered over the rim of his glass at Brooklyn as he sipped the champagne. He couldn't believe his luck. The star client that he was trying to woo was standing before him. Landis would have never guessed in a million years that the woman he had admired from afar at a Grammy after-party was the same person he had gone to college with. Brooke's drastic transformation had him intrigued.

"Why don't you two catch up while Michael and I tie

up a few last-minute details," Pepper said, tugging Michael out of the room by the arm.

Once they were alone, Landis stood there for a moment trying to decide what to say. He remembered her manager mentioning that Brooklyn didn't want to discuss business while she was on holiday. Although Landis was anxious to land her as a client, he wasn't going to broach the subject—at least not yet.

"So...you and Pepper have stayed in contact over the years," Landis finally said.

"Yes, we're close, like sisters."

Landis wasn't going to mention his agency vying for her business, but ignoring the fact that she was a megastar felt like trying to ignore a roaring tiger on the loose. "I must say that I'm a huge fan of your music."

"Thanks."

Landis watched as she finished her champagne. As her ruby lips touched the glass, he envisioned them brushing softly against his cheek. He felt like a nervous schoolboy trying to strike up a conversation with the prom queen. Landis took a moment and also finished his drink. He then asked, "Would you like another glass of champagne?"

"Sure."

He crossed the room, retrieved the bottle and returned to where Brooklyn was standing. "May I have your glass?" As he took her flute, his hand lightly touched hers, and this time when their skin touched, a spark of excitement rushed up his spine. There was no denying his strong attraction to Brooklyn.

"Here's to Michael and Pepper and their impending nuptials."

"I'll drink to that," Brooklyn said, clinking her glass to his.

As they stood there toasting, Pepper appeared in the doorway. "Hey, guys, come into the living room. The other guests have arrived."

Landis and Brooklyn followed Pepper out of the lounge, into the festively decorated living room where Christmas carols were playing softly in the background and a uniformed server was carrying a silver tray of seared ahi tuna on toast points. Another server was passing around crystal flutes of champagne. Landis recognized a few faces from college, but the only face he was interested in was Brooklyn's.

He watched Brooklyn glide across the room, greeting the other guests. The slinky red dress she wore hugged her body in a sensuous way, and the towering heels made her legs look a mile long. Landis quickly imagined those legs wrapped around his back while he and Brooklyn made mad, passionate love. His eyes were fixed on her. He decided right then and there that he wasn't going to make the same mistake that he had made at the cocktail party a few years back and allow her to slip away without at least engaging in a conversation.

Landis waited for the right moment to approach her. After speaking to the other guest, Brooklyn made her way over to Pepper. The two women had their heads together, talking softly. He couldn't hear what they were saying, but whatever it was had Brooklyn blushing.

After a few minutes, Brooklyn and Pepper had finished their conversation, and now Pepper was standing in the middle of the room with Michael by her side.

"Hello, everyone, and thanks for coming out on this cold, snowy night. Michael and I are elated to have you guys be a part of our wedding. Tonight is all about having fun before the big day arrives. To help kick off the night, I've created a game called Tied Up in Tinsel," she said, holding up a handful of long silver tinsel.

"That sounds naughty," Michael said, with a sly grin on his face. "What are the rules?"

"Well, for starters, the game is played in pairs," Pepper said, looking around the room. Everyone was already coupled up, either married or in long-term relationships, except for Brooklyn and Landis.

After surveying the room, Landis made his way over to Brooklyn and whispered in her ear, "Looks like we're the only two single people here."

"It appears so," she responded.

Pepper put the handful of tinsel on a nearby table, except for one elongated strand. She then took Michael by his right hand and tied the tinsel around both of their index fingers. "The object of the game is to go through the entire evening together without breaking the tinsel. The couple who remains tied together wins."

"Sounds interesting," Landis whispered. He was standing so close to her that he could smell her perfume. The fragrance was fresh and sexy. In her heels, Brooklyn was almost as tall as Landis. He moved a bit closer to her and took a deep breath, savoring the intoxicating scent.

Brooklyn smiled.

"Don't be shy. Step up and get tied," Pepper said with a laugh.

Landis didn't want to seem too eager to play the game, so he held back and waited for Brooklyn's lead. He watched as Pepper, with Michael's help, joined the couples one by one until he and Brooklyn were the only ones left.

"What are you guys waiting for? Get over here," Pepper said, waving them over with her free hand.

Landis gently took Brooklyn's hand and made his way over to Pepper with Brooklyn following closely behind.

"Okay, Landis, let me have your right hand, and, Brooklyn, I'll need your left hand," Pepper said, taking hold of their hands. She then tied the tinsel around their index fingers. "Let the game begin."

"How am I supposed to do anything? I'm right-handed," Landis said, looking at the silver bow around his finger.

"You have a partner, remember? Brooklyn, are you left-handed?" Pepper asked.

"No."

"Problem solved. Brooklyn will be your right hand. Now go enjoy yourselves," Pepper instructed and flitted away with Michael by her side.

Landis's arm was now touching Brooklyn's, and the unexpected closeness was a welcome surprise. He glanced into her hazel eyes, and she stared back at him. As the seconds ticked by, it felt as if they were the only ones in the room. Landis cleared his throat.

"Do you want a drink?" he asked.

"Sure."

They made their way over to the server, careful not to break the tinsel. Landis reached for a flute of champagne with his left hand and handed it to Brooklyn. He then took another glass for himself.

"Here's to getting reacquainted," he toasted, clinking his glass to hers. Landis eyed her over the rim of his glass like he had done earlier and could feel himself getting excited with each passing second.

Chapter 5

"Well, looks like we're bound for the rest of the evening," Landis said.

Brooklyn was silently thanking her lucky stars. She was finally spending an evening with the man she had admired for years. His arm was pressing against hers, and she could feel his muscles. Being this close to Landis was making Brooklyn moist with desire. She wanted to break the tinsel right then and there and jump his bones. Brooklyn hadn't made passionate love in nearly two years. She was on a self-imposed hiatus from sex. Her last relationship with a record producer had ended badly when she caught him in a compromising position with an intern, promptly ending their six-month relationship. Brooklyn was now long overdue for some heated, in-the-buff, body-to-body affection.

"Are you hungry?" he asked.

Yes, hungry for you! she thought. "No, not really. Can you excuse me? I need to go back to my room. I forgot to put Pepper and Michael's gifts under the tree."

"Uhh…I would, but we're tied together, remember?"

She glanced down at their fingers and smiled coyly. "Guess you'll have to come with me."

Brooklyn led the way through the living room, down the long hallway that led to the guest wing of the penthouse. She put an extra sway in her hips as she moved, hoping that Landis was watching. When they reached the room, Brooklyn opened the door and went inside.

The massive bedroom was decorated in all white with a silver metallic duvet covering the king-size bed. White Christmas lights adorned the windows, creating a soft glow.

"The gifts are in my luggage," she said. Brooklyn had started walking toward the closet, but Landis stopped her.

"Wait a minute. I've been dying to do this all night."

He reached out with his free hand, brought her close and wrapped his arms around her waist. Landis then leaned in and gave Brooklyn a soft kiss on the lips. He then stepped back and said, "I can't believe you're the shy, chubb—I'm sorry."

"It's all right. You can say chubby, because it's the truth."

"But now look at you." Landis stood back and gave her an appraising look. "You're gorgeous. And please let me apologize."

"For what?"

"For not recognizing your beauty when we were in school. I was a dumb jock back then, but I'm a wise man now, and I sincerely apologize."

"No apology necessary."

"You're so sweet." He kissed her again, but this time more passionately.

Brooklyn's heart began beating a mile a minute. Although she had fantasized about this day for years, she hadn't expected him to move so fast. She returned his kiss and soon their tongues were taking over, doing a duet all of their own.

Landis ran his left hand down her back and didn't stop until he reached her ample rear end. He began massaging her ass, pressing her into his groin.

Brooklyn could feel his rising manhood, which was getting harder by the second. She pressed firmly against him and began grinding her hips.

"I want you," Landis whispered in her ear.

Brooklyn nibbled on his earlobe, stuck her tongue in his ear and then said, "I want you more."

Landis untied the belt on her wrap dress, allowing it to drape open. He stood back for a moment and admired her sculpted body. She wore a red lace thong with a matching low-cut bra, which accentuated her breasts.

"Wow, you're beautiful," he said, rubbing his hand down her taut midsection.

"You're not bad yourself."

Brooklyn hesitated for a moment. She had never been the type of woman to give in to a man on the first date, but Landis wasn't just any man. Besides, she reasoned that they had known each other since college. She threw caution to the wind and started unbuttoning his shirt. Once it was open, she mirrored his moves and ran her hand over his well-defined pecs. His chest was hairy, but not overly so. She touched his dark nipples and rubbed them until they firmed up.

"Mmm...that feels good. You think we can make love without breaking the tinsel?" he asked.

"I'm up to the challenge if you are."

"Challenge is my middle name." He chuckled. Landis reached into his pocket, retrieved his wallet and produced a condom.

"Look at you, Mr. Ready For Action," she teased.

"It's the Man Code to always keep at least one condom on you at all times."

"Oh, I like that code."

Once they made their way over to the massive bed, Brooklyn kicked off her heels and wiggled out of her thong while Landis unhooked her bra with his free hand, releasing her ample breasts.

"You'll need to unbuckle my belt," he said, taking off his Gucci loafers.

"Gladly," she said, smiling.

Brooklyn unbuckled his belt and unfastened his pants, allowing them to fall to the floor. She tugged at the waistband of his black boxer briefs. "You need to take those off."

"With pleasure!" Landis unleashed his massive member and rubbed the head of his penis against her smoothly shaven triangle.

Brooklyn was so moist with excitement that she could barely contain herself. "Stop teasing me and start pleasing me!"

Landis tore open the foil wrapper, took out the prophylactic and rolled it onto his engorged manhood. He eased Brooklyn down on the bed and covered her body with his. Landis spread her legs wide and eased his way into her slippery canal. Once he was inside, he began pumping, going deeper and deeper.

"Oh, yes!" she yelled softly, careful not to be over-heard. "You feel so good."

"So do you," he said, cradling her head with his left hand.

Brooklyn wrapped her legs around his back and rode his rhythm, matching him pump for pump. He was making love to her so good that her back arched, her toes curled downward and she thrashed her head back and forth on the verge of ecstasy.

"Are...you...coming?" he asked in between heated breaths.

"Yes...*yes*...YES!"

Landis clenched her left hand with his right hand, ensuring that the tinsel remained intact.

Brooklyn couldn't hold back any longer. She let go on his latex-covered penis.

Landis followed suit and came hard into the condom. After a few seconds, he was the first to speak.

"That was beyond fantastic!"

"It was worth waiting all these years for," she admitted with a huge smile plastered on her face.

"I didn't really know you back in college, but I'm oh-so-glad I know you now," he said, hugging her tightly with his free arm.

After making love, they were too exhausted to return to the party, and drifted peacefully to sleep.

The early-morning sun beaming through the slits of the miniblinds disturbed Brooklyn's slumber. Normally, she wore an eye mask to bed so the sunrise wouldn't ruin her sleep. She tried to turn away from the source of the light, but there was something preventing her from moving freely. Brooklyn blinked her lids open, and there was Landis resting soundly next to her. She glanced down at their hands, and their fingers were still bound together. He was so close that she could smell the faint scent of his cologne. She inhaled deeply. The fragrance was a reminder of their heated lovemaking and she began blushing.

Brooklyn lay there and wondered what the aftermath would be like. As she ran different scenarios through her mind—would he act indifferent as if she were just another conquest? Would he make an excuse and leave as fast as humanly possible?—he began to stir. Brooklyn's breath caught in her throat. She looked over at him and watched his eyes open. He stared at her for a moment.

"I'm so glad it wasn't a dream," Landis said in a groggy voice.

A puzzled expression painted her face. "Excuse me?"

"I was afraid that last night was a dream, but looking at your beautiful face this morning, I know it was real."

"Yes, it was real all right." She blushed.

Landis leaned in and kissed Brooklyn good-morning. He caressed the back of her head with his right hand, finally breaking the tinsel.

Chapter 6

It was Christmas Eve, and Brooklyn and Pepper were strolling down crowded Fifth Avenue amongst the holiday shoppers.

"I love Manhattan during the holidays," Brooklyn commented. She had left her bodyguard at Pepper's place and was in disguise, wearing oversize dark shades and a down maxi coat with the hood flipped up around her face.

Store windows displayed various holiday scenes, from a winter wonderland of yesteryear, to a futuristic space scene with a robotic Santa and reindeer soaring through the solar system. The buildings lining the avenue were also decked out for the season. The exterior of Saks Fifth Avenue was wrapped in its traditional humongous red ribbon and gigantic bow. The smell of roasted chestnuts being sold by street vendors permeated the crisp air. Brooklyn and Pepper had just completed some last-minute shopping before they headed off to Bridgehampton to celebrate Christmas and prepare for the wedding.

"That's not all you love," Pepper said, cutting her eyes at her friend. She hadn't had a chance to have a little girl talk during breakfast, since Landis and Michael were present.

"What's that supposed to mean?"

"I'm guessing you also loved being tied up in tinsel."

Brooklyn began smiling from ear to ear. "When you introduced the game, I thought it was a lame idea, but was I ever wrong. If it wasn't for your ingenuity, Landis and I would have never gotten so close so fast."

"How close did you get?"

"Close enough for me to want more. I didn't intend to skip out on the party. We went back to my room so that I could get your gifts and put them under the tree. Once we entered the room, Landis didn't waste any time making a move."

"Don't worry about missing the party. I'm just glad you two finally hooked up."

"So am I. It's refreshing to meet a man who doesn't have a hidden agenda. Some of the men I've met in the past were only interested in dating me so that I could help advance their music careers. Thankfully, Landis has a thriving business and doesn't need any help from me."

"Sounds like you're falling hard for him."

Brooklyn exhaled. "Actually, I fell for Landis the first day I laid eyes on him back in college. And now, after all of these years, we finally have a chance to bond. Landis is everything in a man that I've ever wanted. He's smart, handsome, successful and great in bed!"

As they were talking, Pepper's cell phone rang. She dug it out of her pocket and answered. "Hello?"

"Hey, babe, are you and Brooklyn still shopping?"

"No. We just finished up."

"Good. Why don't you guys meet me and Landis at Rockefeller Center?"

"Hold on a second." Pepper took the phone away from her mouth and turned to Brooklyn. "Michael wants us to meet him and Landis at Rock Center. Do you want to go?"

Brooklyn smiled broadly. "Of course!"

"We're on our way."

Brooklyn and Pepper walked arm in arm up Fifth Avenue and over to Rockefeller Center. The popular landmark was abuzz with activity. Tourists were snapping pictures in front of the gilded statute of Prometheus. The colossal, seventy-six-foot-tall Christmas tree, decorated beautifully with a multitude of lights and ornaments, towered over the ice-skating rink, which was crowded with skaters.

Brooklyn glanced over the throng of people and spotted Landis and Michael cutting through the crowd. The sight of her handsome lover brought a smile to her face. Landis wore jeans, black biker boots, a black wool beret and a navy peacoat with a burgundy knit scarf tied around his neck. The closer he came, the faster her heart began to beat.

"You disappeared on me after breakfast," Landis said after kissing Brooklyn on the cheek.

The four friends had had a leisurely breakfast at the penthouse the morning after the party, with eggs Benedict, fresh fruit and mimosas. As they sat across the table from each other, Landis and Brooklyn stole glances at each other and played footsie underneath the table, secretly flirting.

"Pepper wanted me to do a little last-minute shopping with her."

Landis stepped a bit closer and whispered, "I was hoping to get in some last-minute lovemaking before you left."

"You didn't get enough last night?"

"Nope, did you?"

Brooklyn quickly flashed back to the night before. Landis's sculpted body had left an indelible impression on her, and the thought of him wedged between her thighs made Brooklyn want him all over again. "Not really."

"Hey, do you guys want to go ice-skating?" Pepper asked.

"I'm not much of a skater. I'm too clumsy," Brooklyn replied.

"Falling down is half the fun. Come on. It'll be a blast!" Pepper said.

"I'm game, if you guys are," Michael chimed in.

"Me, too," Landis said.

Brooklyn cut her gaze to Landis and said, "I can think of better things to do, but since it's your weekend, Pepper, how can I say no?"

"Oh, goodie!" Pepper clapped her hands.

The four friends marched inside the building to check their belongings and rent skates. As they waited in line, Landis stood close behind Brooklyn and began whispering in her ear.

"Last night was magical."

Brooklyn turned her head slightly and whispered, "Yes, it was an unexpected surprise."

"I hope I wasn't too forward."

"No, not at all. I truly enjoyed every minute."

"What did you like most?" he asked.

His baritone voice reverberating in her ear sent an erotic chill up her spine. Landis had taken her out of her comfort zone, and she was reveling in her sexual liberation. Brooklyn found herself getting aroused as she replayed their maiden night together. "I loved the way you felt inside of me," she said brazenly.

"Did I fill you up?"

"You sure did." Brooklyn backed up into him so that their bodies were touching. "And now I want more."

"Your request is my pleasure."

As they were talking, Landis's cell phone rang. He dug the device out of his pocket and read the caller ID. It was the associate marketing director of his company. Landis unlocked the phone and answered.

"Hey, Robert, what's up?"

"You didn't get back to me on the Brooklyn deal. Did you speak to her manager about trying to close the deal before the end of the year?"

Landis glanced at Brooklyn as he spoke. "Yes, I talked to him. Unfortunately, closing that particular project isn't going to happen in the next week," he said, trying to sound vague.

The line began moving, and Brooklyn stepped ahead.

"Too bad. We really need Brooklyn's star power to get the agency to the next level."

"Yeah, I know. Look, Robert, I've gotta run. I'll be in touch if there are any changes in the next few days."

"Okay. Have a good Christmas."

"Thanks. You, too." Landis disconnected the call and moved closer to Brooklyn.

"Work?" she asked.

"Yes. The wheels of progress keep moving even during the holidays." He chuckled.

"I love your phone. I've been wanting the latest smartphone but keep forgetting to have my assistant order one."

Landis looked down at the phone still in his hand. "Thanks. I love it, too. This phone does everything a tablet does and more."

"After the holidays, I'll call my assistant and have her order one."

The line moved quickly as they were talking, and soon they were lacing up their skates. Michael and Pepper were the first to hit the ice. Brooklyn watched Michael hold Pepper's arm as they made their way around the crowded rink.

"I don't think I can do this," Brooklyn confided.

"Sure you can. Don't worry. I'll be by your side the entire time. I promise I won't let you fall."

Listening to Landis's words gave Brooklyn an assurance that she hadn't felt from a man in a long time. Although they were not officially a couple, she was 90 percent certain that they would have a future together.

As they were ready to enter the rink, some of the skaters had skated over to the side and stopped. At first Brooklyn thought that she had been spotted and the crowd was eagerly awaiting her appearance. She tucked her head into her chin, trying to further hide her face, and then she heard Landis say, "Hey, look! That guy is down on one knee. I think he's about to propose."

Brooklyn surveyed the ice, and sure enough, a couple was front and center. The man had produced an aqua-blue box out of his jacket, opened the lid and was holding a diamond ring. Brooklyn couldn't hear them, but she could see pure joy on the woman's face. Once the man put the ring on her finger, the crowd erupted in cheers and applause. Obviously he had proposed and she had said yes.

Brooklyn peered over at Landis and couldn't help thinking that one day she would be the recipient of a proposal. Touring around the country performing had indeed been a dream come true. She was now ready to figure out what the future held for her and Landis.

Chapter 7

Snow was coming down fast and furious, creating a blizzard effect, blanketing the city and surrounding areas with mounds and mounds of fluffy snow for a white Christmas. Pepper and Michael had rented a vintage railcar to transport their guests to their home in Bridgehampton—one of the quaint towns outside of New York City located on Long Island—where they were celebrating the holiday together before their wedding. Though a replica of an antique train, the railcar was modernized for convenience; nonetheless, it was complete with wood paneling, lace curtains and quaint private quarters.

The wedding party was in the dining car being served a hearty breakfast of blueberry pancakes, uncured bacon, applewood-smoked chicken sausage, fresh-squeezed orange juice and gourmet coffee.

Landis was seated next to Brooklyn at a small, white-linen-covered table, enjoying the meal as well as her company. He couldn't believe how well they gelled. Being with Brooklyn was effortless, unlike his past relationship with a young woman with whom he argued all the time. Although Landis was a tiger at work who rarely took no for an answer, in his personal life he was just the opposite—kind and gentle. Landis had grown up watching his father dote on his mother. His parents had a loving relationship and never argued in front of their two children. Landis had adapted his father's gentlemanly ways and as a result was nonconfrontational and didn't like being at odds with his partner. Though his ex-girlfriend was beautiful on the outside, she was mean-spirited. After two months of walking around on eggshells, he couldn't take her outbursts anymore and called it quits. Landis glanced over at Brooklyn and couldn't help but smile. She was the complete package—beautiful, easygoing and smart.

Maybe now is a good time to bring up my conversation with her manager, before we arrive in the Hamptons and get wrapped up in Christmas and the wedding, Landis thought. He opened his mouth to speak, but was interrupted.

"Why aren't we moving?" Brooklyn asked, looking out the window.

The train had slowed to a complete stop.

Landis peered past her for a look. The snow was now coming down so hard that all he could see outside was a white blur.

"Excuse me, ladies and gentlemen," the train attendant said, coming into the car. "The conductor has stopped the train due to the weather. This unexpected snowstorm has caused a complete whiteout, and visibility is zero. For safety's sake, we'll be sitting idle until the snow lets up. I'll keep you posted. And thanks for your patience."

"Oh, bummer! I wanted to have Christmas dinner before sundown," Pepper said.

"I know you did, but better safe than sorry, honey," Michael said, putting his arm around her shoulder.

The rest of the wedding party grumbled slightly and then settled back for what was sure to be a long wait.

"How about mimosas for everyone?" Michael asked. He then ordered champagne for the group.

"I should have brought a book with me," Brooklyn commented.

"Why is that?" Landis asked.

"To occupy my time. I get antsy if I'm sitting too long."

He leaned across the table and whispered. "I can think of a few things to keep you busy."

"Oh, yeah? Like what?"

Landis looked over his shoulder before continuing, and lowered his voice even more. "Like a repeat of the other night, minus the tinsel."

"Sounds interesting...but where? We are on a train."

"I noticed a few empty private staterooms in the next car. Are you game?" he asked with a wicked grin on his face.

"I sure am. Why don't you leave first and I'll follow in a few minutes. That way we won't look obvious," Brooklyn suggested.

"Okay." Landis took a white linen napkin off the table. "I'll put this in the doorway so you'll know which room I'm in."

He causally stood up and walked out of the dining car. Excitement gripped Landis as he waited for Brooklyn. His appetite for her was insatiable, and he wanted her more with each passing second. He still couldn't believe that Brooke Lynn from school was now Brooklyn the international singing sensation. However, his desire for her had nothing to do with the fact that she was now a celebrity. Their chemistry was magnetic, and he would have been attracted to Brooklyn no matter what she did for a living. Landis hadn't felt this way about a woman in years, and the experience was refreshing.

"What took you so long?" Landis asked, pulling her into the room and closing the door once she arrived.

"It hasn't even been five minutes."

"Even a minute away from you is too long." He took her face in both of his hands and kissed her soft lips. Landis then wrapped his arms around Brooklyn's waist, bringing her closer until their groins met. He began grinding into her, pressing his manhood firmly against her pelvic region.

"You are a naughty boy, Mr. Keates." She giggled.

He kissed the side of her neck. "I just can't help myself around you."

"Maybe we shouldn't be doing this with everyone in the next car," Brooklyn said, stepping back a bit.

Landis stepped forward, closing the space between them. "Don't be silly. We're old pros at making love with people in the next room. I can be quiet, if you can."

"I can be as quiet as a church mouse moonwalking on cotton."

They both laughed.

"And you have a sense of humor. I love it! You can sing, tell jokes. What else can you do?"

"Let me show you." Brooklyn unbuckled his belt and unzipped his jeans, allowing them to fall to the floor. She rubbed her index finger around the waistband of his black boxer briefs before slipping her hand into his underwear. She fondled his package until she felt him firm to her touch. "Somebody's getting excited."

"We sure are. Don't stop! That feels good."

Brooklyn increased the pace, kneading him until he had a full-blown erection. She then knelt down and put the tip of his penis in her mouth. She kissed the head several times, then licked the side of his shaft like a luscious lollipop before taking the full length of him in her mouth. She sucked and sucked, applying pleasurable pressure to his manhood.

Landis put his hands on the top of her crown of auburn tresses to steady himself. "Damn, girl, where did you learn those skills?"

Brooklyn didn't respond; she just kept sucking and licking and sucking some more. Her head was now bobbing back and forth like it was on an automatic spring.

"You…you're…going to make me come," Landis said in between breaths. He was on the verge of coming and could feel his soldiers marching to the finish line. He quickly extracted his member from her mouth and relieved himself onto the floor.

Brooklyn wiped her mouth with the back of her hand and stood up.

"Wow! You are something else, Brooklyn."

"I aim to please."

"And you certainly did. I'll be right back."

Landis headed to the small adjoining bathroom. He returned a few moments later carrying a warm towel.

He gently wiped the edges of her mouth and then leaned down and cleaned up the evidence of their naughtiness.

"Now let me return the favor," he said, pulling her toward him.

Brooklyn kissed him on the lips. "I'll wait until we get to Bridgehampton. I want to think about you going down on me. The anticipation of your tongue on me will be enough to keep me wet until we get to our destination."

"Oh, you're such a tease."

Brooklyn smoothed her hair, winked at him, opened the door and slipped out.

Landis leaned against the back of the door and exhaled hard. "Damn, what a woman!"

Chapter 8

Pepper and Michael's country house in Bridgehampton was aglow. White Christmas lights framed the outside of the two-story home as well as the surrounding trees. The lights twinkled in the darkness, making the home look like a vision out of a storybook. The group had finally arrived well after the designated time. Brooklyn peered out of the limousine window and marveled at the illuminated miniature manger, replete with three wise men, on the snow-covered lawn.

The caravan of three black limos parked in the circular driveway discharged the weary guests.

"Come on in, everyone, and welcome to our home away from home," Pepper announced.

"I thought your penthouse was decorated to the hilt, but this is spectacular," Brooklyn commented, walking from the marble foyer into the grand living room. A ten-foot-tall pine tree was adorned with gold metallic bows, silver ornaments and ribbons of lights. Brooklyn inhaled, taking in the smell of fresh pine. "Hmm, and it smells good, too. This is my first time seeing your Hamptons house in the winter. It's spectacular!"

"Thanks. But I didn't have time to do these decorations. I hired a crew to get the house ready for Christmas."

"They did an awesome job," Landis commented.

"Now, come on, everyone. Let me show you to your rooms. After you settle in, come back downstairs in an hour for dinner. I had the chef prepare a special meal for tonight."

Brooklyn was so thankful to have been included in Pepper and Michael's holiday plans. She hadn't had a real Christmas in years. She was usually on tour and had spent many a Christmas evening in a hotel suite ordering room service. Now, not only was she with her best friend during this special time of the year, she had also found that special man to spend the holiday with. Brooklyn couldn't have been happier. She bounced up the stairs and followed Pepper as she showed everyone their sleeping quarters.

Landis and Brooklyn were the last two left. Pepper turned to them and asked, "So, do you two want to share a room?"

Brooklyn wanted to shout *Yes,* but she held back to hear Landis's response.

"I would love nothing more—that is—" Landis reached for Brooklyn and hugged her against his side "—if it's all right with you."

Brooklyn blushed. She could feel her cheeks becoming rosy as she stood there in his embrace. "Sure, we can share a room," she answered casually.

Pepper opened the door, walked inside and flicked on the lights. The room was huge, with a king-size sleigh bed and antique furnishings. "Nice digs," Landis commented and put their bags down.

"Thanks. I bought most of these pieces in Europe and had them shipped over. That settee over there," Pepper said, pointing to a cream-colored silk damask minisofa, "is from the late eighteen hundreds."

"It's gorgeous," Brooklyn replied.

"Okay, you guys settle in and I'll see you in an hour," Pepper said, leaving and closing the door behind her.

"First things first. You need to take off that coat," Landis said, coming up behind Brooklyn and helping her out of her luxurious sable fur. He tossed the coat onto a nearby chair. "That's better, but you still have on too many clothes."

"Oh, I do, do I?"

"Yep," he said, taking off his peacoat and tossing it on the same chair.

"Well, it is winter, and turtlenecks and cashmere slacks are appropriate attire for this weather."

"Now that we're inside, I can think of a better outfit."

Brooklyn looked at Landis with dreamy eyes, batted her lashes and asked, "Oh, yeah, and what is that?"

"A thong and low-cut lacy bra."

"That's not an outfit."

"Let me be the judge of that. Now take off your clothes."

Brooklyn was always comfortable in her skin, even when she was overweight. She may have been shy around Landis in the past, but that unsure teen was long gone. She removed her boots, unfastened her belt, unzipped her gray cashmere slacks and stepped out of them. She then pulled the black turtleneck over her head. Now wearing only her underwear—a black thong and matching bra—she put her hand on her hip and struck a pose. "You like?"

Landis quickly made his way toward her. "I do. You look like a Victoria's Secret model. You're breathtaking." He reached out and touched her stomach, running his hand up and down her midsection. "And your skin is so soft and smooth."

The feel of his strong masculine hand on her skin sent goose bumps up her arms. Landis was turning her on with just a simple touch. *What is this man doing to me?* Brooklyn was falling hard and fast. A part of her was saying, *Hold back and tread lightly.* And yet another part was saying, *Go for it, he's a good man.* Brooklyn went with the latter thought, drowning out the doubt.

"So…have you been thinking about me putting my tongue on you?" he asked.

"I sure have."

"Is the thought making you wet?"

"It sure is, but now that we're here, I shouldn't have to fantasize about you any longer."

"And why is that?" he asked, roaming his fingers down her stomach and into her sexy underwear.

"You're supposed to make my fantasy a reality."

Landis didn't say another word. He took Brooklyn by the hand, led her over to the bed and sat down. He spread his long legs, took her by the hips and brought her close. He peeled her thong off, exposing her lady parts. Landis stared at her, intently admiring her body. "You're beautiful here."

"Thank you. Do I look good enough to eat?"

He licked his full lips. "You sure do."

Landis reached around, took her by the ass and pulled her closer. He then stroked the perimeter of her clit with his firm tongue.

Brooklyn spread her legs farther apart, allowing him better access, and put her hands on his shoulders to steady herself.

Landis licked and licked until he uncovered her tiny piece of pleasure-pleasing flesh. He took her clit in his mouth, sucking it softly at first and then increasing the pace.

"Mmm," she moaned and then shifted her hips slightly to the right so that he could hit her spot better.

Landis kept up his rapid pace, licking and sucking, with his saliva dripping from his chin.

"Oh, that's it!"

Landis slipped his middle finger into her vagina and pumped it up and down as he continued with his oral fixation.

"I'm…I'm…coming!"

Brooklyn exploded, and her knees buckled as she came.

"Are you okay?" Landis asked, steadying her.

"I'm perfect! And so are you. That was amazing."

"Better than the fantasy?"

"Much, much better. We'd better get ready for dinner. I'm going to hop in the shower." She crossed the room, picked up her tote bag and made her way into the adjoining bathroom.

While Brooklyn stood underneath the pulsating water, she replayed their day of oral pleasures. She had given him an expert blow job, and he had returned the

favor in spades. A broad smile spread across her face.
Landis was turning out to be better than she could have
ever imagined. It had taken years to finally connect with
him, but the wait had been worth the lost time. Brooklyn thought that being with Landis now as opposed to
when they were in college had worked out for the best.
In college, she had been a shy coed who wasn't in touch
with her sexuality. Fast-forward twelve years and she had
not only settled into her womanhood, but wasn't afraid
to ask for what she wanted.

After lathering up and showering, Brooklyn stepped
out of the marble shower and toweled off. She dressed
in a simple black Michael Kors dress with a deep neckline that accentuated her cleavage, a strand of pearls
and a pair of black patent leather pointed-toe pumps.
Brooklyn spritzed her neck and wrists with perfume
and made her exit.

"Wow." Landis whistled. "You look like a superstar."

"That's because I am." Brooklyn giggled. "I'm just
kidding. Thanks for the compliment."

She glanced over at the bed. Sitting in the middle of
the crimson silk duvet was a box, beautifully wrapped in
teal foil paper with a perfectly tied silver bow. "What's
that?"

Landis picked the box off of the bed and handed it to
Brooklyn. "Merry Christmas."

A shocked expression registered on her face. She
wasn't expecting a gift from Landis. "You didn't have
to buy me anything."

"I know I didn't, but I wanted to. Open it."

Brooklyn untied the silver ribbon, tore open the gift
wrapping and exclaimed, "Oh, wow! Just what I wanted!
When did you have time to buy me a smartphone?"

"I called one of Santa's helpers and put in an express order."

"Thank you so much!" Brooklyn hugged Landis around the neck and gave him a tender kiss.

"The phone is just like mine. It has all the bells and whistles."

"You'll have to show me how to work it. I kept my last phone way too long because I didn't want to deal with the learning curve of operating a new device."

Landis hugged her to him. "Don't worry. I'll be your very own personal tutor. I'd better get in the shower so we won't be late for dinner."

"Okay."

Brooklyn watched Landis strut across the room and admired his strong physique. He was so handsome that she felt like following him, stripping off her clothes and sexing him up in the shower. Her sexual appetite for Landis was insatiable. She just couldn't get enough of him. Not only was he an excellent lover, he was kind and generous. Brooklyn sighed and said in a low tone, "This man is definitely a keeper."

Chapter 9

"Merry Christmas, everyone!" Pepper said, standing at the head of the table with Michael by her side.

"We want to thank each and every one of you for spending the holidays with us and for sharing our joy on our impending nuptials." Michael raised his champagne flute. "Cheers."

Crystal flutes were filled with chilled Veuve Clicquot and the group of eight held their glasses high and toasted. They were seated on opposite sides of an oblong table, which was filled with a Christmas feast, featuring a rib roast with winter vegetables, a golden roasted turkey and chestnut stuffing, homemade cranberry sauce, garlic mashed potatoes, and a whole roasted salmon over a bed of sautéed spinach.

During dinner, Brooklyn stole glances at Landis. She was still marveling at his surprise Christmas gift. His thoughtfulness was amazing. Landis had logged in to his memory bank that Brooklyn wanted a smartphone and had taken the initiative and bought her one, as if he were her man.

"This food is delicious," Landis leaned over and said to Brooklyn.

"I can't wait for dessert," she replied.

"What's on the menu?"

Brooklyn whispered into his ear, "You."

"Mmm, sounds delicious. I can hardly wait, either."

Brooklyn and Landis were in their own world, having a naughty exchange as if they were the only ones at the table.

"You were amazing upstairs," she whispered.

"And you were wonderful on the train."

Brooklyn reached underneath the table and rested her hand on top of his mound of manhood. She gently began massaging his crotch.

"You better stop or I won't be able to stand up without being embarrassed."

Brooklyn giggled. "I guess you have a point. It would be out of place at Christmas dinner to say the least." She removed her hand and continued eating.

After dinner, the chef presented dessert, which was a perfectly sculpted yule log cake adorned with green leaves of icing.

"Let's go into the den for after-dinner drinks," Michael announced once everyone had finished.

The den was large, yet cozy, with polished wood paneling, ivory tufted-leather furniture and hardwood flooring covered with a huge bearskin rug. A hewed stone fireplace framed a roaring fire. Michael stood at the bar and poured hefty portions of port and cognac. Once everyone had their drink of choice, the men lit cigars and were talking in a group. Some of the women were smoking petite cigars and sipping port. Pepper excused herself from the women and went over to Brooklyn, who had just returned from the restroom.

"Look at you. You're glowing."

Brooklyn wiped her forehead. "I'm just hot. The fire is blazing."

"Oh…I don't think it's the fire. I think it's Landis that has you burning up."

Brooklyn peered over Pepper's shoulder at the group of women to make sure they were out of earshot. She was a private person and didn't want to expose her private business to people she hadn't seen in years. Since everyone in the room was enjoying their own conversations, Brooklyn felt comfortable sharing an intimate conversation with her friend.

"You're right. Landis has ignited a need in me that I haven't felt in a long time. We can't keep our hands off of each other," she whispered.

"Do I need to call the minister and tell him we're going to have a double wedding?"

"I wouldn't go that far. Do you think he's into me now that I'm a world-renowned singer?" Brooklyn asked with a sudden twinge of doubt.

"Of course not. Landis isn't shallow or starstruck. I've grown to know him better over the years and have seen him work diligently to build his agency. And now that he's a successful businessman, I'm sure he's looking to settle down and get married."

Brooklyn digested Pepper's words and hoped that her friend was right. She had experienced a man trying to use her to advance his career, and she didn't want to go through that unpleasant experience ever again. "I guess I'm just a little paranoid."

"I can understand your position. If I thought Landis was trying to use you, I'd be the first one to speak up." Pepper put her arm around Brooklyn. "You're my girl after all, and I've got your back."

"Thanks. I appreciate your friendship."

"I value yours, too. And I'm truly grateful that you're singing at the wedding. Oh, and don't forget, your rehearsal at the church is tomorrow."

"Okay, great."

"Hey, what are you two gabbing about over here?" Landis asked, approaching them.

"You," Pepper spouted.

Landis pointed his finger at his chest. *"Moi?"*

"Yep. I'm putting you on notice right here and now. If you hurt my girl, you'll have me to answer to," Pepper said, placing her hand on her hip.

Brooklyn stood there and shifted her eyes from Pepper to Landis; she couldn't believe that Pepper was totally speaking her mind. She felt a little embarrassed, but also relieved that Pepper had said what she herself had been thinking.

"I have no intention of hurting Brooklyn," he said, hugging Brooklyn close to his side and giving her a kiss on the cheek.

"Good." With that said, Pepper crossed the room to where the other women were standing and joined in their conversation.

"Wow, what did I just walk into?" Landis asked.

"Pepper is being overprotective. We were talking and I mentioned how this one guy I dated only wanted to use me to advance his career. I thought he had genuine feelings for me, but I was mistaken."

"Oh...I'm sorry you had to go through that experience. Trust me. My feelings for you are real."

Brooklyn exhaled slightly, letting out a sigh of relief. Hearing Pepper voice her opinion was one thing, but listening to the words come out of Landis's mouth was the reassurance she needed to quiet the doubt lingering in the back of her mind.

Chapter 10

Landis was downstairs in the expansive gourmet kitchen preparing breakfast for his newfound love. He had risen with the sun, bathed, quietly dressed and crept out of the room while Brooklyn was still fast asleep. He wanted to shower Brooklyn with not only great sex, but genuine kindness.

He busied himself at the stove making scrambled eggs and bacon for two. Landis wasn't much of a cook and had a limited repertoire of dishes that he could prepare without burning, and scrambled eggs and bacon was one of them. There were bagels in the bread basket. He toasted two of them and smeared them with butter and cream cheese. Landis even sliced and sectioned a large pink grapefruit.

He searched the cupboards and found a wooden bed-tray table. He arranged the food on a large china platter and placed it on the tray with two glasses of orange juice, two mugs of steaming hot coffee and a small container of cream.

He made his way up the back staircase and down the hallway, carefully holding the tray with both hands. When he reached their room, Landis eased open the door and slipped inside.

Brooklyn was curled up underneath the covers. Landis stood at the side of the bed and watched her sleep for a few moments. She looked angelic and peaceful.

You're one lucky man, he thought.

She began to stir.

"Good morning," he said, putting the tray next to her.

"Good morning. What's all this?" she asked, sitting up against the headboard.

"Breakfast in bed for my beauty," he said, sitting down.

"Oh, how sweet. I didn't know you were a chef."

"Far from it, but I can manage breakfast." He picked up a forkful of eggs and fed them to her. "Here, take a bite before they get cold."

"Hmm, these are good. What did you put in them?"

"White cheddar cheese, garlic powder, salt and pepper, but the key is a little half-and-half."

"Oh, listen to you sounding like a chef on the Food Network. I'm impressed."

"Thank you, my beauty. Do you want me to make you a breakfast sandwich?"

"A breakfast sandwich?"

Landis put his eggs and bacon between the bagel slices. "See." He took a bite. "It's really good."

"Looks delicious, but I'm watching my carbs."

"You're perfect just the way you are. You don't need

to lose a single pound, but I understand your need to stay fit, especially in your line of work. Here, try this grapefruit. It's naturally sweet." Landis took a section and held it to her lips.

Brooklyn took a bite. "Mmm...succulent." She took another piece, and this time, instead of biting the grapefruit, she slid the piece of fruit between her lips, moving it in and out of her mouth until the skin broke and a stream of juice began flowing down her chin. She then popped the section in her mouth.

Landis watched as she played with the fruit as if it were a sex toy. Looking at the juice drip from her mouth was turning him on. "I like the way you eat grapefruit."

"Oh, you do, do you?" She took another section, rubbed it across her lips and then reached over to Landis and put the fruit in his mouth.

"Juicy, isn't it?" she asked.

He nodded his head. "Almost as juicy as you are."

Brooklyn put her hand underneath the comforter. "Yes, I'm juicy all right. Wanna see?"

Landis removed the tray, put it on the nightstand and pulled the covers back. "I sure do." He rubbed her sweet spot. "How did you get so wet so fast?"

"I was dreaming about making love to you before I woke up."

"Oh, really? Were you on top?"

"Yes. I was riding you like you were a prized pony."

"I'm a thoroughbred, baby."

"That's even better. I love a big, strong stallion."

Landis rose, went over to his duffel bag, took out a condom, returned to Brooklyn, disrobed and said, "See how excited you've got me." He tore open the foil wrapper, took out the rubber and slid it onto his firm penis.

He then lay back on the bed. "Let me see your jockeying skills."

Brooklyn didn't waste any time stripping off her nightgown and mounting Landis. She took his stiff shaft, slid it inside her wanting canal and started pumping back and forth.

Landis held her knees and spread them open a bit more. He rotated his hips, all the while pushing himself farther inside her.

Brooklyn grabbed hold of the headboard and rode him harder and harder. "Damn, that feels so good!"

Landis reached around, took two handfuls of her ripe ass and flipped her over, reversing their position. He wedged himself in between her legs and went to work, pumping and grinding, until beads of sweat formed on his forehead. He could feel himself on the verge of coming, but held back. "I want you to come first."

Brooklyn had her legs wrapped around his back and was matching him move for move. "O-okay..." she panted.

"Tell me when you're coming."

Landis ramped up the pace, working feverishly.

"I'm...I'm...coming," she said, in between breaths.

Landis watched her mouth twist and her head whip back and forth as she reached the pinnacle. Now that she was satisfied, he allowed himself to let go and came hard into the condom.

"That was awesome!" Brooklyn said, resting back on the pillow.

Landis rolled over. "Yes, it was. Every time we make love, it gets better and better."

"There's no denying that we're sexually compatible."

Landis kissed her on the lips. "Yes, we are. You're addicting." He began rubbing her nipples.

"Don't tell me you're ready for round two?"

"I sure am. Just give me a few minutes." He took off the used condom, wrapped it in a tissue.

"We're going to have to wait until later. I have to go to rehearsal."

Landis looked at her oddly. "Rehearsal for what?"

"I'm singing at Pepper and Michael's wedding."

"Oh, I didn't know that. I thought you were one of the bridesmaids."

"Actually, I'm the maid of honor and I'm also singing a solo. I'm meeting with the church pianist today."

"So, this is a working vacation for you?"

"No, I wouldn't say that. I'm not working, per se, just singing for a friend. Let me hop in the shower. I don't want to be late."

"Okay."

While Brooklyn was in the bathroom, Landis leaned back on the headboard and pondered whether or not to broach the subject of his agency vying for her as a client. *Since she's going to a rehearsal and in a semiwork mode, she might be receptive to talking about the prospective deal.*

As he was thinking, Brooklyn came out of the bathroom wearing a pair of cream-colored leggings, a cream cashmere sweater and a pair of thigh-high ivory boots. "Wow, you look like a vision in winter white."

"Thanks. What are you doing today?"

"I don't know yet. I have to check with Michael and find out what he has planned for the groomsmen."

Brooklyn gave Landis a peck on the lips and picked

up her new phone, which was right next to Landis's on the nightstand. "Okay, I'll see you later."

She rushed out before he had a chance to say anything. He then remembered that her manager hadn't told Brooklyn about the deal yet, so even if Landis had brought up the subject, she wouldn't know what he was talking about.

Landis began to feel as if he was being deceitful by not disclosing the fact that he was in talks with her manager.

"She needs to know the truth, so there won't be any mix-ups," he muttered.

Landis reached for his cell phone. He dialed her manger's number, but got his voice mail. Landis hung up and decided to send a text message instead.

Malcolm, we need to talk about the deal with Brooklyn. There's been a new development. Call me ASAP. It's extremely important!

He waited a few minutes, but received no return text. Landis began to feel uneasy. He couldn't have possibly known a few days ago that the client he was trying hard to land would land in his bed. Brooklyn had been burned before by an ex-boyfriend, and Landis wanted to be clear that he had no intentions of using their new-found relationship to advance his career.

Chapter 11

Brooklyn's rehearsal went well. The church pianist had years of experience under his belt and was extremely professional. He didn't make an issue of Brooklyn being an international star. He treated her like just another choir member, which she appreciated. Although she was an award-winning singer, Brooklyn didn't like being fussed over. She was singing "Ave Maria" in Italian for the ceremony and wanted to ensure that she and her accompanist were completely in sync. After only an hour of rehearsing, they had the song perfected. She thanked him and left.

Brooklyn was meeting Pepper at the bridal shop for a fitting. The rest of the bridesmaids already had their dresses. Due to Brooklyn's rigorous touring schedule, she couldn't make the previous fittings. Instead, she had texted Pepper her measurements so that the seamstress could start on her maid-of-honor dress.

The bridal shop, Wedding Bliss, was located on Main Street in Bridgehampton. Brooklyn's bodyguard chauffeured her through the quaint town, which was decorated with a huge menorah as well as a Christmas tree. The lampposts were wrapped with garland, and old-fashioned colored Christmas bulbs were strung high over the main thoroughfare.

The limo pulled in front of the shop, and Brooklyn stepped out, wearing a pair of dark Prada shades and her ankle-length brown sable coat over her winter-white outfit.

"Hey, how did rehearsal go?" Pepper asked once Brooklyn walked into the shop's private room.

Brooklyn took off her coat and sunglasses. "Great. Mr. Vance is awesome! He knew exactly what key to play for my pitch."

"Isn't he a lovely older gentleman? He's been with the church ever since I was a little girl. I knew you would like him."

"Excuse me, Ms. Daniels, would you and your guest like a glass of champagne?" the saleswoman asked, peeking her head in the door.

"That sounds great. And can you also bring in her dress?" Pepper asked.

"Sure thing."

"So are you getting nervous?" Brooklyn asked.

"Not at all. I knew I was going to marry Michael the first time I saw him during freshman registration. Even though he was a little dorky back then, with his wire-frame glasses and starched khakis, I knew he was the man for me. Sort of like you and Landis."

"Not really. I admired Landis, but no way did I ever think he would give me the time of day, let alone propose marriage."

"Look at the two of you now. You guys are inseparable, and you make the perfect couple."

Brooklyn's face lit up. "You think so?"

"No doubt! You're gorgeous and he's so handsome. Not only are you guys beautiful on the outside, but you both have kind hearts."

As they were talking, two saleswomen came into the room. One was carrying the dress and the other woman had a bucket filled with ice and a bottle of Moët & Chandon. She poured two glasses of bubbly and the other woman hung the dress on the fitting-room door.

"Here's to you and Michael—may you guys have a long, healthy, happy marriage," Brooklyn said, raising her glass once the saleswomen left the room.

"And here's to you and Landis. May you two grow closer with each passing day."

The BFFs toasted and sipped.

"Go try on the dress. I'm excited to see how it looks on you," Pepper said.

"Yes, ma'am." Brooklyn rose, took the dress off the door and went into the fitting room. A few minutes later, she emerged wearing a one-shoulder lavender silk shantung dress that stopped just above the knee.

"Wow! It fits perfectly!" Pepper squealed. "I'm so relieved, especially since there's little time for alternations. Do you like it?"

Brooklyn turned in the floor-length mirror to look at herself. "Yes, it's elegant, no crazy ruffles or huge flowers. I'll definitely wear this dress again."

"I'm glad you like it. Even though I had emailed you

a picture of the dress, there's nothing like seeing it in person."

Brooklyn's phone rang as they were talking. She crossed the room, dug the device out of her tote bag and looked at the caller ID. It was Malcolm, her manager, calling. Brooklyn hit the ignore button. She was enjoying the moment with her best friend and didn't want to interrupt their time together discussing business. Whatever he had to say could wait.

"Nice phone," Pepper commented.

Brooklyn blushed and rubbed the front of the phone. "Thank you."

"Is it new?"

"Yep! It's my Christmas present from Landis."

"Christmas present?" Pepper asked, wrinkling her nose.

"That day at Rockefeller Center, I admired his phone and mentioned that I needed a new smartphone. The next thing I know, the phone was wrapped up in a box and sitting on the bed Christmas evening."

"That's so sweet!"

"Isn't it? He's a keeper for sure."

Brooklyn was beaming as if she were the bride-to-be. She couldn't have been happier. She had finally met her match. Landis didn't have any hidden agenda. He had let his intentions be known the first night they met. Brooklyn remembered Pepper's words about Landis wanting to settle down and hoped that her friend was right.

"Maybe Landis and I will be next at the altar."

Pepper picked up her flute and touched it to Brooklyn's. "I'll toast to that."

Chapter 12

"Oh, it's so cold out here!"

"Walk faster and you won't feel it."

Brooklyn and Landis were out on the private deck that was right outside their bedroom. The early-evening temperature had dipped down into the low thirties, but that didn't prevent them from venturing out onto the deck in white terry-cloth robes, boots and nothing else. Landis had the bright idea to relax in the hot tub before the rehearsal and dinner.

"Why did I agree to coming out here in the freezing cold? This is ludicrous!" Brooklyn whined.

"Oh, come on. Stop being a baby." Landis had made his way to the hot tub; he took off his biker boots and dipped his toe in the water. He had gone out earlier and turned on the hot tub. "The water is perfect." He dis-

robed, revealing his sculpted body, and eased himself
into the bubbling water.

Brooklyn stopped in her tracks momentarily to stare
at his nakedness before he submerged himself up to his
neck. Landis still had a toned athlete's body. His thighs
were firm, his chest was well defined without being
too muscular and his biceps appeared strong and powerful. Admiring his body had motivated her, and she
picked up her pace, nearly running. When she reached
the hot tub, she tore off her robe, kicked off her boots
and quickly stepped in.

"Ahh, that's better," she said, settling into the tub.

"Now you can't even feel the cold. Can you?" Landis
asked, with a fog of condensation emanating from his
mouth as he spoke.

"No, you can't, but it's still frigid out here." Brooklyn
glanced around at the mounds of snow in the corners of
the deck and couldn't believe that she was sitting in a
hot tub in this frosty climate.

"It might be cold out there, but it's warm and toasty
in here."

"I know, but my mind can't get over the fact that I'm
outside, naked in the winter. The last time I was in a hot
tub, it was in sunny California on an eighty-degree day
and I had on a bathing suit."

Landis moved closer to her. "Close your eyes."

"What?"

"Close your eyes for a few seconds."

Brooklyn did as instructed. She could hear the gurgling of the bubbles and nothing else. The night was
still and quiet. She inhaled the crisp air and exhaled.
Suddenly, she felt Landis's lips on hers. With her eyes
still closed, Brooklyn returned his kiss. She slipped her

tongue into his mouth and French-kissed him with abandon. Brooklyn was no longer cold, but was heating up with pheromones. She moved closer, threw one leg over his body and straddled him, all the while keeping her eyes closed.

Landis gently palmed her breasts and began massaging the mounds of soft flesh. He played with her nipples, softly squeezing them between his fingers. "I love your tits. They're not hard like artificial boobs."

"No, baby, I'm all natural," she said, opening her lids.

They stared longingly into each other's eyes, momentarily silent. Their passion was speaking loud and clear.

Brooklyn reached underneath the water and began stroking his manhood, bringing it to attention. She wanted to feel him inside her. She was becoming addicted to making love with Landis. She just couldn't get enough.

"Wait one minute," Landis said. He moved Brooklyn's leg to the side, then reached over the edge of the tub for his robe and fished out a condom from the pocket. He stood up in the middle of the water, rolled on the prophylactic and sat back down. "Okay, where were we?"

"I was getting ready to feel you inside me."

"Oh, I like the sound of that. Come here." Landis held Brooklyn's arm as she resumed her position.

Brooklyn sat on his mound of flesh and started suggestively rotating her hips until she felt him growing beneath her. She opened her legs wider, scooted closer to his groin area and continued grinding.

Landis took hold of his stiff rod and inserted the tip into her sweet spot.

Brooklyn bounced up and down, and up and down, inching his hardness farther into her ready canal.

He held her by the waist, lightly lifting her with each bounce, until they were moving so fiercely that water sloshed around them.

The steam from the hot tub and their lovemaking caused beads of perspiration to sprout up on Brooklyn's forehead. She felt free and liberated, making love underneath the stars in the crisp winter air. She didn't hold back. She gave him all she had.

"I...I...love you...Landis!" Brooklyn shouted out as she came.

Landis held her tightly around the waist. "I love you, too, Brooklyn."

After giving in to their yearnings, they relaxed in each other's arms, staring up at the onyx sky. The moon was full and seemed to hang above them like an exquisite oil painting.

"We'd better get going, or else we're going to be late for the rehearsal," Brooklyn said, breaking the spell.

Landis stepped out first, put on his robe, picked up Brooklyn's robe and held it out for her. After putting on their boots, they strolled back to their room as if it were a balmy ninety-degree day, in love and totally oblivious to the cold.

Chapter 13

The rehearsal at the church was seamless. The wedding party was small, and the ceremony would be simple; no complicated dance steps to learn for a YouTube video, just an ordinary church wedding. After an hour of rehearsing, the bridesmaids and groomsmen had their roles down, and now the group was exiting the church on their way to dinner.

The rehearsal dinner was being held at Tutto il Giorno in Sag Harbor. The quaint Italian restaurant was situated near the harbor and was Pepper and Michael's favorite eatery in the Hamptons. For their ceremonial dinner, they had rented out the entire restaurant for the event.

"Don't you just love this place?" Pepper asked Brooklyn once they were seated.

"It's adorable. I love the canary-colored walls, and the white wainscoting gives the room a warm, cozy feel."

"That's exactly why Michael and I love this place! Besides, the food is amazing."

"Good, because I'm starving." Brooklyn leaned closer to Pepper and whispered, "Landis and I worked up an appetite earlier this evening."

"Do tell."

Brooklyn looked across the table at Landis, who was sitting next to Michael. "Let's just say we gave relaxing in the hot tub a new meaning."

"You guys are like a couple of horny bunny rabbits."

"What can I say? We have insatiable appetites and it isn't just about the sex. Tonight, we admitted our love for each other."

"Oh, Brooklyn, I'm so happy for you."

"I'm ecstatic, too. I haven't told Landis this yet, but I'm thinking about buying a condo in Manhattan so we can be close. Long-distance relationships are hard. In the beginning everything is rosy, but over time, the flame dies out. I don't want that to happen to us. I've waited too long to be with Landis, and I'm not wasting any more time."

"You're making the right decision. You living on the West Coast and Landis living on the East Coast is too long a distance to travel on a regular basis," Pepper commented.

"I'm finished with the tour. After I complete the last two tracks on my new album, I'll have free time and I plan to spend that time in New York with Landis." Brooklyn glanced over at her lover again.

Landis winked at her as he rose and excused himself from the table.

"Good for you. I'm glad you're not taking what you have with him for granted. Landis is a catch and I'm sure he has women throwing themselves at his feet on a regular basis," Pepper commented.

"I can imagine the women are on him like white on rice. He's handsome, smart and successful. What woman wouldn't want him? But he's all mine now, and I'm not letting him go," Brooklyn said with conviction in her voice.

As they were talking, a tall, attractive woman with a short pixie haircut approached Pepper.

"Excuse me, Ms. Daniels. How's the service?"

"Hi, Jesse. Everything is perfect. The server brought our cocktails and we're just chatting before dinner comes out. Jesse, let me introduce you to my dear friend Brooklyn," Pepper said.

"Oh, I know Brooklyn. Well, shall I say I have all of your CDs?" Jesse gushed.

"Thank you," Brooklyn said.

"Brooklyn, this is Jesse, the manager here. She's great! She has planned the entire menu for our rehearsal dinner. All I did was make the phone call."

"It's been my pleasure to arrange this special menu for you and your guests. Let me go back in the kitchen and check on the first course. It was nice meeting you, Brooklyn," Jesse said, before leaving the table.

Landis was coming out of the men's room and bumped smack into his ex-girlfriend. He stopped in his tracks, stunned.

"Jesse! What are you doing here?" he asked, completely shocked.

"Hello, Landis, how are you?"

"Uh…I'm good. What are you doing in the Hamptons this time of year?" he asked, trying to determine why his ex-girlfriend was in this part of Long Island during the off-season.

"I'm the manager here."

"Manager? You don't work on Wall Street any longer?"

"No, I got burned out. Working on the Street was turning me into an evil monster who barked orders at anyone who crossed my path. So I quit my job, and bought a small cottage here in Sag Harbor. A friend of mine is the co-owner of this place. He offered me a job, and I jumped at the chance for a welcomed and much needed change of pace."

"Good for you, Jesse." Landis studied her face. "You look relaxed. I don't see those stress lines that used to wrinkle your forehead."

"Thank you. I'm extremely peaceful these days. Landis, I really need to apologize for the way I treated you when we were dating. I was rude to you for no reason. You're a good man and didn't deserve that type of treatment."

"Thanks, I appreciate your apology."

Jesse leaned up and kissed Landis on the cheek. "Can we be friends?"

"What's going on here?" Brooklyn asked, walking toward them on her way to the restroom.

Landis's gaze darted between Jesse and Brooklyn. For an instant, he felt as if he had been caught cheating. He quickly got that thought out of his head. He had nothing to hide. He reached out for Brooklyn's hand and held it tightly.

"Jesse, this is my girlfriend, Brooklyn."

"Yes, we just met. Landis, I'm so happy for you. Well,

let me get back to work. Goodbye, Landis," Jesse said and walked away.

"What was that all about? And why was she kissing you on the cheek?" Brooklyn asked.

"Jesse is my ex-girlfriend, and she was apologizing for her offensive behavior during our relationship."

Brooklyn reached up and wiped Landis's cheek with her hand. "Just so you know…I don't want any other woman kissing on my man for any reason."

"Yes, ma'am. Don't worry. You're the only woman I want kissing me."

"Good. I'll be right back."

When Brooklyn returned from the ladies' room, Landis clenched her hand and they walked back to the table, quite the happy couple.

Chapter 14

"Harder!" Brooklyn tried to muffle her scream as Landis bent her over the footboard of their bed.

"You want more?"

"Yes, yes!"

It was the morning of the wedding, and Brooklyn and Landis were indulging in their own private honeymoon activities. They had confessed their love for each other and were now comfortable verbalizing during intercourse.

"Is that all for me?" Brooklyn asked, looking over her shoulder at him when he firmly pushed into her.

"Yes, baby!" he said. Landis cupped her rear. "Is this all mine?"

She pushed back against him. "It's all yours. Can you handle it?"

Landis placed his large hands on each side of her hips, brought her closer and pressed himself deeper.

"Oh, yes! Yes! That feels amazing!"

Brooklyn and Landis rocked back and forth. They were working so hard that the headboard began knocking against the wall.

"We're going to wake up the entire house," Brooklyn whispered. "Let's get in the bed."

Landis gave another firm push before ejecting himself. "I think we're going to need another condom before this one breaks." He rolled the used condom off, wrapped it in tissue, tossed it in the trash can and replaced it with a fresh one.

Brooklyn lay on her back in the middle of the bed, with her knees bent and one foot on the nightstand. She crooked her finger at Landis. "Get over here and finish what you started."

"With pleasure." He wedged himself between her firm thighs. "Is this what you want?"

"You know that's exactly what I want." Brooklyn licked her lips in anticipation of the delicious feel of Landis firmly inside her. "Stop teasing me and start pleasing me." She put her other foot on the nightstand, locking Landis between her legs.

"I want you to beg for it," he said, putting the tip of his penis into her opening and then pulling out.

"Please, please can I have some more of that?"

"I don't know." He moved again. "How bad do you want it?"

Brooklyn turned her head from one side to the other. His teasing was driving her crazy with a sexual need that she had never known before. "I've never wanted anything more." She reached up to pull him toward her, but he moved back out of her reach.

"Put your hand down. I'm running this show."

His baritone voice alone was enough to make her juices flow, and she shuddered with yearning. "I love a man who can take control."

"And I love a woman who can handle me."

Brooklyn watched as Landis took hold of himself and stroked her up and down. She groaned at the sight and opened her legs even wider. She had never wanted a man like she wanted Landis. They were evenly matched, sexually as well as intellectually, and the combination was a potent aphrodisiac. Brooklyn arched her back and scooted closer to him.

"Let's wait until after the wedding. I think you've had enough of me for now."

Brooklyn tightened her legs around his thighs, gripping him in place. "Oh, I don't think so, mister."

Landis chuckled. "I do like your persistence. How can I say no?" He inserted his penis one inch at a time until he was all the way inside her. Landis knocked over the nightstand as he began moving.

Brooklyn pulled him on top of her and wrapped her legs around his lower back. She bucked and pumped, matching him move for move. The friction against her inner walls felt divinely erotic. She closed her eyes and totally gave in to him. "Oh, yes, baby!"

"Tell me when you're coming."

"Okay, just don't stop."

"Don't worry, I won't. You feel too good to stop."

Their bodies were intertwined as they passionately made love, giving in to each other with abandon.

"Now, now...I'm coming now!" Brooklyn said with an urgency in her voice.

Landis picked up the pace, ramming himself as far into her as he could go. "I'm coming, too!"

After reaching ecstasy simultaneously, Landis slumped down on the bed next to Brooklyn. "That was amazing! I could stay here with you all day and not leave this room," he said, hugging her close.

"Yes, it was marvelous, but we have a wedding to attend. I need to get going. Pepper wants all of her attendants to dress at the church," Brooklyn said, sitting up.

"Are you sure we don't have time for a quickie?" He stroked her hip. "Give me a few minutes and I'll be ready for round two."

Brooklyn glanced at him, and as tempting as the offer was, she knew that if they started up again, she would be late. "No, I can't. I don't want to disappoint Pepper on her wedding day. But trust me, after we get back from the reception, I promise to rock your world!"

"You promise?"

"Yep."

Twenty minutes later, Brooklyn was showered and dressed. She gathered the maid-of-honor dress that was hanging in the garment bag on the closet door and put on her coat. She looked around for her phone but didn't see it. Brooklyn remembered putting her phone on the nightstand, and then recalled Landis knocking over the table as they made love. She knelt down, picked up the phone and put it in her purse.

"Okay, honey, I'll see you at the church," she said, giving him a kiss on the lips.

He returned her kiss. "Okay."

As Brooklyn made her way down the winding staircase, she couldn't help but think how lucky she was to have found the perfect man for herself.

Chapter 15

The quaint, century-old white frame church was located a short distance from the center of town, surrounded by towering snow-covered evergreens. The first thing Brooklyn saw as the limo parked was a huge Christmas wreath with dark green leaves and bright red holly berries decorating the door. She stepped out of the car and noticed how quiet and serene the surroundings were. The sun was shining brightly, causing the snow to sparkle like diamond dust.

This is a perfect day for a wedding, Brooklyn thought as she made her way inside.

She marveled at how elegantly the church was decorated. Lavender silk organza bows were tied around the edges of the wooden pews that lined the center aisle. Floral arrangements of white and lavender roses in huge crystal vases were placed on white columns near the altar. There was also a unity candle in a sterling-silver holder with a silver lighter behind the altar.

"Good morning. Are you ready for your solo?" Mr. Vance, the pianist, asked as Brooklyn neared the front of the church.

"Good morning, Mr. Vance. I certainly am. I can't wait. Am I the first one here?"

"No, Pepper is in the bridal suite. Come on. I'll show you where it is." Mr. Vance led Brooklyn through a wooden door adjacent to the choir loft and down a short carpeted hallway.

As they were walking, Brooklyn tripped on a piece of the carpet that was a bit tattered. "Oops." She held on to the wall to break her fall.

"Be careful. This church is old and well used. Underneath that carpet where you almost fell is a trapdoor. During the days of slavery, this church was part of the underground railroad."

"Oh, wow! I love hearing facts about those times. It's so interesting to me."

"If you have time tomorrow, I can give you a tour of the entire church and show you the tiny crawl space where the slaves hid."

"That would be awesome. Can I bring a guest?" she asked, thinking that Landis would probably enjoy the tour, as well.

"Of course, bring whomever you like."

"If I can make it, I'll call the church and let you know."

"Not a problem, I'll be here either way. Here's the bridal suite. The bridesmaids will be dressing in the room across the hall."

"Thanks, Mr. Vance."

Brooklyn opened the door and went inside. The room was filled with antiques. A mahogany vanity table and mirror were near the far wall, and a cranberry velvet chaise longue was positioned opposite the vanity table. Brooklyn looked around the room and saw Pepper's wedding dress hanging on a hook behind the door, but she didn't see her friend.

"Pepper, where are you?"

No answer.

Brooklyn put her dress and purse on the chaise longue, crossed the room and knocked on another door, which she assumed was the bathroom. "Pepper, are you in there?"

Brooklyn put her ear to the door and could hear sniffles. She turned the knob and slowly opened the door. Inside, Pepper was sitting on the edge of an old-fashioned claw-foot tub with her head held down.

"What's the matter?" Brooklyn asked, rushing over to her friend.

Pepper raised her head, revealing her tearstained face. "I can't do this," she said, in a soft whisper.

"What? Why are you crying?"

"I don't think I can marry Michael."

"Why? He's the love of your life."

"I know but…" A flood of tears stopped her words.

Brooklyn reached for a tissue and handed it to Pepper. "You're not making any sense. Just the other day, you said that you knew you were going to marry Michael the first time you laid eyes on him."

Pepper wiped her face and blew her nose. "I'm scared, Brooklyn. What if the marriage doesn't work? What if the sex fizzles out and he cheats? What if—"

Brooklyn promptly cut her off. "Look, Pepper, there

are no guarantees in this life, but what you and Michael have is the real deal. You guys have already built a life together. You've been together since college. Now don't you think that if the relationship was doomed to fail, it would have fallen apart years ago?"

Pepper held her hands in her lap and rubbed them together. "I guess you have a point."

"Of course I do. You're just nervous, that's all. I'm sure most brides get the jitters before they march down the aisle, which is understandable. This is one of the biggest decisions you'll make in your life."

"That's what scares me. Suppose I'm making the wrong decision."

Brooklyn sat down next to Pepper and put her arm around her friend. "The wrong decision would be for you *not* to marry Michael. The happiness and sheer joy I've seen from you two over the years is inspiring. I don't have a crystal ball, but if I had to guess, I'd say in years to come, you two will be celebrating your golden anniversary in this church surrounded by your children and grandchildren."

A smile began spreading across Pepper's face. "You really think so?"

"Absolutely! Now stop all this crying and let's get you dressed. We have a wedding to attend."

They both stood up, and Pepper hugged Brooklyn tight. "Thanks for being my friend and snapping me back to reality. I had a momentary meltdown, but I'm back now! Where's my dress? I'm getting married!"

Brooklyn helped Pepper with her hair and makeup, and then into her white, beaded Vera Wang gown. She then slipped on her maid-of-honor dress and refreshed her makeup.

Once they were all dolled up, the two friends stood in front of the mirror and admired their reflections.

"Wow! You look stunning," Brooklyn said.

"So do you. Wait until Landis sees you. I'm telling you that man is likely to propose today, you look so good."

"It's a bit too soon for that, but I wouldn't be opposed to receiving a little robin's-egg-blue box next Christmas," Brooklyn said, blushing. She glanced at her diamond Cartier watch. "It's showtime. Mr. Vance should be waiting for me at the piano. I'll see you out there."

"Okay, and thanks again, Brooklyn, for everything."

"Don't mention it. That's what friends are for."

Brooklyn exited the suite and returned to the sanctuary. She stood at the edge of the doorway and peered out. The wooden pews were now filled with guests. Mr. Vance was playing an old spiritual song as the minister, Michael and Landis made their way to the altar.

A knot formed in Brooklyn's throat the moment she laid eyes on Landis. The black tuxedo he wore accentuated his broad shoulders and fit his body as if it were tailor-made. He was the epitome of style and class. His face was smoothly shaven, and his hair was cut to perfection. Brooklyn's insides warmed at the mere sight of him. She was totally in love with Landis and was excited about their future together.

Suddenly, the fear that had struck Pepper had reared its ugly head again, but this time it was aimed at Brooklyn. She began doubting whether or not what she and Landis shared was a real connection or just hedonistic sex.

Stop it right now! she admonished herself. As she

was thinking, she heard Mr. Vance play her cue to approach the piano.

Brooklyn took a deep breath, arched her back and strutted over to the antique mahogany piano. She could feel all eyes on her. She glanced over at Landis, and he was staring at her with a dreamy expression. Watching the love in his eyes was all Brooklyn needed to ease her doubts.

Mr. Vance played "Ave Maria" while she belted out the lyrics in Italian, giving a stellar performance. Once the song was over, everyone clapped as if they were at an intimate concert. Brooklyn bowed her head and walked down the side aisle to the back of the church where the rest of the wedding party waited.

The bridesmaids and groomsmen were paired off and ready to make their entrance. Once they heard Mr. Vance play a rendition of the Carpenters' wedding song, they began marching toward the altar.

Brooklyn was the maid of honor and didn't have an escort. As she made her way down the aisle, she kept her eyes on Landis. It was as if she were marching straight to him.

After the flower girl did her job of tossing the lavender rose petals along the runner, Mr. Vance switched songs and began playing the "Wedding March." Everyone stood and welcomed the bride as she waltzed in on her father's arm.

The ceremony was short and sweet, with the minister reading from 1 Corinthians and then asking the "do you take" questions. Once the vows were recited, unity candle lit and rings exchanged, a small boy dressed in a tiny tuxedo came ambling down the aisle with an old-fashioned broom that was decorated with lavender and

white bows. He put the broom near the altar and returned to his seat.

"Pepper and Michael have decided to jump the
broom in celebration of their ancestors," the minister
announced.

Michael took hold of Pepper's hand. Pepper gathered
her dress and they jumped the broom into the land of
holy matrimony. The guests cheered and clapped.

"I now pronounce you Mr. and Mrs. Redmond!"

Michael engulfed his bride in a tender hug and they
kissed passionately before making their way to the nar-
thex to receive their guests.

Chapter 16

The exclusive country club was ensconced on an incline overlooking the Bridgehampton Golf Club. Pepper's parents had been members for over twenty years and had reserved the private ballroom for their only daughter. Uniformed servers passed hors d'oeuvres—stuffed shrimp, crab cakes, prosciutto and melon—and flutes of champagne during the cocktail hour before the sit-down dinner was served. The Grecian-style ballroom had multitiered crystal chandeliers, Roman columns, a black-and-white-checkered floor and an antique mural painted on one of the walls. A quartet was playing standard jazz songs as the guests mingled.

"Well, I did it! I's married now!" Pepper exclaimed, holding out her ring finger and mimicking a character from the *The Color Purple*.

Brooklyn took her hand and inspected the diamond-encrusted wedding band. "Wow! This is a beauty. Michael did good."

"He sure did. My husband is the best!"

"Listen to you, using the H-word," Brooklyn teased.

"One day, hopefully soon, you'll be married to Landis and saying, *my husband* this and *my husband* that. It surely sounds better than saying, *my boyfriend*."

Brooklyn tapped her flute against Pepper's. "I'll drink to that." Brooklyn glanced around the room. "Where are the guys? I haven't seen much of Landis since we arrived."

"Michael and the groomsmen are on the patio smoking cigars."

"In this weather?"

"Yep. Michael wanted to have a moment with the guys before dinner and before the after-dinner festivities began. After we have our first dance, cut the cake and toss the bouquet and garter, Michael and I are out of here. We're heading back to the city and spending the night in the honeymoon suite at the Waldorf. In the morning, we're catching a flight to Bora-Bora. I didn't know where we were going on our honeymoon until a few minutes ago. Michael wanted to surprise me."

"That's a wonderful surprise." Brooklyn gave her friend a big hug. "Pepper, I am so happy for you."

"Don't worry, you'll have your big day soon enough."

As they were talking, Brooklyn's cell phone buzzed. She opened her beaded evening bag, took out the phone and looked at the screen. The screen indicated that she had a new text message.

"My mom is trying to get my attention. Excuse me. Let me see what she wants," Pepper said.

"Okay."

Brooklyn swiped the phone's screen to reveal the message, which read:

Hey, Landis, got your text regarding a new development regarding Brooklyn. Call me when you get a chance so we can discuss. Malcolm

She was confused. Why was her manager sending a text referring to her as Landis? Brooklyn examined the phone, turning it over and looking closely at the front and back. The phone had scratches and wasn't as new and shiny as hers.

"This is Landis's phone," she muttered. *Our phones fell off the nightstand and I must have accidently picked up his phone instead of mine.*

Brooklyn reread the message. Clearly, Landis was in talks with her manager that she knew nothing about. A sick feeling washed over Brooklyn. *Landis has been keeping a secret and playing me this entire time!* She immediately thought about her ex-boyfriend who had tried to use her to advance his career. Her temper began rising with anger replacing her feelings of disappointment.

"Hey, babe," Landis said, approaching her.

"Don't 'hey, babe' me. What the fuck is this?" she asked, shoving the phone into his hands.

Landis took the phone. "Uh…I can explain."

"Save it, Landis. Obviously, you were sexing me up for your own agenda, whatever that is!"

"No, it's not like that at all…. I was in talks with Malcolm months ago."

"Yeah, right. Obviously, this is your phone. You must have mine."

Landis opened his jacket, reached into the inside

pocket and took out the phone. He looked at it before handing the phone over to Brooklyn. "This is a total misunderstanding. Please let me explain."

"You've had plenty of time to mention that you're in talks with my manager, but you chose not to mention whatever you and Malcolm have been discussing."

"Excuse me, ladies and gentlemen, can you please take your seats? Dinner will be served shortly," Pepper's mother announced.

Brooklyn turned on her heels and stormed off before Landis had a chance to explain. She had been down this road before, and his deception was hurtful and unacceptable.

During dinner, the wedding party sat together at an elongated table in the front of the room. Brooklyn tried to mask her disappointment and look happy for Pepper's sake, but inside, she was dying. The man she had given herself to physically and emotionally had betrayed her trust. Landis had had ample opportunity to tell Brooklyn the truth, but he had chosen to remain silent. In her opinion, he was no better than her ex.

After dinner, Brooklyn steered clear of Landis as Pepper and Michael danced the tango for their first dance and cut the multitiered red-velvet cake. She watched her friends bask in marital bliss, and a tear escaped her eye. She was crying for their happiness and the demise of her future with Landis. Brooklyn had mistakenly let her guard down and trusted that Landis had genuine feelings for her, but she had been sorely mistaken.

"Okay, can I have all my single ladies over here? It's time to toss the bouquet," Pepper said, waving a dozen white roses as Beyoncé's "Single Ladies" played in the background.

A group of women quickly formed near Pepper, waving their arms, eager to catch the bouquet. Brooklyn stood back and watched them; she didn't budge.

Pepper looked across the room. "Hey, Brooklyn, get over here!"

Brooklyn shook her head no.

"Come on. Don't be shy. I'm not throwing this bouquet until you get in line."

Brooklyn didn't want to cause a scene. She walked slowly over to where the other women were and stood there, stiff as a statue.

"On the count of three," Pepper announced. "One... two...three."

Pepper turned her back, glanced over her shoulder and threw the flowers directly at Brooklyn.

Brooklyn caught the bouquet, but wanted to throw the flowers back at her friend and walk out. But she didn't. The last thing she wanted to do was ruin Pepper's big day. She walked back to her chair with the heavy burden of disappointment weighing her down.

Once the women returned to their seats, an attendant brought a chair to the center of the room for Pepper. Michael came and knelt in front of his bride. He proceeded to lift her dress and remove her blue garter with his teeth.

"Okay, single guys, it's garter time," Michael said, waving the garter in the air.

Brooklyn watched a group of men, including Landis, come front and center.

Michael counted down to three and tossed the garter. Landis reached up and plucked the lace band out of the air.

"Oh...I think we have our next newlyweds. Brooklyn, can you come here, please?" Pepper asked excitedly.

Brooklyn was mortified. She didn't want to be any-where near Landis. Unfortunately, Pepper was unaware of what had transpired between them.

"Come on, Brooklyn," Pepper said, waving her friend to the front.

Brooklyn rose and walked slowly toward Landis. When she reached him, she stood there with her gaze cast to the floor, avoiding eye contact.

"Brooklyn, please have a seat so that Landis can put the garter on your leg," Pepper instructed.

Brooklyn took a deep breath. She didn't want Landis to touch her, but there was no way she could get out of this tradition, so she reluctantly sat down.

Landis knelt in front of her, put the garter in his mouth and slowly eased the sexy material up her leg, all the while staring at her face.

Brooklyn couldn't deny the sensual sensation run-ning up her spine. *He's just trying to entice you. Get a grip!* she told herself.

The moment the garter was firmly on her thigh, Brooklyn stood up, smiled politely and excused her-self. She rushed into the restroom, locked herself in a stall and let out a flood of tears. She cried for Landis's deception and the future they would never have.

Chapter 17

Landis returned from the reception alone. He had searched for Brooklyn before he left the country club, but hadn't found her. When he opened the door to their room, it was dark. He flicked on the lights. The room was empty. Although Landis wanted to see Brooklyn and explain himself, he knew that she wasn't going to return. The way she had avoided his eyes while he put the garter on her thigh told him that she was pissed.

He closed the door and spotted a note on the nightstand. Landis made his way over, sat on the bed and picked up the piece of paper. He unfolded the note and read it silently.

Landis, you have broken my heart. I thought we had a future together, but I see that you were only interested in me for business reasons. I'll never understand why you didn't tell me about your involvement with Malcolm. In any event, it's over between us. And you can forget about any future dealings with my manager.

B.

Landis crumpled the note in his fist and threw it across the room. He couldn't believe the sudden turn of events. He looked down at the tousled bed linens and flashed back to earlier that day when he and Brooklyn had made exquisite love.

Suddenly, he felt sick to his stomach at the thought of losing the love of his life. His pulse began racing as panic set in at the possibility that this could be the untimely end of their relationship. He slumped down on the bed and could feel his underarms beginning to perspire. His nerves were getting the best of him. Landis knew that he had to get a grip—and quick—before Brooklyn walked out of his life forever.

He took the phone out of his jacket pocket and called Brooklyn. The line rang and rang before going to voice mail.

"Brooklyn, I know you're upset, but please call me back so I can explain."

He disconnected the call and put his head in his hands. Landis was at a loss. He didn't know what to do. He started to call Malcolm, but it was late. Landis lay across the bed and closed his eyes. He tried to sleep, but was too wound up. Landis lay awake until the sun began peeking through the blinds. He reached for his cell phone, hit redial and called Brooklyn again, and again his call went to her voice mail.

"Brooklyn, baby, please call me back. This is a total misunderstanding. I would never use our relationship for my own agenda. Call me…please!"

Landis wasn't going to sit back and wait for her to return his call. He needed to act fast if he wanted to salvage their relationship. His next call was to Brooklyn's manager.

"Hello?" Malcolm answered in a groggy voice.

"Hey, man, I'm sorry for calling you so early, but I need you to talk to Brooklyn and explain our business dealings," Landis said in a rush.

"What's to explain? I told you that she's not discussing business until after the holidays."

Landis went on to tell Malcolm the recent turn of events. He started with the fact that he and Brooklyn had gone to the same college. However, he didn't know the shy girl in his statistics class had lost weight, changed her name and was now a superstar.

"Can I be honest with you, Malcolm?"

"Of course."

"I'm in love with Brooklyn and will gladly remove my agency from the list of contenders."

"Really? Are you serious? You do know that the agency that's selected to handle her endorsement deals stands to make a hefty commission."

"I don't care about the money. I care about Brooklyn. I should have told her the minute we reconnected that my agency was vying for her business. I feel like I've misled her, and that was not my intention. Please, can you call her and explain the truth?"

"Man, sounds like you've got it bad."

Landis exhaled into the phone. "She's my soul mate. I can't go through this life without her."

"Wow! That's heavy. I'll call Brooklyn and tell her the whole story, but I can't make any promises."

"Thanks, Malcolm."

Landis disconnected the call, tossed the phone on the covers. He thought for a moment. He wasn't going to leave his fate in the hands of Brooklyn's manager. He reached for the phone and dialed Brooklyn's number. It went straight to voice mail again.

"Brooklyn, if you're willing to give me another chance, meet me at Rockefeller Center on New Year's Eve in front of the Rock Center Café. I'll be there at eleven-thirty waiting...I love you."

Landis closed his eyes and said a silent prayer. This was the season for miracles, and he only hoped that his one wish—Brooklyn's forgiveness—came true.

Chapter 18

The night of the reception, Brooklyn had cried her eyes out while hiding in the ladies' room. After she shed the last tear, she exited the stall, cleaned the smudged makeup from around her eyes, applied some eye drops, reapplied her makeup, put on a brave face and went to find Pepper. Brooklyn had come out of the restroom just in the nick of time; Pepper and Michael were heading toward the door on their way out.

"Have a great honeymoon," Brooklyn had said, giving her friend a tight hug.

"Thanks. You should go find Landis and enjoy the rest of the evening. There's plenty of champagne left," Pepper said, still beaming from the day's events.

"I'm a bit tired. I think I'm going to call it a night."

"Don't be silly. Just because Michael and I are leaving doesn't mean you guys can't stay and party like rock stars."

Brooklyn was dying to tell Pepper the truth as to why Landis had befriended her so fast, but she wasn't going to ruin Pepper's special day.

"Okay, I'll stay," Brooklyn said, only to appease her friend.

"Have fun! We're off." Pepper kissed Brooklyn on the cheek before dashing out the door with her groom.

Once Pepper and Michael's car had driven off, Brooklyn retrieved her coat from the coatroom, called her bodyguard and had him bring her limousine around. She went back to the house, quickly packed and wrote Landis a goodbye note. Brooklyn wanted to get as far away from Landis as possible. There was no way that she was going to stay in the same house, let alone the same room, with Landis after he had deceived her.

That night, Brooklyn checked into a suite at the W hotel in Union Square. After changing her clothes and settling in, she stood by the window and peered out. A light snow had begun falling. The flakes drifted from the sky like confetti, covering the streets. She watched couples stroll hand in hand down the sidewalk. She sighed, crossed the room and opened the minibar.

Brooklyn poured two miniature bottles of Scotch in a glass and took a sip. As she drank, she heard her phone buzzing in her purse. She went over to the king-size bed where her purse lay and retrieved the phone. The screen indicated that she had a voice-mail message. Brooklyn was still shaken up from earlier and fumbled with the phone before hitting the right button. She put the device to her ear and listened to the message.

"Brooklyn, I know you're upset, but please call me back so I can explain."

She deleted the message and tossed the phone on the bed.

"Upset! I'm beyond upset!" she yelled into the air. "He's sadly mistaken if he thinks I'm going to listen to any more of his lies!"

As Brooklyn was ranting to herself, the phone buzzed again. She reached for it and read the screen. She hit the call answer button.

"Hello, Malcolm," she said, in a tight voice.

"Hey, Brooklyn, how are you?"

"I could be better. What's up?"

"I'm calling to talk to you about Landis Keates. He and his agency—"

Brooklyn cut Malcolm off midsentence. "I don't want to discuss Landis *or* his agency."

"Just give me five minutes and let me explain the situation."

Brooklyn sighed. "You have two minutes, Malcolm, and then I'm hanging up."

"Okay. Okay. While you were on tour and busy with the new album, I was lining up marketing agencies. I fired the last agency we had because they were not getting you the endorsement deals that you deserve. Anyway, the Keates Agency went above and beyond storyboards and marketing charts. Landis actually pitched you for an endorsement deal with a major cosmetics company, even though you're not his client."

"Oh, really? Why didn't you tell me any of this?"

"You were so busy that I didn't want to bother you until I had the top three agencies lined up. And then the holidays came and you didn't want to discuss business until after the New Year."

While they were talking, Brooklyn heard a beep in her ear. She took the phone away for a second and glanced at the screen. It was Landis calling. She put the phone back to her ear and continued listening to Malcolm.

"That still doesn't explain why Landis didn't bother mentioning that his agency was vying for my business," she said, anger in her voice.

"Brooklyn, I can understand why you're upset and how you might think that Landis was trying to woo you in order for his agency to get the contract, but you're wrong."

"That's exactly what he was trying to do!" she said, raising her voice.

"No, it's not. I talked to Landis, and he wants to remove his agency from the list of contenders. He's in love with you and would rather lose the contract than lose your love."

"He said that?" she asked.

"Yes, in so many words. Listen, Brooklyn, Landis doesn't care about the commission his agency stands to gain. I honestly believe that he got caught up in his emotions and didn't know how to tell you about our negotiations. I really don't think he was trying to deceive you."

Brooklyn listened to Malcolm's words before speaking. She had known her manager for years and trusted him implicitly. "Malcolm, thanks for calling and telling me the whole story. I'll take it from here."

"Will you be all right?"

"Yes, I'm fine. Good night and thanks again."

Exhausted from all the emotions, Brooklyn rested

her head on the pillow, exhaled and closed her eyes. She could see images of herself and Landis and all the ways they had made love. Brooklyn's resolve began to soften. She opened her eyes and saw a red light blinking on her phone.

She picked up the device and hit the voice-mail button. There were two more messages from Landis. She listened to them both. This time, she didn't delete his messages, but replayed them over and over.

Chapter 19

Landis rushed through the crowds on Fifth Avenue trying to get to one store in particular. It was New Year's Eve and most of the shops along the trendy avenue were closing early. He wove and dodged his way a few blocks until he reached his destination.

He hadn't heard from Brooklyn, but that didn't stop him from making plans. Landis was hopeful that she had listened to his message and would meet him at Rockefeller Center.

After he had finished his errand, he made his way home and impatiently waited until evening. Landis thought about calling Brooklyn again, but didn't. He wasn't going to harass her. If Brooklyn didn't ever want to see or speak to him again, he couldn't blame her.

I should have told her about the agency business that first night before we were intimate, he thought to himself.

"That's water under the bridge now," he said aloud.

Landis busied himself with paperwork from the office, trying to pass the time and get his mind off Brooklyn. Although he hoped that she would show up, he also had to be realistic. There was a good chance that he would never see her again—at least in person.

After waiting for what seemed like an eternity, it was time to leave. Landis gathered the purchase he had made earlier and tucked it in his pocket. He then put on his navy peacoat, hat, scarf and gloves and headed out the door.

The wind was brisk as he walked the long distance to Rockefeller Center. Landis opted not to take a taxi or the subway; he wanted to walk to clear his mind. Tonight could mark the beginning of something special or the end of a dream. Either way, he had to prepare himself for the worst.

The ice-skating rink at Rockefeller Center was extra crowded with people making their way to the New Year's Eve ball drop in Times Square, as well as skaters whizzing by on the ice and people milling about taking in the holiday sights before they were gone. Landis stood in front of the restaurant—their designated spot—and waited impatiently. Five minutes after the appointed time she hadn't arrived, so he walked around looking through the crowd, but he didn't see her. He checked his watch; it was 11:55 p.m.

Landis went back to the restaurant and paced back and forth. He checked his watch again. He quickly dashed inside on the off chance she was there, but she was nowhere in sight.

I guess she's not coming.

He sighed heavily. Midnight was closing in, and he

didn't want to be in the crowd alone when the clock struck midnight, so he slumped his shoulders and hung his head. The love of his life was gone forever and he had to accept that fact. Landis turned and began walking back toward Fifth Avenue.

"Hey, wait up!"

Landis turned around, and running toward him was Brooklyn. He ran to meet her and scooped her up in his arms.

"Oh, baby! I'm so sorry! I…"

Brooklyn kissed him on the lips and then said, "No need to explain. I talked to Malcolm and he cleared everything up. I'm sorry I didn't give you a chance to explain at the reception."

"It's all my fault. I should have been up front with you from the start. Please believe that I wasn't trying to use our relationship to win you as a client."

"I do believe you. Please forgive me for overreacting."

As they were talking, they heard the crowd begin to chant.

"Ten…nine…eight…seven…six…five…four…three…two…one…HAPPY NEW YEAR!"

Landis and Brooklyn embraced and kissed for what seemed like minutes. He released her, dropped down on one knee, reached in his pocket and took out a tiny box.

"Brooke Lynn Samuels, will you marry me?"

Brooklyn stared down at him with her mouth agape and tears rolling down her face.

"I wasn't expecting this, but *yes!* YES! I'll marry you!"

The people around them began cheering as Landis placed the ring on Brooklyn's finger. He stood, wrapped her in a warm bear hug and then gave her a tender kiss on the lips.

"Come on. Let's go home."

* * * * *

REQUEST YOUR FREE BOOKS!

2 FREE NOVELS PLUS 2 FREE GIFTS!

KIMANI™
ROMANCE

Love's ultimate destination!

An unexpected
attraction too strong
to deny…or forget.

National
bestselling author
ROCHELLE
ALERS

Sweet Silver Bells

The Eatons

Designing luxury hotels in Charleston is a career coup for Crystal Eaton.
Meeting charismatic corporate attorney Joseph Cole-Wilson is an unexpected bonus. Until one passion-filled night in Joseph's penthouse
changes her life forever. But Joseph can't accept their liaison as a onetime
fling. And when a chance encounter reunites him with the Florida beauty,
the Cole heir vows he won't let her get away a second time.

"This one's a page-turner with a very satisfying conclusion."
—*RT Book Reviews* on *SECRET VOWS*

Available October 2014 wherever books are sold.